# THERE IS A RIVER

# THERE IS A RIVER

A NOVEL BY

## CHARLOTTE MILLER

NewSouth Books

Montgomery

*F*
*MIL*

NewSouth Books
P.O. Box 1588
Montgomery, AL 36102


Copyright © 2002 by Charlotte Miller
This is a work of fiction. The characters, names, incidents, dialogue and
plots are the product of the author's imagination or are used ficti-
tiously. Any resemblance to actual persons or events is purely
coincidental. All rights reserved under International and Pan-American
Copyright Conventions. Published in the United States by NewSouth
Books, a division of NewSouth, Inc., Montgomery, Alabama.

Library of Congress Cataloging-in-Publication Data

ISBN 1-58838-090-4


Design by Randall Williams
Printed in the United States of America

*To Randall Williams,*
*who always believed.*

# Contents

# THERE IS A RIVER

. . . We will not fear though the earth should change, though the mountains shake in the heart of the sea; though its waters roar and foam, though the mountains tremble with its tumult.

There is a river whose streams make glad the city of God . . . God is in the midst of her, she shall not be moved . . .

The nations rage, the kingdoms totter; he utters his voice, the earth melts . . . He makes wars cease to the end of the earth; he breaks the bow, and shatters the spear . . .

Be still, and know that I am God.

—Psalms 46: 2-10 (RSV)

# PROLOGUE

*Eason County, Alabama*
*October 1939*

$C$ASSANDRA PRICE COULD
*hear the sound of furniture breaking after the old man walked out of*
*Buddy's office. She reached the doorway to see Buddy yank a drawer from*
*his desk and throw it, contents and all, directly at where she was standing.*

*She moved back and the drawer hit the door frame waist high, sending*
*fountain pens, rubber bands, and dozens of boxes of matches skittering*
*over the floor near her feet. She placed one hand on her belly, assuring*
*herself that nothing had hit her there—she could not let anything happen*
*now. Not when she was this close.*

*Not when she was going to have Buddy Eason's baby.*

*She peeked around the doorjamb once Buddy was no longer throwing*
*furniture. He was yanking drawers open and slamming items on the desk.*
*He was cursing, but Cassandra did not take the time to listen—whatever*
*he was saying did not matter. He and his grandfather had fought. But he*
*and his grandfather fought often. It did not usually result in thrown*
*furniture or a bloody face, which Buddy had at the moment, Cassandra*
*noted with distaste—but that did not matter either. She had not bedded*
*him for his looks. She had not bedded him for his personality. She had*
*bedded him for the baby growing inside of her, and for the money and the*
*Eason name the baby would bring her.*

13

"Buddy, are you hurt?" she asked, though she did not care. She was startled to see him take a gun from a lower drawer and lay it on the desktop. He fished in the drawer again, not answering, and came up with a handful of bullets. "Buddy—?"

"What?" he hissed at her, and she stepped back.

She did not say anything as he loaded the gun and set it on the desktop, then watched as he yanked open another drawer. He slammed it, then started across the room toward her, and Cassandra shrank away, though he did nothing but take his coat and hat from the hatrack to toss them on one of the leather armchairs before his desk.

"Are you going somewhere?" she asked.

He did not answer. He set an open briefcase in the chair, then began to rake things from the desktop into it. The gun was dumped in with everything else.

"Are you—" she began again, crossing toward him.

"Yeah, I'm going, if it's anything to you."

"But, where?"

He did not answer.

"But—but, you can't leave—I mean—" She panicked. He couldn't leave. Not now. Not with her pregnant. He had to marry her. That was what was supposed to happen. He had to.

She stared at his back.

"Whatever you and your grandfather were fighting about, it can't be so bad—you need to—"

"The old man is the first thing I'm going to settle."

That made no sense. Buddy squatted before the credenza and yanked open a door.

"But, why—"

"What does it matter to you?"

"But, you can't leave—I—I'm pregnant—" she blurted out. "You've got to stay and—"

He turned to look at her. "I don't have to do anything."

"But—it's yours; the baby, it's yours," she said, and could hear the desperation in her voice. No, it was not supposed to happen like this.

"So? What if it is?"

"But, you can't—you—you have to marry me! You have to! Your grandfather won't let—"

"Do you think I would marry some mill village whore like you?" he asked, and Cassandra was surprised to hear his snorting laugh. "Do you think the old man would let me marry somebody like you, even if I wanted to?"

And suddenly she understood.

He never would have married her.

The railroad tracks that cut the town in half had decided it after all. Cassandra was from the mill village. Buddy Eason was from town. And he would never marry her.

The memory of something her mother said about a pregnant, unmarried cousin came to her—rather dead and buried than to disgrace the family.

If Buddy did not marry her, she knew that her self-righteous mother, Helene, would put her out the minute she learned Cassandra was pregnant. There was no doubt—better dead and buried, Cassandra told herself. Better dead.

Cassandra's eyes moved to the gun in the open briefcase, and she reached for it almost without thought—better dead. Better not to have people laugh at her and call her trash. She was not trash—she was Cassandra Price—her mother had always said she was better than anyone else living in the mill village.

She had been good enough for Buddy Eason to bed.

She just wasn't good enough to marry.

She was crossing the room before she consciously made the decision— better dead. But she would take care of something first.

When Buddy stood and turned, Cassandra placed the business end of the gun to his crotch—take care of something. Oh, yes.

Panic came to Buddy's eyes. He was shoving her away with one hand, grabbing for the gun with the other, when Cassandra Price—who knew now that she would never be Mrs. Buddy Eason—pulled the trigger.

# PART ONE

~ 1939 ~

# I

THE BOARDS AT THE EDGE of the unpainted porch floor, where it overhung the bare-swept yard, were water damaged and gapped in places, reminding Nathan Betts of the look of rotted teeth. He stopped that Thursday afternoon in October of 1939 just short of the front steps and stared at them, though he knew already he was being watched from behind more than one set of curtains up and down the length of Spring Street. People minded each other's business here in Eason County. Nathan accepted that. It was part of living here, and there was no need to waste thought on something that could not be gotten around.

He walked up the steps and picked his way carefully across the front porch, took his hat from his head, knocked, and waited. He could hear a dog barking behind the house, and another up the street. Nathan knew this house probably belonged to George Marion, the same white man who owned the house where Nathan lived several streets away, as well as so many other houses here in this part of town. Mr. Marion would let a porch fall through before he ever had it fixed—but that was just the way white folks were when they had more money than they had a use for, Nathan told himself. They bought houses here in the colored part of town to rent them out for more than the houses were worth, and they never wanted to spend any money to keep the places safe and decent.

He knocked for a second time, reminding himself that people could do things far worse than that to each other.

That was what had brought him here in the first place, after all.

He held his hat in both hands by the brim, hearing at last the sound of heavy footsteps inside the house.

Esther Tipton opened the door only slightly and peered out. Her face was broad and very plain, darker than his, and it held no welcome for this man who had come uninvited to her doorstep.

"Brother Jakes said that you was comin' by t' talk t' me," she said. "I cain't think what for."

"Can we talk inside?" he asked, realizing that he was now turning the hat.

"No." She gave no explanation, and Nathan knew there would be no choice but to have his say here on the front porch where half the neighborhood could watch him.

He took a deep breath and made himself quit turning the hat. He had done this before, he reminded himself—but he had been a young man then, with no white in his hair. "I come t' ask if you wanted to marry me," he said at last, then watched with no surprise as anger came to her face.

"Why would you want t' ask me that?"

"I got a boy, an' two girls at home who need a momma. I understan' you need a husband just th' same."

Hate came to her face to push aside the anger that had been on it. She pulled the door back fully to stare up at him, and for a moment Nathan was certain she would step out onto the porch and drive him out into her front yard. "Look at you, nigger, comin' here 'cause Old Walter Eason sent you—does he own you body an' soul so much that he can pick a wife for you? I didn't have no choice in what Buddy Eason done t' me—but this is my baby he put inside 'a me an' I'm gonna raise it, an' I ain't gonna be bought off by no sorry excuse for a man sent t' me for a husband."

"Walter Eason didn't send me here," Nathan said, staring back. "I come on my own. Brother Jakes told me that Buddy Eason forced hisself on you an' got you with child. He said your baby's gonna need a name an' you're gonna need a man in th' house, an' he reminded me that my children need a momma—"

"You'd raise Buddy Eason's child like it was your own?"

"It would be my own."

"What if it looks white?" she asked, and the words hung there between them.

"That don't matter. My momma's daddy was white; wouldn't nobody know no difference."

She nodded finally and looked away. She stared at the rotting boards in the porch floor. Nathan watched, thinking she might be a handsome woman if she ever smiled.

But Esther Tipton had little to smile about. Nathan knew she would never have the satisfaction of seeing Buddy Eason pay for what he had done to her. At least she could have some justice in knowing that he was paying for what he had done to someone else. Buddy Eason was in the hospital now, a fat white man under the care of fat white doctors, having been put there by a skinny white woman he had probably wronged as well.

"We could have a good life," he said, his eyes not leaving Esther. "I won't never hurt you like he done," he said, and her eyes rose to meet his at last. "I ain't no kind'a man like that."

∽

"But, that's not possible," Helene Price said for the second time as she settled heavily into a chair near her husband in the waiting room of the Eason County Hospital in Pine.

Walter Eason stared at her from across the room, where he stood before the tall windows that overlooked the narrow front lawn. He saw disbelief settle on her face, and he wondered why she had not shown such utter refusal to believe when she had learned a few days before that her daughter, Cassandra, had tried to kill Walter's grandson, Buddy.

That day Helene had asked only if Cassandra would have to spend the night in jail, or if Helene could possibly take her home "until all this mess gets straightened out."

This time it had taken only the words of a doctor to bring this look of absolute refusal to her face.

"That's not possible," Helene said again.

Cassandra had tried to induce a miscarriage of the child she was carrying, Buddy's child. Walter Eason's first great-grandchild.

"Cassandra is not—she's not—"

The woman waved one hand in the air. The hand slowly settled back to her lap, and her chin rose. Walter then read the look on her face for what it was—sheer defiance to believe that her unmarried daughter would have gotten herself into this situation.

"My daughter is not with child," she said dismissively. Helene straightened her back. She sniffed, her chin still raised, and Walter knew she was trying to be more than she was, more than just the wife of the supply room boss at the cotton mill. More than just the mother of a young woman who had gone wrong. More than the mother of a daughter who had intended to kill Walter's grandson.

Dr. Thrasher stared at Helene, then turned his eyes to her husband. "When she realized that what she'd done hadn't worked, she asked me to do away with the child—"

"Well, do it then," Helene Price said, sitting forward suddenly. The words were hurriedly spoken, quieter than any other words she had uttered since she entered the room. She leaned toward the doctor now, her hands clenched into fists in her lap. "Get rid of it. No one would ever have to—"

"Helene!" Bert Price rose to his feet. He was a little man, hardly taller than his stout wife, and so thin it appeared he was in the process of wasting away, as if living with Helene Price and that daughter of his had drawn all the life out of him. Walter could remember Bert Price in his younger years, could remember him vital and strong, before life—and Helene Price—had beaten the desire for living out of him. Bert stood swaying on his feet, staring at his wife, his mouth slack and open now, as if he could think of nothing more to say.

"But—no one would know, and we certainly wouldn't tell any-one," Helene Price continued.

She looked from her husband to the doctor, cold reason now on her face. Her hands smoothed the fabric of her skirt. The garment was picked in several places, and badly nappy along one side where she had repeatedly brushed against some object over the years she had worn it. It must have been expensive when it was new, though too tight for the woman wearing it, as most garments appeared when Helene Price was in them. She sat primly now, her hands folded lady-like in her lap.

"Cassandra was having female problems," she said. "That was why Dr. Thrasher was called in. Young women her age are always—"

"That's enough," Walter said, unable to listen to her any longer. He was not surprised when silence fell over the others in the room, though Helene Price fidgeted nervously, picking at an invisible bit of lint. Walter stared at her then his eyes moved to Bert Price, and an unexpected feeling of pity came over him—what could it be like to live with such a woman? Walter could think of very few men who deserved that particular hell.

"I'll take care of this," he said at last, his eyes settling on Helene Price. Very few men, indeed.

Buddy did not acknowledge his grandfather's presence when Walter Eason entered his hospital room that evening. His eyes were fixed on the silent radio across the room, one hand resting on an open *Life* magazine on the bed beside him. Seeing him, Walter thought of all the hopes he had once had for his only grandson—but those hopes had vanished one by one through the years, culminating in the afternoon Buddy was shot, when Buddy had dislocated Walter's left shoulder in the course of an altercation between them. Walter had no doubt that Buddy would have killed him that afternoon if not for the small pistol Walter had had the foresight to conceal in his pocket before he went to Buddy's office that day.

The same pistol he had brought with him in a pocket today.

He walked closer to the bed, thinking that being shot and

believing he would die, even for so short a time, could change a man, and perhaps it could change even his thirty-one-year-old grandson. Walter's gaze fell on the magazine beneath Buddy's hand, and on the photograph of a young woman dressed in a bathing costume—Buddy had drawn grotesque breasts on her picture, and shaded in the nether region with the appearance of hair. Vulgar images had been inked in the sky across the top of the page, depicting—

Walter looked away.

Cassandra Price had intended to shoot Buddy in the groin. Walter knew that, for Buddy had been screaming the words over and over again when Walter had arrived at the hospital no more than an hour after the shooting. Buddy had grabbed for the gun when he realized her intentions, and the bullet had gone into this thigh, hitting a blood vessel. Buddy had been certain he would die. Walter had been told he had screamed over and over again for someone to get a doctor, even before they were able to move him from his office at the mill, which was probably the only thing that had saved Cassandra Price's life.

In the hospital later, once Buddy knew that he would live, he had said he would kill Cassandra.

"That bitch tried to blow my balls off—she's going to wish she had blown my goddamn head off instead by the time I'm finished with her—"

Buddy had refused to press charges, and demanded that Cassandra be released from jail, telling the police the shooting was an accident. He had made certain she would be told to stay in town, however. He wanted to know he could get to her when the time was right.

But Walter Eason had other plans.

He stood beside the bed now, though Buddy had still not acknowledged his presence.

"Cassandra Price is in the hospital," Walter said, but said nothing more.

Buddy's eyes came to him. Walter waited for a moment, hoping that he would speak. When he did not, Walter continued. "She did something to try to do away with the child she's carrying."

Buddy spoke at last, and Walter was not surprised at his words. "Maybe she'll bleed to death," he said quietly, and then looked away again.

"She'll live. So will the child."

"Too bad." And Walter was surprised to see Buddy smile. "But I'll take care of that for her. She won't be worrying about having any brat when I'm through."

"It's your child, isn't it?"

Buddy shrugged, "She wanted bad enough to get laid." He laughed, then winced as he moved the bandaged leg. "She thought I'd marry her—like I'd marry some mill village whore who—"

In that moment, Walter hated his grandson as much as he had ever hated any man.

He had released his walking stick, leaving it leaning against the bed as he placed the fingers of his right hand on Buddy's wounded thigh. He pressed down, twisting with the arthritis-enlarged knuckles of his first and middle fingers. Buddy opened his mouth to scream, and Walter's other hand covered Buddy's mouth.

He kept his hand in place, staring into Buddy's pain-filled eyes. Perspiration was beading over Buddy's forehead now and was slick over his upper lip and cheeks under Walter's left hand. He knew that hand and arm were little better than useless, the shoulder too badly damaged when Buddy wrenched it days before, but its presence alone seemed enough to silence his grandson.

"You will show respect for the mother of your child," Walter said quietly, staring into gray eyes that he knew were very much like his own. There was dampness under his right fingers now, blood seeping through the bandage. "You're going to marry that girl and be a father to her child—"

Buddy twisted his head, freeing his mouth from Walter's hand. "Like hell I will."

"—or you'll get nothing from me, not now or after I die."

"Fuck you, old man—I don't need you."

The words were spoken disdainfully, as if the boy—the man,

Walter corrected himself, though he had never been able to think of his grandson as a man, though he could not think of Buddy as a man even now—gave no thought to what it was he was throwing away.

"Don't you? You have no home, no money. You've spent more than you've ever earned. Even the automobile you drive is one I bought and paid for. How far do you think you'll make it outside Eason County?—and, if you don't marry that girl, you will leave Eason County, and you'll leave with nothing."

He thought Buddy would speak, and, when he did not, Walter continued.

"I thought you'd see reason," he said quietly.

"Why would you want me to marry that whore?"

"Because you're just alike," Walter said. "You deserve each other."

He removed his hand from Buddy's thigh and picked up his walking stick as he started toward the door, not surprised in the least to feel the movement of air against his cheek, the passing of the issue of *Life* as it flew past his head.

"That bitch tried to blow my balls off!" Buddy screamed behind him, and Walter turned back.

"There's always next time," he said. "Maybe once you're married her aim will improve."

# 2

You think they invited
Bert and old Helene to th' weddin'?" The fixer shouted over the
sound of the machinery in the card room of the Eason Cotton Mill on
a Friday afternoon in December of that year. He leaned against one of
the timber supports for the floor above, his eyes on Janson Sanders,
but Janson did not respond. He had no interest in Buddy Eason's
wedding, though the topic had dominated conversation the mill
village over since Helene Price had let slip the news of her daughter's
impending marriage to Buddy Eason.

Janson ignored the man, coughing instead on the cotton dust in
his lungs as he stared at the sliver of cotton that ran from a carding
machine, until the fixer moved on. Buddy Eason had not been seen in
the mill or village much in the past several months since Cassandra
Price shot him—and today Buddy Eason was marrying the woman
who put a bullet into his leg. If ever there was a marriage made in hell,
this had to be it, Janson told himself. It was not that long ago that
Janson would happily have killed Buddy Eason for the things Buddy
had done and said, and even moreso for the things Janson knew
Buddy was capable of doing.

Now he wished him a long life spent with Cassandra Price at his
side.

Dying hurt only once, Janson told himself. Hell itself had to be
waking up every morning knowing there was a snake in your bed.

He looked down the row of cards to where his brother-in-law,

Stan Whitley, was stripping cotton lint out of a machine. In many ways, he and Stan were far different men. His brother-in-law had more in common with the Easons than he ever would with Janson or with any other hand at work in the cotton mill. He had been born to money and luxury, as had Buddy Eason. Even now, in his faded workclothes and worn-out shoes, with the light reflecting off the round lenses of his eyeglasses from the electric fixtures high overhead, Stan looked as if he should be at work in the mill office alongside Walter Eason, and not here in the card room. Stan had never been meant for this kind of life, but, then again, neither had Stan's sister, Elise, when she had agreed to become Janson's wife. Time and circumstances had brought them all—including Janson—to a place they never expected.

There was noticeable lint already collected in Stan's red hair, though his shift had begun no more than an hour before. Janson's own hair, black when he entered the mill that morning, would be gray with cotton dust and lint by the end of his double shift. That would be one of the few times during the day when there would seem little difference between him and most of the other hands who spent their hours here in the Eason Cotton Mill. At the end of those sixteen hours, the mixed Cherokee and white heritage that usually showed so clearly in his face and coloring would be little evident beneath the tiredness and layers of cotton dust.

Janson drew his attention back to the machinery in the noisy card room. He knew it was not safe to let his attention wander while working—it was just that he was tired, feeling older than his thirty-two years. There would be seven hours to go before the end of this second shift of the double, and—

There was a sound, something he was always unconsciously listening for—a scream, horror, as Janson had heard only a few times before, and he knew that someone had been caught in a card—

Janson turned quickly, almost catching his own sleeve in the belt that ran from the machine to the drive shaft overhead, feeling it jerk at him before he yanked it free—then he saw.

It was Stan, his arm being dragged into the card.

~

No one spoke to them, or even looked in their direction. Stan had been taken from the card room to the mill office, what was left of his right arm a bloody mess, and from there he and Janson had been driven to the hospital on the other side of town. A tourniquet had been used to slow the bleeding, and now they waited for the doctor—but the wife of the First Baptist preacher, eight months along with child, had been hit by an automobile along Main Street, and Dr. Washburn and Dr. Thrasher were both working to save the mother and child.

Stan lay still, his face ashen, his lips a thin line. Somewhere along the way his eyeglasses had been lost, and Janson could only think of how young he looked without them, even younger than his twenty-seven years.

Janson stood beside the examination table, holding Stan's good hand as he had since they had arrived at the hospital, trying to keep his eyes from the shredded mess below Stan's right shoulder. There was nothing he could do but stand and wait, nothing but pray silently as he held that lone hand. He wished that Gran'ma had passed on to him her knowledge of stopping blood, wished that someone would come to help, or at least to lessen the pain he could see on the face of the younger man—*God, don't let him die*, he prayed, his head bowed now and his eyes closed. *Elise could never take it. I could never take it.*

"Janson—" The voice was a whisper. Janson opened his eyes to find Stan looking up at him, pain creasing a forehead that Janson had never before seen marked by anything other than concentration at work or reading.

"Don't try t' talk. Th' doctor'll be here in a minute."

"But, I have to, in case—"

"Nothin's gonna happen. You're gonna be all right—"

"I might not."

Janson could not speak. He knew his brother-in-law could die today—his brother, for Stan had become no less than that.

"I want you to know I'm glad about you and Elise—I don't think I've ever said that before. I'm glad I've been part of your family all these years."

"I'm glad, too." Janson nodded and squeezed his hand. There was sweat beading over Stan's pale face, and the hand that Janson held was now clammy and cold.

"Remember when I found you after you'd climbed out of the well?" Stan said, his voice so quiet now Janson could hardly hear it. "Lying there in the rain—you looked so bad. I didn't know if you were alive—"

Silence fell between them and Janson looked away—yes, he did remember. If not for Stan, he probably would have died that night twelve years ago. The family he and Elise had made together—Henry, the son Elise had been carrying even then, and their daughters, Catherine and Judith—Janson would never have known any of them if not for Stan. Stan had been beside them through all the hard years, had sharecropped and picked cotton and learned to plow—Janson wished there was something he could do for Stan now. There was such a presence of death in the room, death so strong that Janson could feel it. He felt a pressure on his hand and he looked down at his brother-in-law to find what he knew to be a forced smile on the younger man's face.

"Don't worry, brother," Stan said in such a light whisper Janson was not even certain that he understood the words. "I won't give up without a fight."

~

Elise Sanders opened her door to find Walter Eason on her front porch, and a large, black car pulled up on the street before the house she and her family shared with the Shelbys. She gripped the edge of the doorframe, fear filling her—it had to be Janson. She knew how dangerous it was for the men who worked in the card room, had seen men in the mill village who had been mangled in the machines, men missing hands, fingers, arms—God, not Janson.

The words that came both relieved and horrified her. "Mrs. Sanders, there's been an accident in the card room. Your brother's been taken to the hospital—"

Walter Eason drove her across town, and she ran from the black car the moment he stopped it before the building there alongside a sign that read *"No Parking."*

"Stan Whitley—my brother—he was hurt in the mill; where is he?" she demanded of the first person she saw in white inside the building.

The nurse pointed down a hallway and opened her mouth to speak, but Elise ran past her before the woman could bring voice to the words. She found Janson standing in the hallway just outside a closed door and she ran to him, then stood swaying on her feet as he caught her arms and held her. An awful, grim look in his eyes made her heart rise into her throat, and, for a moment, she was certain that her brother was dead.

"Stan, is he—"

Janson held to her arms for a moment, looking at her, and she thought she would scream if he would not speak. "He's alive."

The relief came to her with such an impact that she would have collapsed to the floor if not for his hands beneath her elbows—but there was more. She could see it in his eyes, and she felt her heart rise to choke her again.

Elise opened her mouth, but no words would come out—she did not want to know. She could see it in his eyes, but she did not want to know.

"He lost his arm, Elise." His supporting hands gripped her harder, as if he could feel the weakness coming into her knees that would have taken her to the floor. An awful medicine smell filled her head, making her dizzy.

"No—that can't be. It—" Her voice sounded lifeless, numbed.

She stared up at him, swaying again, even though he held her. "Stan can't have—"

"He has." His voice was gentle, a worry for her on his face, but the words cut her like a curse.

The door behind them opened and Dr. Washburn came out. He looked at Janson, then stepped back. Elise stared past him into the room, clenching her hands against her chest, then walked toward the bed. Stan lay with his eyes closed, his face pale, a grayish cast to his skin. He looked like death, and Elise would have thought there was no life within him but for the shallow rise and fall of the thin chest beneath the sheet.

Her eyes moved from the gray face to where his right arm should be, but there was only a stump, bandaged in white. Only a—

Her face felt hot and flushed, her breath becoming difficult. A humming filled her ears and she could feel the weight of the hospital suddenly about her. She moved quickly from the room to stand swaying in the hallway again with one hand against the wall, her head down.

Janson stood behind her. He seemed to know what would happen. When she fainted he caught her in his arms.

<br>

<br>

<br>

<br>

# 3

<br>

<br>

<br>

<br>

CASSANDRA PRICE'S WED-
ding day began with her in tears, and it ended just the same. The white
dress she had bought only weeks before was too tight now over her
breasts, and through the waist as well—she was over four months
pregnant now, and getting too big too fast. She would look as if
stuffed into the garment, but she was going to wear it, if for no other
reason than to spite Buddy Eason.

He had laughed at her and her mother when Helene told him
Cassandra would marry in white.

"Is white the color for a knocked-up whore to marry in now?" he
asked, making Cassandra strike out at him even before she thought.
He blacked her eye for that, even with her mother standing there to
witness.

But Helene was no help.

"You can't treat Buddy like that," her mother told her afterward.
"He's going to be your husband, and you have to treat him with
respect—after all, he is Mr. Eason's grandson."

Buddy's grandfather and her parents were there to see the marriage
take place, although old man Eason left as soon as the vows were
exchanged—but that did not matter to the new Mrs. Buddy Eason.
She and Buddy would be leaving to spend a week in Atlanta, and the
thought of being in a big city with Eason money to spend was an
intoxicating prospect for the former Cassandra Price. There was such
excitement in Atlanta at the moment with the premiere of the *Gone*

*With The Wind* movie taking place there that very day, that Cassandra could think of no other place on the earth that she would rather be.

But her honeymoon was not what she imagined.

The streets of Atlanta were crowded. Buddy's car was stopped in traffic several times, sitting once for well over thirty minutes, though Buddy would not let her get out to look at the display of *Gone With The Wind* movie costumes she could see in a nearby store window. As soon as they arrived at the hotel, Buddy left her alone in their room. He stayed out all night, and returned well into the morning. She met him at the door in a fury, having slept very little during the night. His clothes were rumpled, his tie missing, and his shirt untucked and unbuttoned almost all the way down the front. He was drunk and he reeked of more than one kind of cheap perfume—and Cassandra knew that he had spent the night with another woman.

"You spent my wedding night with some whore!" she screamed at him, slamming the door as he walked past her and into the room.

"One whore's as good as another," he said back over his shoulder, as if Cassandra did not matter enough to even look at when he was speaking to her.

She tried to slap him when he turned to her at last, but he caught her wrist and slung her onto the bed.

"You wanting it?" He started toward her, pulling off his jacket. "I'm gonna give you what you want." Suddenly he was on her, his weight crushing her into the mattress, his mouth bruising hers, his body hurting her. She tried to twist free, biting him and trying to push him off, but he hit her, then again, and pinned her to the bed.

He ripped her nightgown down the front, his fingers bruising her flesh—and he took her, using her, violating her in new ways. She screamed into the hand he held over her mouth and tried to get free, but there was no use. He left her hurting and filled with hatred. He was her husband and she hated him—hated him now with a passion beyond the greed for money and power that had made her plan to become pregnant in the first place.

# 4

AT FIRST ESTHER DID NOT
want to look at the child she had just given birth to. She lay staring at
the shadows that moved over the white-painted wall beside the bed,
waiting to hear what the old granny woman would say.

"He's a fine, big boy," Granny Alice said, wiping the crying baby
off where he lay now on the bed beside Esther.

Esther wanted to ask what he looked like, but found herself saying
instead, "He's all right then?"

"He's all right," the old woman said. Her eyes rose to meet Esther's
when Esther looked at her at last, and she stared long and hard. "Your
Nathan's got hisself a fine new son," she said, her hands automatically
continuing the business of cleaning up the baby.

"Nathan," Esther said, the word not quite a question. The old
woman's eyes never left hers.

"Yes, Nathan."

The two women stared at each other, and Esther was certain that
Granny Alice knew.

She looked away just as the old woman picked up the baby and
moved to place him at her breast. He stopped crying the moment that
he was near her heart, and Esther made herself look down at him—
why, he's just like any baby, she thought, staring at the little face, his
eyes puffy and his head slightly misshapen from the birth. She had
feared she would see Buddy Eason staring back at her from that little
face. What she saw instead was her own son, someone who belonged

to her, and she felt a surge of protectiveness come over her at the thought.

"Hello, Andrew," she said, opening one of the little hands to see that it owned five fingers, then moving the blanket aside to look at the other, and to make certain he had ten toes as well. The color of his skin was lighter than her own, but not far different from Nathan's, and she found herself smiling and almost in tears as she touched the dimples indenting the wrists of his pudgy arms. "You're fat, just like your momma," she whispered, to herself as much as to the baby in her arms.

She heard the bedroom door open and she looked up to see Nathan enter the room. She wondered what he would say, wondered what he would think, when he looked into the little face.

He sat at the side of the bed, his eyes not leaving the child in Esther's arms.

At last he looked up at her. "You done real good," he said, genuine kindness in his eyes. "We got us a fine son."

∾

When Cassandra Price Eason went into labor, her husband, Buddy, was nowhere to be found. He had been gone for much of the previous two days, and had come home to his grandfather's house the evening before only long enough to take a bath and to change into a fresh suit.

"Where are you going?" Cassandra demanded, as he took up his hat from the bed and then started again for the door.

"Out. I've got a date."

"You can't go on a date! You're married!"

He snorted. "Married? You call this married?" His outright dismissal made her clench her hands in fury.

She tried to strike out at him, but he caught her wrist and shoved her out of his way. She landed against the dresser, the curved edge of wood catching her hip, leaving what she knew would be an ugly bruise by morning—how she hated him now as she watched him go out into the hallway. She followed him to the door and slammed it shut behind him, then screamed into the empty room, pounding a fist against the outer side of her own thigh in impotent rage. She would have killed him then if she could have killed him and gone back to the mill village, or to prison, or to any other place than the hell she had bought for herself here.

It was early the next morning when the pains began, and she knew somehow she had done it to herself—she had been pacing the floor for most of the night, so enraged with Buddy that she could not sleep. She was somewhat pleased at the commotion her early labor brought to the huge old house on Main Street—but all trace of pleasure left her as the contractions intensified and she really began to hurt.

She was in the hospital by then, driven by his grandfather.

Walter Eason left her alone so that he could go in search of Buddy.

She was still alone when they told her they would have to cut her belly open to get the baby out.

~

Walter Eason found his grandson's La Salle coupe parked in the driveway of the house that belonged to the county whore.

The woman who answered Walter's knock at the peeling front door was unfamiliar to him, but she looked much as he had expected: worn, with smeared lipstick and tousled hair, and she smelled already of liquor there at midmorning. She smiled at him and leaned against the doorjamb, the brightly colored wrap tied about her waist gapping open and causing Walter to turn away.

"Hi, ya, honey—don't tell me you can still get it up at your age," she said, an unpleasant, nasally tone in her voice that spoke of a life lived somewhere other than Alabama. She reached out to run a crimson-painted fingernail down the white cloth of his shirtfront, making him feel the shirt was now soiled. "I got somebody here right now, but—"

"I am looking for my grandson." Walter stepped away from her, not caring what she thought of him or anyone else.

"Is Buddy Eason your grandson?" A smile came into her voice though Walter was no longer looking at her. "Why he's—"

But Walter was already past her and into the house. He moved toward where he thought the bedroom might be, hearing her trail behind. Her voice had risen with indignation.

"Hey—you got no business coming in my house like that, Buddy's granddaddy or not. Hey—"

The bedroom was empty, but Walter could hear water running in what had to be the bathroom beyond. He opened the door to find Buddy sitting in the bathtub.

His grandson stared at him for a moment, then took hold of the sides of the tub and laboriously pushed himself to his feet. He stood naked and dripping as he stared at Walter. A smile came to his face. He reached down to touch himself below his sagging belly, that smile never wavering, but all Walter saw was a glaringly white body already gone to fat.

"You want something, old man?" Buddy asked, still touching himself. Walter could hear the woman just behind him now, a shrewish voice demanding that he leave, and he reached back to shut the door in her face without ever turning. All he could think about was the girl from the mill village Buddy had gotten into trouble, the girl who was in labor even now to give birth to his child, and the Negro woman he had raped who had delivered a son Buddy did not even know he had fathered. Buddy's member was rising, short and ludicrous beneath the rolls of fat on his belly. He was stepping out of the water now, that smile never leaving his face.

"Come on in here, Adele," Buddy called to the woman through the door. "I've got something just about ready for you," though his eyes never once left his grandfather.

His voice was quieter when he spoke again.

"Old man, you can stay and watch if you want."

Walter did not know what he was going to do until it was already done. He struck his grandson across the face with his walking stick, leaving an angry red welt against the white skin—then he was shoving him backwards, turning him and forcing him down as Buddy's feet went out from under him on the wet linoleum, to drive him headfirst into the tub of running water. Buddy's arms flailed, his feet, then his knees, sliding on the slick floor.

Walter knotted his hand in the thick hair at the back of Buddy's neck, taking a better hold only to push him down further, until he could feel Buddy's forehead slam against the enamel at the bottom of the tub. There was a wet sound, a drowning sound, a fight for life and air and desperation—he released Buddy suddenly and stood back, almost sliding himself. Buddy slung himself backwards and out of the tub, sending water everywhere, then drove himself back against the front of the facilities with his feet until they came out from under him again and he landed on the floor.

He was drawing in deep drafts of air, his eyes on Walter, a knot swelling now beneath his left eye and a reddening mark on his forehead. In that moment Walter did not know if he would find more regret in letting him live or in making him die.

"Your wife's in the hospital having your baby this morning," he said, staring at the fat mound of nakedness lying against the commode. "I thought you might want to know you're about to be a father."

~

It was a tiny, and very ugly, girl child who kept her much larger brother from being born. She had been in the wrong position, blocking the way—Walter did not understand what the doctor told them little more than an hour later when they reached the hospital, and he really did not care. Dr. Thrasher had delivered both children by Caesarean section, and he said even the smaller should survive, though Walter wondered how something so tiny and pinched-looking could be all right as he stared down at the baby girl in the nurse's arms.

A thin, fretful crying was coming from the female child, almost drowned out by the healthy wails of her twin brother in another nurse's arms—Rachel Elizabeth, Walter thought as he stared at the tiny girl, remembering the name told him by Cassandra weeks before. Well, let her name the child, he told himself; the ugly little thing looked just like her anyway.

The boy had reminded him at first look of Buddy shortly after his birth, and Walter already knew he would hold the same name— Walter Matthias, the same as his father, and his grandfather. And his great-grandfather before him.

There was a disruption behind Walter, where the other nurse had been allowing Buddy to see the boy child.

"No—Mr. Eason—really you shouldn't," she said now, and Walter could hear strain in her voice as well. He turned to see Buddy trying to take the child from her arms. "No, Mr. Eason, please—"

At last he managed to wrest the child from her, and then stood staring down at it as its wails increased and the nurse clenched her hands helplessly at her sides.

"I'm its father," he said at last, almost to himself, the glaring overhead lights making a stark contrast of the dark knot showing now beneath his left eye, turning the heavy face ugly with the words. "This one belongs to me."

# 5

IF ANYTHING IN THIS
world, Janson Sanders was dependable. Every Friday afternoon, at the
end of his shift in the cotton mill, he received his pay envelope for the
week's work. Every Friday afternoon he double-checked the figures
on the envelope, counted the money inside, verified the correct
amount had been taken out for rent on their half a mill house and for
the charge at McCallum's Grocery, then put it away into a pocket of
his dungarees or overalls for the walk home.

Janson reached his front porch by three on Friday afternoons; he
ate his dinner, held his wife, and then counted his money again with
Elise as they sat at the kitchen table. On Friday afternoons they
decided what would be needed for them to live on for the next week,
and then he added the remainder to the money he had hidden in a
cigar box in the back of a kitchen cabinet, for Janson Sanders no
longer trusted any bank after the bank failure that had taken their
savings in 1930.

Janson's Fridays were always the same, and had been the same
since they moved back to the village, and that is why, on an overcast
evening late in June of 1940, Elise Sanders was worried when he did
not come home.

By the time darkness began to fall, Elise was unable to take the
worry any longer. She left the three children to eat their suppers and
started toward the cotton mill, determined to make certain Janson
was okay.

The clay streets in the mill village were quiet. She could smell suppers cooking, and hear the distant sound of a radio playing from a house or two as she passed, the electric lights showing through the windows of the mill houses still odd to her after the years they had spent here before electricity was brought to the village. A dog barked, jerking at a chain in a yard as she neared, and she found herself wishing that she had not come alone. She had asked Ruth Shelby, who lived in the other side of the mill house, to listen for the children while she was gone. Henry had just turned twelve, and hardly considered himself in need of watching, but Catherine was only ten, and Judith eight. Henry had wanted to come with her, and his stubbornness reminded her so much of Janson as he stopped her in the doorway, with the same black hair and green eyes, and the coloring that had come from Janson's Cherokee mother.

"You can't go out walking by yourself after dark," he told her, as if he were the parent and she the child. He was as tall now as she, and it seemed so odd to Elise to meet her son on her own eye level, seeing pigheadedness within him that reminded her of herself at times.

He only said the same thing his father would say anyway—oh, she would give Janson Sanders a piece of her mind if he was working a double without having sent her word. He knew better than to make her worry for no reason. She could think of enough things to worry about on her own, without any help from Janson—Buddy Eason had threatened to kill him on more than one occasion, for one thing, and had tried to carry through with that threat just the year before. He had threatened to harm her and the girls as well, and that thought hurried her pace. Janson had kept a loaded shotgun in the house for her since they had moved back to the mill village, but it was locked into a chifforobe to which only Elise had a key.

She found Walter Eason getting into his car in the lot before the mill. He appeared surprised to see her. There was concern in his expression as he stared at her, his snow-white hair a stark contrast to the darkness around him, his gray eyes set on her face from below bristling white eyebrows that met over the bridge of his nose.

"Mrs. Sanders, you shouldn't be out by yourself after dark, and especially not here at the mill," he said, and she knew that he was also thinking of his grandson. It had been Walter Eason who had kept Buddy from killing Janson that year before, and who had afterward stood by and allowed Janson to administer a beating that Buddy had earned long before.

"I'm looking for Janson. Is he working a double?—he didn't send me word. If he did, no one told me."

Her worry was so obvious that even deeper concern came immediately to Walter Eason's face—but Janson was working no double, she learned, after Mr. Eason accompanied her into the mill, and Stan, who had been given a job sweeping on the second shift after the loss of his arm, had no idea where Janson was either. Elise left the mill filled with worry, refusing the ride home that Walter Eason offered her, and that he had insisted she take.

When she reached the bottom of her own street she found a strange truck parked on the street before her house, and she started to run. A man was getting out of the vehicle, and it took her a moment to realize it was Janson. He held a box in his hands, which she almost knocked away in her rush to touch him.

"Where have you been?—I was so worried—" she said, looking up at him, clenching both his shirt sleeves in her hands. She was almost crying now from relief.

"I didn't think it would take s' long. Mr. Fluellen offered to give me a ride, an' there was groceries to deliver on th' way. We got th' truck stuck in th' mud over on th' other side of town, an' I thought we'd never get it unstuck—be careful, Elise, you're gonna make me drop it—" he said, interrupting himself.

The man behind the wheel reached across the seat to close the door after Janson, waving politely to her as the truck started away. Elise recognized the truck at last, and the man to be Bob Fluellen, who ran Fluellen's Grocery downtown.

She looked up at Janson, still not understanding.

"I bought you a radio, Elise. I always swore I would."

She was crying in earnest now, seeing at last what was in the box he held in his hands. He had worried her to death to bring her a radio, and that extravagance when all he usually did was save money made her cry all the harder—he had sworn he would when times were better, had sworn it to her so many times during the years they had done without.

"Elise, you shouldn't be out walkin' by yourself after dark," he said at last, his face filled with concern.

In the midst of the crying she could not help but to laugh.

He had said just exactly what she had known he would.

∽

War was going on in Europe, but it seemed very far away.

There had been problems in Europe and Asia for years—first Germany and Austria, Italy and Ethiopia, Hitler and the Sudetenland, Mussolini and Albania, Japan and China. The past fall, Germany had invaded Poland, and Britain had declared war on Germany; since then, the talk of war seemed to be everywhere. By the time school let out that summer, most everyone was saying that the United States would be in the fight before the next term began, but Henry Sanders did not believe it. Europe was an ocean away on the maps at school, and America was so nice and safe on the other side of that expanse of blue.

The summer of 1940 was proving to be a good one for Henry. People at last had a little extra money in their pockets, money they could use to hire a boy to do odd jobs about the village and town, money he could save to go to the picture show, or to buy the occasional candy or sweets when his mother did not catch him, or even to bribe his sisters to do his chores at home.

On Thursday, July 4th of that year, Henry got up early, even though he had developed the habit of sleeping late while summer was on. A family had moved into the three-room shotgun house across the street a few days before, a house that had been empty since Henry and his family had moved back into the mill village the previous October. Henry had been eager to go over and introduce himself, hoping they might have work he could do to earn enough money to go to the picture show on Saturday. People just moving in were always good for some bit of work or another, if they had money, but, as usual, his mother would not let him "bother" the new family until they at least had the chance to settle in.

Henry figured that two days was enough settling in time for anyone. Besides, he told himself, the man he had seen across the street would be of little help in getting his house in order. His hair was mostly white, which meant that he had to be old, maybe too old to move furniture or to help hang curtains.

The man's wife was sweeping her front porch when Henry crossed the street. She was short and plump, with curly brown hair and an apron with ruffles around the sides and bottom.

She did not acknowledge Henry's presence as he walked up her front steps, so he said, "Ma'am?" then was sorry he had spoken as she jumped at least two inches at the sound of his voice. She looked younger up close than she had from across the street, and he decided she had to be the mother of the girl he had seen at a distance, instead of her grandmother, as he had originally thought.

"Oh, Lord, you gave me a fright!" she said, smiling now though she had one hand clutched tight to her bosom.

"I'm sorry. I just wondered if you might have some work for me. I could clear a garden spot for you, plant it if you like, move stuff around, whatever you need—my name's Henry Sanders; I live over there," he said, motioning with one hand back to their house across the street where it sat on its stacked stone pillars.

"Mrs. Morgan," she said in introduction, smiling again as she nodded her head, and Henry decided he liked her, even if she was jumpy.

"Anything that needs doing, I can help you with," he said, not wanting to let her get off the subject.

"I'll have to ask my husband, but I'm sure there's something you can do—come to think of it, I know there is," she said, and turned and opened the screen door. "There's something I need help moving. Lewis says he's too tired when he gets in. Jimmy—that's Lewis's son, my step-son—said he would come move it, but he hasn't yet."

She led him inside and through the front and middle rooms of the house and to the kitchen as she talked.

"My daughter and I tried, but it's too heavy for us to move it by ourselves—oh, this is my daughter, Olivia. Olivia, this is—oh, I've forgotten your name—"she said, turning, the hand clutched to her bosom again as she stared at Henry.

"Henry Sanders," Henry said, looking past her and to the girl sitting at the eating table with a book open on the wooden surface before her. The girl was about his age, with brown hair that she pushed behind her ears as she stared up at him.

"Henry's going to help us move the big chifforobe in the front room," Mrs. Morgan said, but Henry hardly paid attention to her. He smiled, and the girl smiled in return.

He helped to move the chifforobe, then stood on a chair to hang curtains over the tall windows in the kitchen. Olivia helped with the curtains, which he found made it very difficult to think about it what he was supposed to be doing.

When the work was finished, it never once occurred to him to ask to be paid.

~

As 1940 drew toward a close, it seemed clear that the world was changing. Business was picking up, and there were more people at work than there had been in many years, throughout all the Depression, but the growing prosperity had come at a harsh price. News of the war in Europe sat heavily within everyone. October had seen the first peacetime draft ever, and most people were saying now that it was only a matter of time before the United States would become involved in the war.

There were more hours available at the mill for Janson and Stan both, bringing extra money home to the family, and Elise supplemented their income even more with additional sewing she was taking in. Times were getting better in Eason County. There were jobs to be had, and more opened up as the months passed. Social Security monthly payments had begun during the year, bringing needed money to many older people who had before been dependent on their children, or on the kindness and charity of relatives or friends just for survival. Elise heard the critics of Social Security, but she also heard so many others who understood—the payments had brought back some measure of dignity to so many people, dignity that old age and hard times had taken from them.

President Roosevelt was entering an unprecedented third term, after a battle at the polls with Republican Wendell Wilkie, and the country was settling in for another four years under FDR—if only they could stay out of the war.

Empty houses in the village filled again as the months of 1941 passed and the mill took on a third shift for the first time since the early years of the Depression. Mill hands had been worked hard in the past months, Walter Eason trying to avoid taking on new workers even though an increase in business had seemed to demand it. Like so many others, he knew how easily prosperity could turn to disaster, but at last the workers were taken on, and life in the village seemed again much as it had been in the years before the Crash in 1929—but Elise knew there were some things that would never be the same. Electricity now lighted their rooms, where kerosene lamps had had been the only light they had known years before. Electricity had allowed them the radio with its music and programs, its news reports, and the seemingly constant news of the war in Europe and the activity of Japan.

War filled the news broadcasts, glared at her from the headlines of newspapers, and filled the newsreels that were shown before the few picture shows Elise saw. War seemed to be all that anyone could talk about, and Elise could do nothing but pray—please don't let it come. Please—things are so much better now. Please—

The years of sharecropping were left far behind them, the years of worrying whether they would be able to feed the children through the winter, the years of threadbare clothes and freezing feet in the cold months were all gone. They had money hidden in that cigar box in the kitchen. They had food. They had decent clothes and shoes on their feet. There would be a good Christmas this year, and they had money to face hardship if it came again—and there was Janson's dream of regaining his land.

On the first Sunday afternoon in December, Elise entered the kitchen to find Janson at the table, the cigar box open before him. Judith was at a friend's house for the afternoon, and Catherine at church to practice for the Christmas play. Henry was across the street with Olivia, where he seemed to be now most of the time, so she and Janson were alone, which Elise realized they were so very rarely.

Janson smiled up at her, looking almost embarrassed at having been caught in his frequent counting of their savings.

"Do you think it grows when you're not looking?" she asked, sitting down beside him on the bench.

He ignored her words, and said instead, "In a couple more years, we might have enough t' see about buyin' th' land, even if we have t' take out a mortgage." He looked happier than she had seen him in years, and she knew he had to feel hopeful about the future to even consider taking out a mortgage for the farm he had lost so many years before. He hated credit. It was what had taken the land from him in the first place.

"Do you think the man who owns it now will sell?"

"He will—I swear we ain't gonna get this close an' him not sell t' us. He don't farm it all, an' there's a tenant in th' house—I think he'll sell it. He has t'." He smiled and closed the cigar box, then ran his fingers over the top of it. "In a few years we could be on th' land, Elise, ready t' get a crop in th' spring of '45, or maybe even '44 if times stay good."

He looked so determined, so happy, and she loved him so much. After all the years of work, of struggle, of doing without, after the

Depression and the years of sharecropping—it was so close, his dream, what had kept him fighting through all that time.

She smiled and reached out to touch his hand, but stopped as the front door slammed open. Henry was yelling, "Pa!" as he ran through the rooms, sending doors crashing back against walls and upsetting the rocker in the middle room as he ran past it.

He burst into the kitchen, his black hair in disarray, his young face a mixture of shock, disbelief, and excitement.

"Have you heard?—it was on the radio at Olivia's. The Japs just bombed us, someplace called Pearl Harbor, in Hawaii!" he panted, looking from one face to the other.

Elise stared at him for a moment, then felt Janson's hand close tightly over hers.

They had known it was coming.

The United States would have to enter the war.

# PART TWO

~ 1941 ~

# 6

*Y*ESTERDAY, DECEMBER 7TH,
*1941—a date which will live in infamy—the United States of America
was suddenly and deliberately attacked by naval and air forces of the
Empire of Japan . . ."*

Hardly anyone was moving about the streets of Eason County that
Monday morning. The quiet Alabama day seemed a haven, a stark
contrast to the hell and destruction that had been visited upon Pearl
Harbor, Hawaii. Throughout the mill village, people were gathered
around radios, listening to the voice of President Roosevelt, of the
man who had seen them through the years of the Depression, and
who would now see them through these trials.

*"It will be recorded that the distance of Hawaii from Japan makes it
obvious that the attack was deliberately planned many days or even weeks
ago . . ."*

Elise sat in her favorite rocker in the front room of her home, her
eyes, as were the eyes of everyone else in the room, on the radio resting
on the table nearby. Janson leaned against a wall only a few feet away,
his arms crossed. Catherine was at Elise's feet on a stool, Henry sitting
on the edge of the old sofa. Elise's friend, Dorrie Keith, and Dorrie's
husband, Clarence, were beside him. Their sons, Steven and Jerry,
both young men now, stood nearby; their older brother, Wheeler
James, was stationed on a ship in the Pacific, and no word had been
heard from him since the attack. His mother sat now worried, as did

Lynette Pierce, the girl Wheeler James had asked to marry him only days before shipping out.

*"The attack yesterday on the Hawaiian islands has caused severe damage to American naval and military forces. I regret to tell you that very many American lives have been lost. In addition, American ships have been reported torpedoed on the high seas between San Francisco and Honolulu . . ."*

Lynette turned away, fighting back tears, and Elise saw Dorrie pat her hand. When Elise looked toward Janson again she saw a muscle twitch in his jaw, but his green eyes never left the radio. At her feet, Judith scooted closer on the braided rug—the girl had wakened the household screaming during the previous night. She had dreamed the Japanese were bombing the village and that the mill houses were on fire. For the first time in her children's lives, Elise had not known how to comfort one of them, but had spent the remainder of the night in her own dreams, had seen the mill burning, and planes flying overhead, planes that had red suns painted on the undersides of their wings.

*"As commander and chief of the Army and Navy, I have directed that all measures be taken for our defense. But always will our whole nation remember the character of the onslaught against us."*

Applause began, gradual but building. Elise saw Stan turn his eyes to the fire in the fireplace near where he stood, his brows lowered and his face angry. Janson's cousin, Sissy, sitting in a chair alongside the couch, looked up to where her husband, Tim, stood beside her, their two-year-old daughter, Nora, in his arms. Tim touched her shoulder lightly and gave her a nod, and a smile that Elise knew was meant to be reassuring.

*"No matter how long it may take us to overcome this premeditated invasion, the American people in their righteous might will win through to absolute victory."* There was sudden applause, loud and deafening, interlaced with shouts of assent. Elise's eyes moved to Janson for a moment, then back to the radio.

She could hardly see through her tears.

"*. . . With confidence in our armed forces, with the unbounding determination of our people, we will gain the inevitable triumph, so help us God.*" Again applause halted the President's words, immediate and prolonged. Lynette cried openly now, and Dorrie got up from the sofa and moved to pat the girl's back comfortingly. No word was spoken in the front room of the mill house, just the sound of FDR's voice over the radio as the applause ended and he resumed, and the words came, words they had all been expecting.

"*I ask that the Congress declare that since the unprovoked and dastardly attack by Japan on Sunday, December 7th, 1941, a state of war has existed between the United States and the Japanese Empire.*"

Janson reached to turn off the radio, ending the applause that greeted the President's words. Silence fell in the room but for the sound of the girl's crying and the popping of logs in the fireplace. Then Judith's voice came, sounding so young and very frightened.

"Are the Japs gonna bomb here, Mama?" It was the same question the girl had asked time and again since she had learned of the attack. There was honest fright in her eyes, fright that Elise felt as well, though not for the same reasons.

"No, they won't bomb here. Don't you worry about that."

"I'm gonna sign up tomorrow," Jerry Keith was saying, his expression filled with rage.

"No, you're not, not yet. You're ma's got enough t' worry about already," his father said, staring at him from the sofa. "With Pete gettin' called off furlough because of the bombin', an' Wheeler James—" His words trailed off, his eyes going to the floor.

"Damn Japs," the young man growled, and his brother Steven put his hand on his shoulder.

Stan had been staring at the stump of his right arm. There was anger and rage on his face as there had been in Jerry Keith's voice. After a moment he drove the end of the stump hard against the mantel. Pain showed in his features as he gripped what was left of the arm and turned away.

Elise stared at him for a moment, thinking she should go to him, thinking she should do something, but her eyes touched on Janson instead—he stood just as he had minutes before when the President's speech ended. A muscle worked in his jaw, his eyes remaining on the now-silent box.

At last he lifted his gaze to her, and Elise caught her breath—there was in his expression something she had seen on the faces of Jerry Keith and Stan.

She thanked God that at thirty-four he was too old to be drafted. She could only pray that he was beyond the age to volunteer as well.

∼

The telegram came within days, and Dorrie's hands were shaking so badly that she could hardly read it. Elise watched her friend's face, seeing the fear that had lived there for days turn to horror. Wheeler James Keith, the bright, intelligent boy who had at one time wanted nothing more in the world than to be allowed to finish school, would not be coming home.

In the days that came, Elise knew there were many such telegrams: *"The Secretary of War desires to express his deep regret that . . ."*

Just weeks before Christmas, and the entire world was changed. Four days after FDR's speech, war was declared on Japan. On December 11th, Germany and Italy declared war on the United States. Only two years before, the country had been operating under a neutrality law, but now we were in the war, and in it for the duration.

The Christmas season took on a hard, forced cheerfulness as families said good-bye to young men they knew they might never see again. Couples rushed to be married before soldiers could ship out, and Elise knew that some women wed near-strangers in the heated rush—it was the boys' duty to fight, they seemed to think, and the girls' duty to give them something to come home to.

The economy took an upsurge as businessmen and ordinary people alike began to stockpile items they believed the war would leave in short supply. The government placed huge orders, and suddenly there was work for anyone who sought it, especially as jobs were vacated by men departing for the war.

War—it was now everywhere. Elise knew few families who were not touched in some way. In the front windows of so many homes hung banners with blue stars, one for every brother, son, or husband taken in the draft or who had volunteered—and, as the months passed, far too many of those blue stars were replaced with gold, as men from Eason County lost their lives.

Everyone wanted to do their part. Conservation was the order of the day, conservation of food, of resources, of whatever it seemed the military might need. Rubber tires were rationed. New wool blankets were unavailable at home so the boys could have warm uniforms and blankets overseas. Scrap drives were held for raw material needed in the war effort. Paper, old pots and pans, unused iron bed frames, rags, old clothing—everything was being collected to help in the war. Wartime production was getting into full swing; people were making money; the Depression was finally ended—but goods were scarce, and what was available seemed to rise in price almost every day. There were shortages of food items as people hoarded anything they thought might become scarce. Prices spiraled so badly that by late April the cost of living had increased by fifteen percent over the days before the war.

In mid-April, Elise heard that the President had sent a plan to Congress for handling the problems of the war economy. They said FDR wanted heavier income taxes, a limit on incomes, wages to be stabilized, and more drastic rationing to take place, as well as a reduction in farm prices, and curbs on the use of credit. The Office of Price Administration set price ceilings on many items at March levels, but few people complained—there was a war going on, they all seemed to say, at least outwardly, *and we all have to pull together if we are going to win it.*

Rationing had begun. Before the war most sugar had been imported; now it was in short supply, not only because of the amounts needed to feed the people at home and the men fighting overseas, but also because it was needed in the manufacture of explosives. On April 27th the sales of sugar ceased. On May 4th, registration began in schoolhouses the country over for rationing coupons, and the following day sales of sugar resumed to those who had received War Ration Book One from the Office of Price Administration. Each person was allowed a half pound of sugar per week, but few people seemed to think that was enough. Elise was certain she knew quite a number of people who had lied when asked how much sugar they had on hand when they were issued their ration books. Elise had told the truth, and had had that amount in stamps torn from the ration book she was given. Now, as she drank bitter, unsweetened coffee—in the rare times she could get it—or had to scrimp and save her sugar rations to make a small treat for the children, she found herself thoroughly hating those who had lied and who were hoarding now, just as she hated all those she suspected were buying sugar in the black market that had sprung into life as soon as rationing began.

It was not long before even what Janson called "long sweetening" could hardly be found. Syrup was bought up, and even sorghum and molasses. In so many ways there was a sense of pulling together in the County, of everyone working to try to help in the war effort, that Elise could not help feeling guilty as she drank her unsweetened coffee and prayed the equivalent of an Old Testament pestilence of ants to infest the sugar of all those who were hoarding—but she knew she was not the only one to complain; there suddenly seemed to be complainers in every walk of life. Farmers did not want a reduction of farm prices; storekeepers did not want price ceilings; labor did not want wages frozen; most ordinary citizens thought price fixing was not drastic enough; and no one wanted rationing—but they were doing it for the war effort, and winning the war was what was important to almost everyone.

To Elise, it was not just winning the war, and it was not just ridding Judith of the nightmares of the mill village being bombed, nightmares that blackout curtains and time had only worsened, it was getting it all over with before things could get bad enough for Janson to be called. He had had to register with the Selective Service near the end of 1940, but, being over the age of twenty-seven, and being a father, had kept him out of it thus far—but what if it kept going? she found herself wondering as she lay awake almost every night. Men between the ages of forty-five and sixty-four had already been required to register with the Selective Service at the end of April, in the fourth national Selective Service registration—if men that age were now required to register, how much longer would it be before fathers Janson's age lost the III-A classification that kept them from being inducted?

Even worse was the thought that came into her mind when she looked at her tall son as he turned fourteen on the next to the last Saturday in June that year—what if it kept going long enough to take Henry.

～

Dorrie Keith slowly cleared the kitchen table on a Friday afternoon in early fall of that year, placing upturned plates on top of bowls of vegetables and putting them away in the refrigerator. She had cooked too much. She always cooked too much these days, with no one but her and Clarence in the house. All of her boys were gone now, Wheeler James lost at Pearl Harbor, Pete and Steven both in the Army, and Jerry volunteered for the Navy. All her boys gone, and the house was so unbelievably empty.

Clarence came into the room and kissed her cheek. "What're you gonna do with all them vegetables?" he asked.

Dorrie sighed. "I was thinkin' I'd carry th' squash t' Lynette, an' maybe th' beans t' Elise an' Janson."

He nodded and began to pull on his jacket.

"You goin' t' th' civil defense meetin'?"

"Yeah, I'll be home soon as it's over."

He kissed her cheek again and headed out of the room. She

watched him go, hearing the screen door slam shut behind him as he left the house, then she turned back to her clearing of the table, forcing the worry from her mind. Clarence had had to register with the Selective Service at the end of April, along with all the other men his age and older, men who ought to be thinking about grandchildren and old age, and not being called to fight in a war. It did not matter that the government said men his age would never be called into combat—she had already lost one son in service to her country, had three more in the service. She was terrified now they would take her husband as well.

She finished putting the food away in the refrigerator and closed the door, then stood staring at it. She had wanted an electric refrigerator so badly, and Clarence had finally bought one for her no more than weeks before war broke out, replacing the old icebox she had used since she and Clarence first married—but now she missed that old icebox, with its handles worn smooth from children's hands. She missed the daily visits of the iceman who now passed by their house in his truck. She could remember how in the summer when the boys were little, they would run out to the ice wagon as soon as it was on their street, to get chips of the ice as a treat from the iceman. Wheeler James had usually been the first one there, leaving the shade of the front porch of the mill house with his finger in a book to mark his place. Wheeler James had never gone anywhere without a book. He had never—

Wheeler James—

She choked back tears and turned away from the refrigerator. Her first-born son was dead now, and there was nothing she could do to bring him back.

What else could be asked of her in the war effort? She had already given what was dearest to her heart.

The house was so silent without the sound of boys' voices as she moved from the kitchen into the middle room of the house. She had found herself wishing lately she were young enough to have another baby, several babies. But they would probably be boys and a war would come along and take them as well. She was glad she would never have a girl. Men could go off and fight wars, but women were left behind to put back together the pieces of whatever world they had shattered at the time. Women were left to clean up the mess.

And to bury them too often.

Dorrie was afraid now she might never have grandchildren. All four of her sons had left sweethearts at home, Wheeler James a fiancé. If he had only married Lynette before he shipped out, then there might have been a grandchild. He had felt the war would come, and had not wanted to leave a widow and family behind, and so they had not married—but he had left them behind anyway. A grandchild would have meant so much to her and Clarence, and it would have been a comfort to Lynette. As it was, there was nothing left to them of Wheeler James but memories.

Dorrie moved slowly through the middle room and into the front one in their half of the mill house, too tired to sit still, and too tired to work. She had pulled down doubles every day this week until the overseer had sent her home, telling her to rest—but she could not rest, any more than could any woman in the village who had sent even one son off to the war.

She sighed and went out on the porch in the cool, early darkness, then sat in a rocker to watch people move about on the street as she set the chair in motion slowly back and forth. She was soon chilled, but she could not make herself get up to go back into the house for a sweater.

Children ran and played in a yard across the way.

Young girls walked arm-in-arm down the road.

A young man passed in uniform, and she watched him until he left her sight.

On the window behind her was all that was left to her of her sons, a flag bearing stars. Three blue, one each for Pete, Steven, and Jerry, and a gold one that stood in the place of Wheeler James.

⌁

"That's outrageous!" Helene Price said on an afternoon in February of 1943 as she stood in the living room of her daughter's home, staring into the arrogant face of her son-in-law.

"That's the price for sugar without ration stamps; take it or leave it," Buddy Eason said, returning her stare.

Helene looked to where her daughter sat on the nearby sofa applying red nail polish to her fingernails, but Cassandra did not even acknowledge her presence. Helene had bragged openly only that morning in Fluellen's Grocery—after all, she could not shop in McCallum's in the village any longer, not now that she was Buddy Eason's mother-in-law—that she could get whatever she wanted, rationing or not, shortages or not, war or not. And she could—she only had to pay the price, just as did everyone else. Since the war began, she had had to do without few things. The money she could extract from her husband—even when Bert said they could not afford it—along with the connections she had through her daughter's marriage to Buddy, had allowed her to buy sugar without rationing stamps, meats when grocers told others that they were unavailable, butter, cigarettes—it just took money.

Helene bragged to anyone who would listen of how wise she had been to store a supply of things she had believed would become shortened or unavailable—and it was not hoarding, she told herself. It was only being smart, looking after yourself because no one else would look after you. She had told no few people that her son-in-law could get her anything she wanted, and that Buddy was happy enough to do it for her—she just did not tell anyone that he did not do it out of respect for her and love for her daughter, as he should, but because Helene paid him, just as did everyone else.

"You didn't charge me that much two weeks ago."

"Prices are going up, haven't you heard?—and the OPA can't put price ceilings on the black market." He smirked at her—he actually smirked, she was certain of it—one side of his mouth rising in a tight, little half-smile that made her furious.

"Well, I won't pay it!"

"Suits me fine."

He turned away, shrugging in an off-hand manner, as if her clear stand on common principle did not matter to him.

"If you don't want to pay the price, other people will."

And they would. For all the self-righteous patter that everyone spread about so freely, Helene was certain that almost everyone dealt in the black market at one time or another. There was only so much sugar one could buy with ration stamps, only so much gasoline allowed with the ration sticker each person had been issued, only so much meat available because of scarcity, and Helene knew that even the black market had its limits—but Buddy was being ridiculous. He was profiteering off of a family member, off of his own wife's mother, the grandmother to his children, a woman who he should—

But Helene had to have the sugar. She had begun to attend First Baptist on Main Street shortly after Cassandra married Buddy—after all, she was Buddy Eason's mother-in-law now, and she could not be expected to continue to attend church in the mill village as if she were nobody. A number of ladies from First Baptist and First Methodist were supposed to come to her house the following day to discuss plans for a paper drive. It had taken Helene weeks to get herself placed in charge of the drive, and days more to get the women to agree to come to her home in the village—why Bert insisted on living there now was beyond all good reason, Helene told herself, and she wondered sometimes if he did not keep them there just because he knew it annoyed her. It was no different from his having refused to attend church with her uptown. She always had to face the First Baptist women alone on Sundays, just her against their ranks, for Bert had never once gone with her. He continued to attend the little church in the mill village, and called her "uppity" for her choice of First Baptist. Cassandra and Buddy did not attend any church—although Helene knew she had raised Cassandra better than that—and the twins went to First Methodist with old Mr. Walter, his frail wife, Patricia, and that great cow of a woman who was Buddy's widowed mother.

They were all against her; Helene was certain of it, but she would show each and every one of them. She would make a cake the likes of nothing those First Baptist and First Methodist women had seen anytime recently. She would serve them real coffee in her best cups, and give them ready-made cigarettes to smoke, luxuries they could find nowhere else with the war going on. They would see she was indeed a woman to be respected.

Buddy was turning away, dismissing her completely, as if she were no longer even in the room.

"Oh—all right, I'll pay it, and I need cigarettes, and coffee, too," she said, opening her purse to take out her week's allocation of grocery money. Bert would be furious, but she would not worry about that now. She counted out the amount she was told and handed it to Buddy, watching as the smirk returned to his face. Then he left her alone with Cassandra as he went to fetch her purchases from wherever it was he kept goods stored there in the huge house his grandfather had at last moved him and Cassandra into not long after Wally and Rachel were born. Helene wished she could take the time to see the twins before she left, but she knew they would only muss her hair and dress, and there were other errands she had to run to get ready for the First Baptist women before tomorrow.

The children were probably with their nurse, Georgia, anyway, for Cassandra spent very little time with them. They were practically being raised by that Negro woman, Helene told herself, and she had meant to speak to Cassandra about it. Helene had at least taken the time to raise her own daughter herself.

She tapped her foot impatiently as she waited for Buddy's return, and turned her eyes to Cassandra. The younger woman was blowing on her newly painted nails—red as a hussy's, Helene told herself. Cassandra would never have dared to paint them that color when she had lived in her mother's house, or to wear all that makeup, or such a tight dress. One of her eyes was noticeably black even through the makeup—she'd never keep Buddy happy if she couldn't learn to be a better wife and mother, Helene told herself.

"Cassandra, you ought to look at yourself in the mirror. I've always told you—"

"Mind your own fucking business," her daughter said, glancing at her only briefly.

"Cassandra Marie Price, don't you ever talk to me like that again! If I ever—"

"You're in my house; you can't tell me—"

"Shut up," Buddy said, entering the room. He had not even glanced at Cassandra, but she immediately fell silent, though there was an obvious look of anger on her face as she turned her eyes to him. He handed the sack of sugar to Helene, along with the cigarettes and coffee, then watched as she shoved them down into the box she had brought for that purpose, covering them with crumpled brown paper she had brought as well.

The look on his face annoyed Helene—he thinks I'm just like the rest of them, she told herself. She was not like the other people who bought on the black market, and she knew it. They were all selfish, trying to get more than they had any right to—but Helene was not like that. She had no selfish motives behind the cake she would make from the sugar she was buying today; she had no selfish motives behind the coffee and cigarettes she would offer the First Baptist and First Methodist women as they planned the paper drive. Helene had only the best intentions, she told herself—and, really, when you came right down to it, what she was doing was for the war effort anyway.

Oh, but wait until they see the cake I'll make, she thought as she left her daughter's house that afternoon with her black market goods safely hidden from sight. Just wait.

～

It was not long into the following afternoon when Helene Price realized that things were not going at all as she had intended. The women from uptown sat in her living room, speaking to her rarely, their hands busy knitting socks or baby booties, or sitting quietly in their laps, leaving her lovely cake virtually untouched. The fine coffee she had made, coffee that was so hard to come by, set cooling in cups, her scarce, ready-made cigarettes remaining unsmoked on the coffeetable.

There was a two-year-old roaming around the edges of the room, handling and dropping each whatnot she had placed out on display, causing Helene to have to go after him again and again to rescue a treasure. Already he had forced one pudgy hand into the side of her cake, leaving a huge imprint there, almost pushing it, plate and all, from the table—the horrid mother had only tugged him away, had told him "mustn't touch," but had not offered one word in apology. The child had licked the icing from his hand, then quite purposefully, Helene was sure, smeared his messy prints all over the insides of her front windows—Helene would be cleaning up after him all afternoon, she told herself, but at least Bert would have to realize that he would have no choice but to hire some help for her now that she would be entertaining regularly.

There was another child as well, the two-year-old's elder brother, Helene believed, though no one had laid claim to him, for reasons Helene could clearly understand. He stood near Helene's chair almost all afternoon, picking his nose only to occasionally examine his find, staring at her and asking questions.

"How old are you?" he asked once, though Helene did not answer him. He rubbed the toe of one shoe repeatedly into a spot in the rug, until she thought he would leave a thin place there before he was finished with it.

"I bet you're old," he said a little later, moving closer to her as he examined her face, one hand resting on the skirt covering her lap. He leaned in, pointing with a finger only recently removed from his nasal cavity, to the skin alongside one of her eyes, once actually drawing a line from the edge of her vision and up into her hairline.

"You got lines by your eyes that looks like bird's feet."

The twisting of the toe of his shoe into her good rug resumed and he studied her even more closely. Helene made a face when she was certain no one would notice, but even that did little good.

She turned her attention instead and tried to follow the conversation around her, bending forward with the intention of cutting another piece of cake.

"Why are you so fat?" the boy asked, leaning now on the arm of her chair, one finger up his nostril again as he stared at her face.

His little brother—if that was who the other miscreant was—sent a lamp crashing to the floor, but none of the ladies bothered to right it. Helene stared at him, until Annabelle Fitzgerald—eighty years old if she was a day—dragged her attention away. The woman took a pipe from her handbag, filled it with tobacco, then lighted it. Helene rose quickly to offer her the tray of ready-made cigarettes, bending completely across the coffeetable to do so, holding them out as she thought a proper hostess ought to present them.

"Thank you, but no," the old woman said, clenching the pipestem between her teeth in the midst of the wrinkled face, her lips sinking into a pucker as she puffed. She stared at Helene for a long moment, and Helene wondered if she would ever look away—she's as mad as a hatter, Helene told herself, thinking she would rather be dead than to live long enough to become an embarrassment to those around her.

She offered to make another pot of coffee, said she had another brand of cigarettes, and tried even to offer cake to the nose-picker, though his mother would not allow him to take it.

"Won't you have a slice of my cake?" she said again, talking now to no one in particular. She took the knife up to cut a piece from her lovely creation. Already several slices set on plates there on the coffeetable, and not one of them had been touched. "It really is a lovely cake. I worked all morning to—"

"Thank you, but no," Frances Garrett said, sitting so stiffly in her chair that she never once came to rest against the seat back. Mrs. Garrett was one of the most influential women in the church, a cousin to Walter Eason—by rights she and Helene were related now, at least by marriage—and still she could not support Helene even in this one little thing. All she had wanted was to have a lovely party. All she had wanted was to give them a nice place to discuss the paper drive, and they could not even—

She sat down on the sofa, took up her coffee cup to take a sip, then immediately set it down so hard onto its saucer that it clattered loudly, sloshing its contents out over a lace doily on the table.

"Is there something wrong with the refreshments?" she demanded. "None of you have taken even one bite of the cake I baked for you, and you've let your coffee sit until it's stone cold. You won't even have my cigarettes. I went out of my way to invite you over here, fixed refreshments for you, had a lovely cake and real coffee—something I'm sure you couldn't get anywhere else—and you won't touch one bit of it. Do you all think you're too good to accept my hospitality after I worked so hard to have a nice party for you?"

Frances Garrett had looked ready to explode with indignation at Helene's words, but it was Alice Talbot, seventeen years old and with a fiancé in the Navy, who had spoken. She sat on the edge of her chair, her hands clenched tightly in her lap.

"I wouldn't eat a cake made with black market sugar if Eleanor Roosevelt herself served it to me in the White House! Don't you think we know you didn't make the cake with sugar you got with ration stamps, and the coffee and the cigarettes, you didn't come by those honestly, either. Did you really think we'd eat your cake and drink your coffee and smoke your cigarettes when we know that what you got on the black market might have been something needed to help in the war effort? It's people like you and your selfishness that make things only harder on our boys."

Mrs. Garrett reached over to pat the girl's clenched hands, whether out of an approval of her words, or in an effort to calm her down, Helene could not tell, and at the moment she did not care.

"Well, if you feel that way, young lady, then you can just leave! There is absolutely no excuse in this world for being rude! I tried to be a good hostess, tried to give you something you couldn't have anywhere else, and look at the thanks I get. You can just leave my house this minute if you feel that way, and that goes for any of the rest of you that feels the same." She expected an apology, expected a look of embarrassment on more than one face because of the girl's outrageous behavior, but before her astonished eyes every woman in the room rose almost as one.

They gathered their knitting, their handbags, the bothersome two-year-old and the nose-picker, and left the room one after the other, until she was left alone with her ready-made cigarettes, her fine, real coffee, and her lovely, uneaten, cake.

# 7

GODDAMN IT—YOU BETTER keep me out of it!" Buddy Eason shouted as he paced back and forth in his grandfather's office the afternoon he learned that fathers would no longer be excluded from the military draft. The flab on his cheeks vibrated with every step.

"I'm not going over there to let some damn Kraut put a bullet into me!"

Walter Eason sat behind his desk, his fingers steepled before him as he listened to Buddy's latest tirade. The first was when the draft was instituted and he had to register. The second came when the upper age range for induction was raised to include men his age. Since then, Walter knew his grandson should be thanking his good fortunes daily that he had impregnated Cassandra Price and produced the twins, for Wally and Rachel had been enough in themselves to keep their father out of the military.

It was hard for Walter to admit his grandson was a coward, but, after all, Buddy had been a disappointment in every other way. He had proven himself a failure as a son, as a grandson, and as a husband and father. He was a failure as a man as well.

It had taken all Walter's control to keep Buddy from refusing to register or registering as a conscientious objector in the first place. Buddy had said he would rather go to camp, or even to prison, than go into the military. He had already done more than his grandfather had ever thought possible to destroy the Eason name, but displaying his cowardice so openly was one thing that Walter would not allow. There were Walter's great-grandchildren and their future to think about.

"You haven't been drafted yet," Walter said, staring at Buddy. He knew it would not be difficult to keep Buddy out of the military. The mill was, after all, producing materials essential to the war effort. Buddy could easily be classified as II-A, doing critical civilian work, although Walter knew the only work his grandson did was to show up at the mill office in the mornings. Buddy was blinded to his own luck, blinded by cowardice and total self-concern, and Walter was in no mood to salve his fears.

"Goddamn it—I mean it, old man, you better keep me out of it!"

Sweat beaded over his upper lip and across his forehead, one of the few times Buddy ever broke a sweat, for Walter was certain he had never broken one doing any work. He leaned across Walter's desk, staring at the old man with what Walter knew was meant to be a threat, and Walter had the momentary and almost irresistible temptation to see to it that Buddy did not receive the II-A classification. The military could do Buddy a world of good, Walter thought. Away from here, away from the influence of the Eason name, where he would have to at last stand or fall on his own, where he would have to face discipline and men with more power than he had, Buddy Eason might at last become a man.

But Walter could not risk the life of his only grandson.

He had already buried two sons.

He would not now bury his grandson as well.

Walter sat behind his desk and stared at Buddy, listening as Buddy cursed the Japanese, as he cursed the Germans, as he cursed the government. And God as well.

He remained silent and he waited, wishing somehow that fear alone had the power to make an overgrown boy into a man.

~

Tim Cauthen did not want to be inducted into the Army, but, when the telegram came extending his government's "Greetings," Elise and the family knew that he was willing to go. It made it harder knowing he was leaving a wife he loved dearly, a small daughter, and another child yet to be born.

"If something happens while I'm over there," Elise heard him tell Janson and Stan the day he received the telegram, "you look after Sissy and Nora for me, and the new baby as well."

Janson nodded, as did Stan. Elise watched them, thinking that sometimes men did not use words for the things women would outright say: I may be injured; I may not come home whole and in one piece. *If I don't come back . . .*

She stood in her open back door, watching the three men where they sat on the steps that descended to the back yard. Tim was silent now, staring at the cottonwood tree that grew between this house and the next, then beyond it, toward where his own family lived just down the way.

"My folks never did like the idea of my marrying Sissy, and they don't think any kinder on it even now," he said quietly, the sun shining in his brown hair. "If something happens while I'm gone, they might—"

"Won't nobody take Nora an' th' baby away from her," Janson interrupted, "not so long as me an' Elise either one have breath."

"Or me," Stan added, seeming willing himself to take on Tim's family in a fist fight, though he had only one arm.

Tim nodded, and then rose from the step. "I better get home," but he lingered, continuing to stare toward his home, as if he were missing it already. "Sissy's a good woman," he said quietly. "We've had some good times together."

He brought his eyes to Janson for a long moment, and then he turned and walked away.

~

The entire family accompanied Tim to the depot the day he was scheduled to report. Elise watched as Sissy clung to him, knowing she was afraid to let him go.

Tim smiled at Sissy and chucked her under the chin when she released him at last. "Don't you worry. The war'll be over soon and I'll be coming home."

But Elise saw his face as he drew Sissy to him again, his eyes meeting Janson's in a look that said clearly . . .

*If I don't come back . . .*

Elise and Janson walked Sissy to her door. Her mother-in-law had taken Nora home with her, saying she wanted to play with the baby for just a while.

"Why don't you and Nora come to our house later for supper?" Elise invited. Sissy seemed so young, and she had never been on her own, not once in her life. Elise kept remembering how people had always said Sissy was slow, though Elise had never been able to think of her in that manner. "You can even stay the night, if you'd like," she offered.

"No, we're gonna stay here," she said, staring in the open doorway to the empty three rooms in her half-a-house.

She seemed so lonely already without Tim that Elise wondered how Sissy would ever survive, especially if Tim were—

"Tim's comin' home," Sissy said, almost as if she had read Elise's mind. "Tim's comin' home."

Elise found herself talking of the past after she and Janson reached their house that afternoon. She gathered up their clothes that had been worn the day before, that had been left lying across a chair at the foot of their bed, then started into the middle room of their three to put them with the pile of laundry she had begun to gather earlier in the day.

She could hear the floorboards creak in the front room, then

Janson's favorite rocker as he sat down, a comfortable sound she knew
from the years they had been living in this house. She had learned
many sounds in the places where they had lived through the years,
sounds that were now a part of her, such as the wind whistling
between the wallboards in the old sharecropper house on Stubblefield's
land, or the sound of the squeaking porch step leading up to the first
house they had lived in in the mill village, and especially the sounds
that bedsprings could make before the children had been born and
they had had to learn to be quiet.

She had been with Janson for over sixteen years now, half of her
life, and she could not imagine a day spent without him—how could
Sissy ever live without Tim? How could any woman live with her
husband so far away, and with the knowledge that he might never
come home? Elise thanked God that she had been spared that, and she
wished Sissy had been spared it as well.

There was a knock at the front door and she heard Janson get up
to answer it. Elise could hear the vacant sound of his rocker moving
against the floorboards, so different than when he was sitting in it, and
a moment later the sound of the door opening. There came a man's
voice and the sound of the spring stretching on the screen door.

"Who is it?" Elise called from the middle room when Janson did
not say anything in response to the man. She picked up an armload of
clothes to take to the wringer washer out on the rear porch. "Janson?"

She moved to the open doorway between the front and middle
rooms, thinking that he must have gone outside—but he was standing alone in the front room. There was a paper in his hands, and Elise
did not have to see the back of the man now descending the front steps
or the first words of the telegram he had delivered, to know the
meaning of the look on Janson's face.

His eyes rose to meet hers, and there was a mixture of satisfaction
for himself, as well as concern for her, in the expression that passed
over his features.

He crossed the room to give the telegram to her where she stood
now in the drifts of laundry that had fallen from her arms.

She stared up at him, refusing to take the paper into her own hands.

He could read now. She did not have to tell him what it said.

And she had already read the first word in his eyes.

*"Greetings . . ."*

Like so many others, Janson Sanders was going to war.

# 8

ELISE HAD BEEN BY HERSELF before, but she had never been alone. In the days that followed Janson leaving, she learned what being alone truly was, and what being lonely was all about. There were the children. There was Stan, Sissy, her friend Dorrie, the church, and more sewing than she could possibly get done—but she was still alone.

She had never thought to live a day without Janson, but now she found such days her reality. And, as days became weeks, and weeks became months, that loneliness only grew, leaving an emptiness inside of her. She got up each morning—alone. She went to bed at night—alone. And every moment in between just seemed to remind her that Janson was not there.

His letters helped, letters filled with his missing her, with memories of the past, his love for her and the children, stories about other soldiers he met, letters saying he was doing fine and not to worry. For all the misspellings and uneven script, those letters were gold to her, waited for, read over and over, cherished, gently folded away and tied in a blue-ribboned bundle she kept at her bedside, to be read again and again at night when sleep would not come. They were her only contact with him, and she clung to them, writing him almost every day, knowing he had to feel the same.

And then his letters stopped.

Day after day she waited for the mail. Day after day she was disappointed. Another week passed, and then another. Fear filled her, and she tried to keep herself from worrying.

"Don't worry if you don't hear from me for weeks sometime," he had told her the day he left. He would write every chance he could get, but the letters might not get through, might be delayed, lost—*don't worry if you don't hear from me. . .*

But, she was worried. As the days passed, she could think of little else.

It was the next-to-last Tuesday of June, Henry's sixteenth birthday, and Elise sat in the kitchen, looking at the remains of chocolate icing from his birthday cake. It had taken the last of her sugar to make the small cake, but it had been worth it to see the look of delight it had brought to Henry's face. Chocolate—his favorite—really too small even for the three children and Olivia, who was never far from Henry's side, but still Henry had halved his piece with his mother.

"No, Henry, it's your birthday. I want you to eat it; I made it for you," she had protested, even as he put half of his prized slice on a plate for her.

"It's my birthday. I can do what I want."

"But, Henry—"

"No, Ma, I want to."

So much like his father, less than four years younger than Janson had been when she met him, and almost as tall already as his father. Janson—her mind returned to him no matter what else she was doing. Where was he? Why had he not written? She still wrote him daily, dutifully mailing each letter, praying the next day would bring something from him, something to say that he was okay, that he was thinking of her—that he lived—and she thanked God each day that no telegram came: *The Secretary of War desires to express his deep regret that your husband . . .*

Her letters were chatty, full of gossip, full of stories of the children, of what was happening in the village, and the things people were saying—and that she loved him in every line. She never told him of the unending waiting and the horrid loneliness that made her lie and listen to the darkness at night, of the shortages of food and meat items. There seemed to be a shortage nowadays of everything but loneliness. Sugar could be purchased only with ration stamps. Meat was virtually unavailable, except to those the butcher considered his "best custom-ers." Butter was scarce, replaced by cakes of margarine with color packets to tint it a shade of yellow—Elise knew of no one who did not hate the margarine. Anything could be gotten on the black market with enough money, but Elise had sworn that she would starve before she would buy from the black market. Whatever she bought there might be the one thing needed overseas to save Janson's life.

There was more than rationing and shortages and the lack of word from Janson to trouble her mind during the days and throughout the long nights. There were money worries as well. She hadn't realized how much it cost to feed and clothe and support herself, the three children, and Stan, but she learned quickly after Janson left for the war. Even with Stan's wages from the mill, what she received from Janson, and what she made sewing, she found it hard to make ends meet.

She had never had to pay bills, for there had been first her father, and then Janson, to do it for her—but she found herself handling money now, paying bills, budgeting how they would make it through each week. Stan would have done it for her, but it was not his job—it was her family, the family she had made with Janson. Until he came home, it was her place to handle things.

Elise got up from the kitchen table to put the plates in the dishpan on the counter, then she moved about the house, straightening things that were already straightened, dusting places that held no dust. After a few minutes she found herself in the front room alongside the bed she had shared with Janson, the loneliness filling her until it was an ache.

Laughter and talk came through the open window beside the bed and the screened door. Stan sat in the porch swing with a young lady at either side. He had become very popular with the girls in the village over the months of the war. He was good looking and unmarried, and the injury he had suffered in the mill gave ample reason why he was not in uniform.

For a moment music from next door drowned out the voices on the porch. Ruth Shelby had her radio turned up too loud again. Elise could hear a male voice over the music, and laughter, and she knew Ruth was entertaining again. Bill Shelby was in the Navy, and he had been gone from home since the early days of the war. His wife was rarely lonely these days, however. When she was not at work in the mill, she dated as if she were an unmarried woman, had men over to her side of the house, men who often did not leave until early the next morning.

Loneliness could change a lot in people.

There was a sound next door as if a table had been knocked over, and laughter, loud and drunken, over the din of the radio. "Hussy," Elise muttered as she stood now in the open doorway, staring through the screen door at the chimney sweeps darting about in the lowering sky. There was noise all about her, life all about her, but she felt no part of it. She stood alone, her arms folded over her chest, staring across the way. She felt isolated, homesick, though she stood in her own doorway, wanting so badly just to see and touch Janson—why had she not heard from him? Why—?

After a moment she moved across the room to her sewing machine and went back to work on a dress she had begun early that morning. Her eyes were tired and she felt unbelievably older than her thirty-three years. She tried to concentrate on her work, tried not to think about Janson, about the long days since the last letter she had received from him. She reached with one hand to give the wheel on the sewing machine a turn and get it going, then operated the treadle with her foot to keep it in motion.

The constant whir of the needle moving in and out of the fabric, the sound of the machine, dulled the other sounds into the background—the laughter of the two young women, Stan's voice, the radio next door—then she stopped, listening, and the sound of the sewing machine died away.

She could have sworn she had heard Janson's voice, the sound of her own name—after a time she took a deep breath and then reached to set the machine back in motion, shutting her ears to the sounds around her.

~

The mail was late the next afternoon. The damned mail, always late.

Elise sat in the front room, picking the basting out of a skirt with a pair of scissors. She jabbed her finger, then almost started to cry from frustration—she got up and moved to the screen door, then stood staring out with her arms crossed before her chest, breathing deeply to regain her composure.

Every day was like this now. Every day was nothing but hours to endure waiting for the postman to come, and then only minutes until it was time for bed, minutes until she would have to lie alone to make it through the endless night. It did no good to tell herself that she would have been notified if something had happened to Janson. It did no good to know she would have gotten a telegram.

She caught sight of the postman, Mr. Ware, as he made his way up the street, and she stopped, gripping the door frame so hard that her knuckles turned white. She forced herself to stand there, not to run out onto the street, not to behave like a madwoman.

Mr. Ware came abreast of the house and saw her in the doorway, then waved before passing on down the street. Elise stood with her hand raised in greeting, a dull emptiness settling over her again that she had known throughout the past days. She turned at last and made her way back to her chair, picked up the skirt, and began again to pick out the basting.

Another day, and no word.

She felt too empty even to cry.

She finished the skirt that afternoon, then resumed work on a wedding dress for Dorrie's niece, Rosie. She worked at the sewing machine until her neck and shoulders hurt, until her eyes felt strained, until the calf of her right leg ached from operating the foot treadle, and still she did not stop. Late afternoon came, and Elise busied herself fixing supper, preparing Janson's favorite foods without thought, then she sat as Henry, Catherine, and Judith ate, unable to eat anything herself for the very fact that Janson was not there.

Later, she left the girls washing the supper dishes, though Catherine was complaining through every moment of it, and went back to her sewing, resuming work on the wedding dress, a dress that would bring them needed money. She had saved for weeks to buy new shoes for Judith, so badly tempted to go into their savings for the purchase—it was getting harder and harder to make it without Janson's wages from the mill and all the doubles he had worked in the months before he left for the war. She wondered how they had ever made it during the height of the Depression, when Janson and Stan had both been without a job, and especially in the years they sharecropped. Money was so important, so very important, and there never seemed to be enough of it. Never.

She could not touch the savings. They had lost it twice before— once when her oldest brother had stolen it, once when the bank collapsed—they would not lose it again, and she would not eat it up slowly in the time Janson was gone. It would be there when he came back, and they would then buy his land, the home he had dreamed of for so long, the home he had promised her. She thought about it so often in the long nights, about that white house that seemed so big to her now with its six rooms, compared to their three in the mill village—what had her family ever done with all those rooms in her father's big house in Georgia? That seemed a world away, a lifetime away.

As the hour grew late, Elise stopped work at the sewing machine so the noise would not keep the children awake. She moved about the house quietly, straightening up, tidying the kitchen again, although that had been another of the tasks she had given Catherine and Judith to do after supper. Half of the room was only partially done, with crumbs under the table along with an unwashed fork and a small portion of a biscuit, telling Elise which side of the room had been Catherine's responsibility. Her eldest daughter never did anything more than half way, apparently having concluded that to prove herself capable would only mean that she would be expected to do more often.

Catherine was fourteen now, and sometimes reminded Elise so much of herself at that age that she was sorely tempted to slap her. Elise had been only two years older when she ran away with Janson, and she found herself watching her daughter at times now wondering how she could ever have been so young.

Elise sat down at the kitchen table after she finished straightening up, taking out paper and a fountain pen to began another letter to Janson, though she had mailed one to him only that morning—she just needed to talk to him, to be near him for a moment. Line after line was filled with senseless chatter, Elise writing so rapidly that it was barely readable, then she stopped, stared at the paper for a moment, and wrote: *"Janson, where are you? Are you okay? I miss you so much. Oh, please—"*

Then she crumpled the paper and left it on the table as she rose to pull on the drawstring hanging in the middle of the room to shut the light out.

She moved through the middle room, careful not to wake the children, then entered the front room and closed the door. She sat in her rocker and stared around the room for a moment, looking at the big, empty bed before she took up her knitting—but it was too easy to think as she stared at the stitches made, so she set the work aside and reached for a book, knowing it could occupy her mind.

She had wanted to read *Gone With The Wind* for years now, but had not come across it in at the library until the day before. Everyone had talked about it back in '36 when it was first published, and there had been even more talk when the movie came out in '39—Scarlett O'Hara and Rhett Butler, she knew all about them already, as if they were real people she had heard gossiped about, and not just characters in a book or on a movie screen.

Elise opened to the first page and began to read, then almost closed it when she saw the first mention of the word "war"—but by then she was already caught in the story. She read until late in the night, delaying going to that empty bed until she had to. She read until her eyes hurt and she could barely hold the book, then she marked her place and laid it aside. After changing into her nightgown, she sat on the side of the bed to look at the photograph of Janson on the night stand. The bundle of letters she had received from him lay alongside the photograph, and she took the top one out, pulling it from beneath the blue ribbon. She touched it, running her fingers over the familiar, uneven script, flattening it on her lap to read it for the thousandth time:

*"Dear Elise, first off I love you tell the kids pa sais high . . ."*

The last—most recent, she corrected herself—letter from him. He always began them the same, and she longed to receive a new one, to read that line again, written in a fresh hand and not worn from re-reading upon re-reading:

*"Dear Elise, first off I love you tell the kids pa sais high . . ."*

She gently put the letter away and looked at the photograph again, touched a finger to her lips then to the image of his face, then shut off the light and laid back to stare at the dark ceiling.

She had been wrong, the woman who had written that book. She should have told how bad it hurt to be alone, how bad it hurt to worry if your husband would ever come home. She should have told—but who would want to read about loneliness, about an empty bed and long nights and—

Sleep would not come and Elise lay staring at the darkness. She tried to remember what it felt like for Janson to hold her—then she tried to forget, tried not to think about it at all. There were footsteps on the back porch, the sound of the back door opening and closing, Stan coming in long hours after his shift in the mill ended, coming home to his bed in one corner of the kitchen. His shoes hit the floor and then there was silence.

Elise lay and listened to the darkness, to her own breathing, to the sounds of loneliness and worry, until sometime in the early morning hours just before dawn, when sleep came at last.

~

The next afternoon, Elise sat with Dorrie and a number of other women from Pearlman Street Baptist Church there in the village. They were having a housekeeping shower in Dorrie's kitchen for Hettie King, a girl from the church who would be marrying her boyfriend before he shipped out for the merchant marines. The exclamations over presents had died down, and now the women sat talking about both their neighbors and the privations of the war, enjoying honey-sweetened lemonade and the last of the cake Dorrie had managed to concoct without benefit of white sugar, butter, eggs, or milk.

Women bragged of husbands and sons overseas, photographs of handsome young men in uniform were shown, and a letter read that had come from a son in the military. One woman told of the victory quilt she was piecing for her eldest daughter. Another lady compared the taste of sweetening with honey, syrup, or molasses in the absence of sugar, and still another advocated the careful use of salt to bring out the natural sweetness in foods. There was talk of victory gardens, scrap drives, and first-aid classes; of rationing, the latest issue of *Life* magazine, and the lovely ruffled blouses in a store window uptown. More than once there were comments about the censors who read every word from their husbands, and quite a few ladies talked of jobs taken in the mill for the duration of the war—they all seemed to be doing so much, accomplishing so much more than Elise was accomplishing.

Women who had never worked outside their homes had gone to work in the mill. They were taking up the slack left by the men and boys who had gone to fight, working now beside women like Dorrie who had been in the mill for years, as well as the old men and boys classified as 4-F and unfit for military service. The women worked as hard as their men ever had, pulling long hours, knowing that what they did only helped in the war effort—and Elise was ashamed to think of herself sitting at home with her sewing and her children, while these women went to work in the mill everyday to help in their own way to win the war, bringing home needed paychecks to support their families, and giving themselves something to help to pass the time. The mill was constantly hiring, hungry for workers in the shortages of war, paying good wages—and what she could do with the money! Janson had always said he would not have her working—but these were unusual circumstances, unusual times, and what did he think sewing and picking cotton were, anyway, if not work.

She went to the mill the next day and was hired, and did not think again of how mad Janson would be until she was on her way home—but he could be as mad as he wanted, for she was at last doing something. She had not felt so good about anything in a long time—she would be helping in the war effort. She would be helping to pass the time. In her own small way, she might even do something that would help to bring Janson home—it just felt right.

But Stan was not so sure, and even Henry tried to dissuade her.

"You can't take that job—"

"Pa will be furious—"

"You know how Janson feels about women working."

"What about Dorrie and all the other women who work in the mill?" Elise demanded of her brother.

"Yeah, and none of them are married to Janson," Stan said, looking at her over the tops of his eyeglasses.

"I am going to do it," she stared back.

I am—she repeated those words over and over in the days to come. I am—as she tried to learn the job she was given in the mill. She was supposed to run drawing, and supposed to learn from an old man who seemed to resent her very presence in the mill. If she had thought through all these years that the area outside the mill was hell, with the sounds of its machinery and the sight of flying lint, then the interior of the building was the deepest pit, with its machines and noise, and the lint and cotton dust-choked air.

"I know your husban'," the old man who was supposed to be teaching her said in her first hours in the mill. "I'll tell you what he'd say, that you ought t' be home with your cookin' an' your young'ns, seein' after th' house 'til he gets home, not out tryin' t' do a man's work." He spit a stream of tobacco juice into a nearby spittoon, then wiped at his mouth with the back of one hand as he squinted at her.

He made it as difficult on her as he possibly could, and Elise knew it, but there was little choice for him or for anyone else working in the mill. There were fewer and fewer young men available to take jobs, because of the war, leaving the grizzled old men, the women, and the underaged kids who were being worked against the child labor laws. Elise had been surprised to see the kids there, and even more surprised to see them hidden, sometimes lowered out of windows or sent to stay in bathrooms when the government people came through, but they were always put back to work as soon as it was clear.

Elise hated the mill even before her first shift was over. She was terrified of the machinery, terrified because of what it had done to Stan and to so many others, and that fear was only compounded by the horror stories the older men told Elise and the other women who had come into the mill. She hated the noise, hated the lint and the cotton dust that stuck to her hair and clothing, and did not know if she could make herself set foot in the place even one more time—but she did. She stuck it out, determined to prove to herself, and to the old men, that she could do it, that they couldn't drive her away, and each day it became easier. At the end of each shift she could only think—one day closer to the end of the war. One day closer to Janson coming home. One more day.

Such a long time had passed since she last heard from Janson. She kept telling herself that she would have been notified by now if something had happened to him, that she would have been sent word—but it didn't help. Nothing helped.

At least she was doing something now, she told herself. At least she could return home at the end of a shift, ready for bed, ready for sleep, if sleep would come, her body too exhausted, her mind too numbed, to think of him more than a thousand times each day.

~

One afternoon a few weeks after Elise had gone to work at the mill, Sissy and Dorrie were at her house for the evening. Sissy had been rocking her new baby in Elise's favorite rocker, but Dorrie had laid claim to little Timmy the minute she entered, taking him from his mother and sitting in a near-by chair as she cooed to him. "My, how precious you are—yes you are," as Sissy smiled and watched.

Elise sat on the side of the bed there in the front room, watching her friends as Sissy showed Dorrie a photograph of Nora and her baby brother, which she said she would be sending to Tim. Judith was in the front yard with Nora now, for once enjoying not being the youngest. Catherine and Henry had found things to interest them elsewhere. Catherine, at fourteen, had little patience with either children or babies, and little interest in anything not male and in a uniform. Henry, Elise knew, would be with Olivia, wherever they might be.

It had grown quiet outside. Judith's voice had stilled, as had Nora's laughter. Elise got up from the bed and started for the door, hearing someone coming up the steps now and onto the porch. There was a knock, and then silence. She reached the doorway and looked through the screen door at the man who stood on the porch, and then at what was held in the man's hand—she caught at the doorframe for support, feeling almost as if she had been struck. She could hear Dorrie's voice behind her, and she knew that Judith and Nora were now on the porch behind the man, but all she could see was what he held. A telegram—no, she did not want to know. No—

She swayed, fear gripping her, tightening her stomach muscles into knots. There was a humming in her ears, a humming she knew could not be there, for everyone had fallen silent, from her own daughter, staring now down at the telegram, to Sissy and Dorrie in the room behind her.

Elise made herself breathe, made herself think, make her lips form the words: "Yes—wh—what do you want?"

Her voice was a whisper. She felt Dorrie's hand beneath her elbow, keeping her on her feet.

"Mrs. Sanders?"

She nodded, unable to speak, the room beginning to spin about her, the edges of her vision darkening—*no, I won't faint. I would know it if he was dead. I would know it. I won't faint. I can't. I've got to know. Dear God—not Janson. I can't—*

The man looked at her, and Elise knew that he could see the fear in her eyes, knew that he had delivered news of death and heartbreak so many times before.

"There was nobody home, ma'am. The neighbors said I could find her here."

*Her*—for a moment the word did not mean anything.

*. . . nobody home . . . neighbors said I could find her here.*

*. . . her . . . find her . . .*

Then she felt Dorrie stiffening, and a sound from Sissy in the room behind her, both now waiting for the blow to fall on one of them instead. Comprehension came—*not Janson. Not my Janson. It's not—*

The spinning slowed. She could breathe. She could think.

"Who are you looking for?" she asked, realizing she was trembling.

"Mrs. Timothy M. Cauthen—"

"Tim—" Sissy's voice was small and frightened. Elise turned and saw the look of fear on Sissy's face, saw her rise slowly to her feet, the photograph she had been holding fluttering from her lap and to the floor. Sissy walked to the door and accepted the telegram in shaking hands. She stared up at the man for a moment, and then looked down, at last holding the telegram out for Elise to read it to her.

Elise's eyes fixed on the page, but she could not make herself say the words. She looked at Sissy.

"Tim—he's—" Sissy said quietly, one hand rising to cover her mouth.

Then she sank to the floor.

For a time there was only concern for Sissy.

It was not until later that Elise read her the words: "*. . . regret that your husband . . . was killed in action . . .*"

She was ashamed of herself, but she could not help thinking, *thank God it wasn't Janson. Thank God it wasn't Janson.*

# 9

Janson's handwriting—
Elise stood on the porch a few days later, staring at the letters Mr.
Ware had just put into her hands, four letters with Janson's handwriting. Four letters—

Her hands were shaking so badly that she could hardly hold the
first one steady enough to read it, her vision clouding suddenly:

*"Dear Elise, first off I love you tell the kids pa sais high. . . ."*

She leaned against the nearby wall for support, feeling suddenly
drained, realizing that she had been existing on worry and force of will
alone—but no more. Janson was alive! He had been thinking of her
when he had written the letters now in her hands. He was alive!

She clutched the letters to her and went through the door and into
the front room. Judith sat before the radio there, tuning it to a
program.

"From your father—letters from your father," she said, holding
the letters out to the girl, but refusing to allow her to take them when
she reached for them excitedly. "No, let me read them first," Elise
said, trying to move away and sit on the bed where she could read
them in peace—they were hers, and she had been waiting for so long.

"But, mama—" Judith said.

"No," Elise said, refusing to be distracted.

There were words blacked out of the first letter, an entire line out
of another, the censors at work between her and Janson, but that did

not matter. He had said that he missed her, that he missed even her cooking, though she was fully aware she had never quite learned to cook. The third letter talked about foods he dreamed of at night.

"They must not be feeding him very well," she muttered to herself, surprised not to be annoyed that he talked about what he wanted to eat for the entire duration of a letter. His spelling had not improved, and neither had his handwriting, and punctuation was something he used sparingly, if at all—but those letters were gold, each word the most beautiful thing she had ever read in her life.

"He got the cake we sent him," she told Judith as she continued to read, hearing the girl drag a chair closer to her across the wooden floor. "He said the icing stuck mostly to the paper, but they scraped it off. Mackey and the other men said it was the best cake they had ever eaten—"

"Pa ought not let the other soldiers eat his cake. We made it for him," Judith protested and Elise looked up at her briefly, then the girl's tone changed. "Maybe Mackey could have a piece; he did let Pa have some of the fudge his mama had sent him. I remember that Pa said it was good—"

Mackey was often mentioned in Janson's letters, as were other soldiers he knew over there. Elise thought Mackey had become a real friend to him, perhaps one of the few real friends Janson had ever made in his life—it was funny that war could make friends of men who otherwise would never have met, for Janson had never been outside of Alabama and Georgia before the war, and Mackey, from what she had learned in Janson's letters, had rarely seen the outside of New York City.

Elise started reading the final letter of the four, not wanting to finish it too quickly, for that would only mean the start of waiting again for the next to come. She reached the last line and had to blink back tears, reading words she had read many times before.

Beneath the words "your husband," spelled his own particular way, Janson had signed his full name.

~

At times Janson thought he spent half his days now digging holes, and the other half lying in them. There were also days he spent moving through towns that had been shelled apart, tensed against being shot at by some sniper in a standing building. There was waiting and rare mail calls and mud—more mud than he had ever thought to see in his life, mud to lay in, to taste, to wear in the creases of his body and caked in his clothes and on him until it seemed a part of his skin. There were cold meals and K rations and the goddamn chocolate bars that could break your teeth. There was dysentery and wet feet and mud—always more mud—and being shelled, lying in a hole with metal fragments and wood splinters raining down.

There were nights that never seemed to end, listening, keeping watch, then laying in a hole and trying to sleep, thinking of home—and mud, slogging through it, sleeping in it, trying to dig a place that might be safe for the night. There was killing and being afraid to die and seeing men who were no more than boys being blown apart—and mud, mixed with blood and bodies in the fields they had passed through. Sometimes he wondered if he would ever go home to Elise. Sometimes he wondered if he should. Sometimes he knew he had to no matter how many he might have killed or what he had seen or the sounds that seemed to stay inside of him—and the silence in the long nights, and the waiting, and the coarse edge that had come on him now as it had on all the others.

He sat in the bottom of a foxhole he and Mackey had dug late the day before, his spare pair of socks knotted together and hanging around his neck to dry. This was the same place he had passed the night, at least the little part of it when he had been sleeping. There had been a mail call the day before. He had received a bundle of letters, and that was the reason he was furious now—he could not believe Elise was working in the cotton mill. She knew how he felt. She knew—

He sat trying to write a letter, holding the paper on a book he had borrowed from Mackey, trying to keep the book balanced on his knee as his pen scratched furiously at the paper. Writing was hard enough to do when he was not angry, and he was angrier with Elise than he had been in all the years since he married her. He had written two letters yesterday since he had gotten his mail, one to Elise and one to Stan—she was going to quit that job, no matter what she had to say about it. He would not have her working in the mill. He would not, and if she would not quit on her own, then he would make certain that Stan would make her quit.

*"I mean you quit,"* he wrote. *"I tolt Stan to make you quit if you would not on your own so I mean you quit before he hasto I mean I wont have you work in the mill I wont. You quit write now and dont go back so help me you better quit."*

He stopped and stared at the paper for a moment, then wrote:

*"I mean it you better quit,"* then underlined the last word two words for good measure. *"You quit,"* he wrote again. He did not know how she could have gotten such a fool idea in the first place. She knew how he felt about her working, and for her to go to work in the cotton mill, for the Easons—he didn't care if Dorrie Keith and all the other women in the mill village went to work in the mill. He didn't care if Eleanor Roosevelt herself were to come to Eason County and go to work for Walter Eason. Elise was not going to. Of all things—

But she probably wouldn't listen to him. She never had. There was not once in her life she had ever listened to anybody.

If she had she would never have married him in the first place.

He sat thinking of the days when he had first known her, long ago in the place she had grown up in Georgia, at a time when he had thought the only thing they had to do to be together was to get out of Endicott County and away from her father. He had never thought anything could tear them apart after that. War had never entered his mind.

All he wanted to do now was to see Elise. All he wanted to do was to be a husband and a father and to work for his land. All he wanted was to go home.

And sometimes he was afraid he never would.

"*I miss you,*" he wrote, his eyes never leaving the paper, though his anger had left him for the moment. "*Dont worry about me I am fine you take care of yoursef and the kids and Ill be home when its over. I love you,*" he wrote at last, though he knew he did not have to. "*I love you,*" he wrote again, then stopped himself before he wrote what it was he had really been thinking.

That he hoped he lived long enough to see her again.

∽

December 1944 meant a Christmas without Janson home.

Elise walked toward the mill on a chilly morning late in December, hoping that at the end of her shift she would be too tired to do anything but sleep. She had lain awake for hours the night before staring into the darkness, worrying about Janson over there only God knew where, about Henry who was growing older every day with his father gone, Catherine who fancied herself in love with a boy who would be leaving for overseas, and Dorrie whose youngest son was now missing in the war. Elise just wanted it to end. She just wanted Janson and all the other men to come home. She wanted the world to be normal and life to go on and things to be like they were.

She was doing all she could, everything she could, to help in the war effort. She was pulling her shift in the mill. She was buying war bonds. She was conserving cooking fats and cooperating with rationing and not complaining too much. She had planted a victory garden in the spring, and canned vegetables in the fall, had given to scrap drives and bought even more war bonds and written to Janson every chance she could. They were doing their part, they were all doing their part, all the women who had gone to work in the mills or in war plants throughout the country, all the old people pulling shifts again when they should be enjoying their rest, and the kids growing up while their mothers worked and their fathers were at war.

They were all doing their part—or at least almost all of them were,

Elise thought as she neared the front of the mill to find Buddy Eason standing at the edge of the sidewalk arguing with a man who was carrying a clipboard.

"I'm sorry, Mr. Eason, but that's the best I can give you," the man said calmly, then visibly flinched as Buddy began to yell at him again.

"Well, goddamn it, I've already told you it's not good enough!" Buddy shoved the smaller, badly balding man with the last words, then stood with his fists clenched, as if he thought the little man would fight.

"There's a war going on, Mr. Eason."

"Fuck the war!" Buddy shouted, and Elise saw several women who were nearing the gated entrance to the mill hurry their steps to get on past the two men. "I don't give a damn about the war; it's not good enough!"

Elise had no idea what the confrontation was about, and it really did not matter. Little excuse was needed for Buddy to go into a rage.

No—not everyone was doing his part. There were people such as Buddy Eason who used the circumstances of war to make themselves rich. Buddy controlled the black market in Eason County, which Elise and most other people in the mill village knew, but which no one did anything about. It was said that Buddy could supply anything, to anyone, for the right price—he could even supply women, or so Elise had been hearing, for people said he was openly involved with a "lady" who ran a "house" out in the country.

There were few areas where Buddy did not seem above the law, but there was one law that even Buddy Eason seemed unable to get around. Buddy had attempted to sell second-rate goods to the government, but somehow his grandfather had found him out. Walter Eason had made restitution, and now Buddy was on the outs even with his family—but Buddy did not seem to need the protection of grandfather or his family name any longer. The war had brought him money of his own, along with the power and influence that only money and fear can combine to give. He had gone to fat in the past years, and the added bulk had made him more imposing—but it was the knowledge of what he was capable of doing that gave him the power he wielded so freely.

Everyone had no doubt that Buddy Eason could do just about anything, to anyone, if he so chose.

Elise continued down the sidewalk, though she refused to look in his direction. His voice had stilled in the argument, and, even when the other man spoke again, Elise heard little response from Buddy. She glanced back at him as she stepped to the end of the short line of people waiting for entrance at the gate, only to find his eyes on her, a look of absolute hatred on his face—but it was a look she had expected to see there, and it was one she returned with equal feeling.

She showed the badge pinned to her dress when her time came at the gate, although the man standing there knew her face. Security had been tight since the cotton mill had begun to manufacture for the war effort. They were making nothing more than heavy ducking for tents, and material to be used in parachutes, but still the security measures were constant. The grounds had been fenced off, and entrance was to be gained now only through the guarded gates by showing a badge. All the millhands had been fingerprinted, and there were rumors that the FBI had been called in to investigate them all. Elise had nothing to hide, and she could not help but to think—I wish someone would really check into Buddy Eason. Oh, I wish someone would.

She stared up at the red brick of the mill, knowing the end of the eight-hour shift would at least bring her that much closer to the end of the war.

~

Janson could no longer remember what it felt like to be warm. His hands were numb, his fingers aching and stiff from digging through snow and frozen earth to make a hole for the night. Then they had had to move out, leaving their overcoats and packs behind so they could struggle through knee-deep and even deeper drifts of snow, cold and so hungry that his stomach was gnawing away inside of him. The snow had started again, light at first, and then heavier as the wind picked up, driving into his face with a stinging, brutal force that made him want to close his eyes. He fell, then struggled to his feet again, so cold that his teeth were chattering—the world looked like a Christmas card, he thought, but it was a Christmas card from hell, because he knew that somewhere in that dark, snow-driven blindness were German soldiers who were just as cold and hungry as he was, and who would kill him and the men with him if they had a chance.

They were moving through the open, nearing the edge of woods, but still he could hardly see the man ahead of him in the darkness. The snow stung his eyes, the wind and cold hitting him in the face so hard that he found it difficult to breathe—there was a sudden rattle of gunfire from the cover of trees at the side of the field, causing him to hit the ground, his face in snow, the mess up his nose and filling his mouth. He spit it away, then made himself crawl on his belly in the direction of the woods, fighting the urge to dig in where he was, for he knew he might very well die here in the open before he could manage to dig his way through the snow and several feet of frozen ground. He came on another soldier sprawled on his belly in the snow at the edge of the woods, unmoving, and it took him only a moment to realize the man was dead. He pushed himself on, reaching the woods and the cover of the trees.

They were returning fire now, and hurried orders were being given, a group of men to flank the enemy, through the woods and along a ridge to their rear. Janson's name was called, and he was moving out—but he had a bad feeling about this, a very bad feeling, the same as he had had the day Mackey died, caught by sniper fire in a town that was supposed to be cleaned out, or only minutes before the green kid of a replacement sharing his foxhole had taken a bullet between the eyes—he had watched the boy die, had seen the life leave him, and since then had known his own time would come. He had been too close, had seen too many men die, had been wounded twice, though not seriously either time.

He kept thinking of Elise as they moved through the woods, of the letter in his pocket, a letter he had received several weeks before at the last mail call—he just wanted to go home. He just wanted to see Elise, to see his children, and he wanted the war to end before his own son could be here as well—he had seen boys die who were little older than Henry, German boys and Allied boys, boys who had not lived to be men, and who had never known the pleasures of a wife or a marriage bed.

He just wanted it to be over.

They were moving up behind the German positions now. The sound of the machine guns were loud from the nest ahead, and it seemed they would make it without being seen. The men spread out, a few taking positions behind trees, Janson and two other men leaving cover to move in closer. They could see the Germans now, uniforms in the darkness, helmets below the reach of return fire—suddenly one of them turned, his eyes meeting Janson's over the distance. He was a kid, big and husky, with a look of fear on his face—then he raised a cry of warning, his gun coming up. There was gunfire from beside Janson, and again just to his rear. The soldier beside the German kid was hit, his helmet sliding down over his face. The kid was firing, the look of fear still on his face, and Janson tried to move to cover even as he returned fire—but he could not. He was going down, landing on his face in the snow. He tried to struggle to his feet, tried to get to the protection of a tree, but one leg would not move, and the other only pushed at the snow. There was gunfire all around him, and he was hit again, feeling the bullet pass through his upper arm even as the pain washed up from the pit of his belly and down one leg.

He was bleeding, blood on his hands when he put them to his side—where was his rifle? Had he dropped it? Thrown it aside? His mind was not working. The world was dark. And he could not feel the snow. He had wanted to see Elise again. He had—

# 10

ELISE SAT ALONE IN THE front room of the mill house, trying to write a letter to Janson. Usually the words came easily to her. Usually there was so much to say, but this afternoon all she could do was sit and stare at his photograph on the dresser top, and then beyond it to her own image reflected in the mirror. She could think of nothing more to write other than: *We're fine. We miss you. I love you.*

The house was quiet. Henry and the girls were not home from school yet, and Elise had done nothing since finishing her shift in the mill but sit at the dresser and try to write her letter. The house was too quiet.

*We're fine. We miss you. . . .*

There was a knock at the door and she got up, thinking it might be Dorrie running late on her way home after her own shift, or possibly Sissy stopping by with the baby. But when she opened the door, she found a man her mind did not want to recognize.

Then she saw the telegram in his hand.

"Mrs. Janson T. Sanders?" he asked. She was clinging to the knob of the door as she held it open, her free hand clenched into a fist against her chest. She knew that she did not answer him, but suddenly the telegram was in her hands and he was leaving the front porch, the screen door now shut behind him. She was shaking as she shut the door, shaking as she crossed the short distance to the dresser to sit again, holding to the back of the chair as she made her way past it, shaking as she placed the telegram on the surface there before her and tried to take up her pen and make herself continue her letter to Janson—*he won't be dead if I don't read it*, she told herself. *He won't be dead—I'll write a letter and I'll go fix supper and I'll read the telegram later and it won't be for me. It's for someone else. Janson's not dead. Janson's not—*

She was taking the telegram up in shaking hands, the trembling moving through her arms and into her body until she was quaking and chilled all over. A knot was rising into her throat to choke her, the paper rattling in her hands so badly that she could hardly read the words.

Henry's voice came from behind her as the door opened, and then Catherine's, and Judith's. "Mama, Mrs. Shelby said—"

But Elise was dropping the telegram, her hands covering her face, the knot in her throat turning into a choked sob as the shaking enveloped her completely.

"Mama—"

"Pa's not—"

"Mama—"

Elise took her head from her hands and looked at the three faces around her. Her voice was shaking so badly that she could hardly speak. "He's been wounded—he's alive," was all she could say. "He's alive."

～

Janson awoke with a start, the sound of the train whistle loud in his ears. He had been dreaming, had been back there again. The cold. The darkness. Realizing he had been hit. Thinking he would die there frozen into a grotesque shape in the snow.

He had thought he would never see Elise again, and it had been with surprise that he had come to consciousness briefly to find himself staring into the blood-streaked face of a medic. He had awakened again some unknown time later in a field hospital, doped up on morphine for the pain, but alive, hearing someone tell him that it was over for him, that he was going home.

Going home—

The sound of the train was constant and welcome in his ears, the feel and sway of it beneath him taking him only closer to home, to Elise, and to his children. Elise had wanted to come to where he was the minute he reached the United States, but he had refused to allow it. She could not leave the children, and he would not have her traveling alone in war time, no matter what else she had to say—he would be home soon enough, he told her.

Soon enough.

He stared out the window, the countryside beginning to take on the familiarity of a long-known face. They would soon be entering Eason County—had it been only a year, no, less than a year, since he left here? So much had changed since then. So much. Tim was gone now, and another of Clarence and Dorrie's sons, Pete. The village grocer, old Mr. McCallum, had lost all three of his grandsons in just the past few months, and the Baptist minister, Reverend Satterwhite, had a son missing and presumed dead. The land he was moving through might not have been forcibly scarred by war, as had been much of the land of Europe that he had seen, land that was torn apart and blood-spattered, hole-pitted and shell-blackened and filled with death—but war had touched here as well. War had taken so many men and boys who had once sweated in fields beneath the Alabama sun, who had worked in cotton mills and walked Main Streets and courted sweethearts, and who were lying now buried in foreign soil so far away from the Alabama clay, dead in a war that had still seen no end. Janson did not know how the world could ever be the same after this.

Most of all, though, he wondered about Elise.

She sounded so different on the telephone when he talked to her. She had been excited and worried and—older, more sure of herself, as if she did not need him now.

And why would she?

She had been alone all these months. She had worked and looked after three children. She had taken a job in the mill and handled money and done things on her own.

And she had not needed him.

She would not need him now, especially not now, a cripple home from the war, one more burden to bear.

He looked down at himself, at how he was sitting, his weight all on one side, the cane resting against his thigh. Dull pain ached in his hip and down into one leg, as it had for much of the time since he had awakened in the field hospital—a bullet had passed through his side and exited through his left hip; two others had torn through that leg. The doctors had tried to tell him what those pieces of metal had done to his body, but all he understood was that he would have a pronounced limp, and that he might need a walking stick for the rest of his life. To him, his body seemed twisted now, his left leg not in alignment with the right. That leg and hip were not as strong as the other side, and he leaned heavily on the cane when he walked. It hurt, a dull ache in the bone that reminded him of a toothache, but seated in that area, and worsening when he walked a lot or stood or sat for long periods of time.

It ached now, and he tried to shift to a more comfortable position, but he knew there was not one. There never was.

The Army nurses had been nice. They had been the first American women he had seen in a very long time, and had brought him paper and a pen so that he could write to Elise. Some had even flirted with him. They were pretty and he had talked to them, had showed them pictures of his wife and kids, told them about home, even about the land he would buy one day—if he could work it now.

He dragged his mind back to the present. There was no need for the land, no need for anything, if Elise did not want him. He could be a husband to her, a man in her bed, a father to his children—but he did not want Elise to feel pity for him. He did not want her to look at him and turn away. He wanted things to be like they had always been, his wife back again, his home as he had left it, Elise to be Elise, not independent where she didn't need him any more. He just wanted his life back.

He stared out the window at the passing countryside. A train had first taken him to her those long years ago. A train had taken them to their life as man and wife in Eason County. A train had taken him away when he had left for the war. A train was bringing him back now to a life he had not known in a very long time.

The train began to slow as it passed through the outskirts of Pine and then neared the depot. Janson leaned forward, staring out the window, his eyes searching for a familiar face, worrying whether he would recognize his children after these months. They were almost grown now. They might not even need him back. Elise might not—

So many nights he had dreamed about coming home. So many nights as he had lain in a hole dug into foreign soil, so many nights in the cold and the rain, lying in the mud, or in snow as he dug through frozen earth—he was home.

As the train came to a stop he saw her standing on the platform, her eyes moving over the train as she searched the many windows of the passenger cars for sight of him, and he hurt inside at the very sight of her—had he really forgotten how she looked, how the simple sight of her could take his breath away?

Home—he thought, as he pushed himself painfully to his feet, leaning heavily on the walking stick. He was home.

∾

Those had been the longest days, the longest weeks, in Elise's life, knowing that Janson had been wounded, receiving word that he would be coming home, waiting for him—but it was over now. She stood on the depot platform, looking for the first sight of him. He had been gone almost a year, and she wondered how much he would have changed in that time with all he had been through.

He had called her as soon as he arrived in the United States, reaching her on the telephone at Sissy's house. Elise knew she would not forget to her dying day the sound of his voice that first time after so many months, sounding so different, so distant, but unmistakably Janson.

"I'll be comin' home," he told her, refusing to let her come to where he was in a hospital up north. "I'll be comin' home—"

When she had talked to him over the past weeks, he had seemed to understand what she was feeling. He had seemed her Janson, but later, over the days of waiting, she had begun to worry, and now she was afraid—would he be different now? How could any man not be different? She knew he had probably killed German soldiers, for that was what he had been sent to do. He had almost been killed himself, had been wounded three times, this last time so horribly that he almost died. He had been cold and hungry and afraid—he had said little about it on the telephone, but she knew, or at least thought she knew, from the little that he had said. How could any man not be different now? The Janson who left here had never taken another man's life, had not even liked firing a gun, though he had done so many times in hunting to feed the family. He had been kind and gentle and—and somehow she knew that the Janson who would come home to her today would no longer be that man. How could he be?

Almost a year. She herself had changed so much in that year. She was thirty-four years old now—God, how old thirty-four had seemed to her when she was sixteen. She had found gray in her hair in the months since he had been gone, had yanked it out again and again, only to find it returned once more. In the time he had been gone, she had never once wanted another man, though she had lain awake so many nights in a bed that had seemed emptier than she had ever thought any bed could feel. In all that time she had never doubted him—but now, as she waited, she wondered. She knew how Janson was. Almost an entire year—could he have waited?

The woman who had said good-bye to him a year before would never have even dared the thought—but she was no longer that woman, and she knew it. For almost a year now, she had depended only on herself. Stan had been there, but her family was her family and she had taken care of them. War had changed her—how badly had it changed Janson? Men over there were fighting, dying, probably living life to the fullest extent possible because they knew how easily it could end. Elise just wanted her husband back. Janson not being Janson was something she did not think she could bear.

There had been a lot of time for thinking, for remembering, in the time since he had been wounded. The years they had spent together, the first day she met him, the struggle just to be together, all Janson had gone through to marry her, seeing him beaten and bloody at her father's hands, their having run away together, the life they had finally begun—those things were never far from her mind. She thought of their first coming to Eason County, of her horror of the life he had brought her to, her fear of his grandmother, her tears over burned pans of cornbread and nearly setting the kitchen on fire—it all seemed so silly, so childish, now. The years in the mill village, even the years sharecropping, had been good years because they had been to-gether—but, of all the memories of their life together, there was one that had stayed with her the most in the past days. That memory was of standing before his grandparents' house not long after he had brought her to Eason County, on a day when she had watched him walk down a long, red road toward Pine to ask for a job he had once refused, from a man he hated—and he had done it for her, and for Henry, the baby she had been carrying at that time. His grandmother had known then that he would never be the same, had said as much to Elise, though Elise had not understood it at that time—and he had been different when he came home that day. He had been a husband, and a father-to-be, and no longer just the boy she had loved and married despite her parents and her own common sense—but he had still been Janson, more mature, accepting of what had been placed on him, but still Janson.

Elise had thought she knew him so well then. She had been only a child herself, barely seventeen. Only over the years since had she really gotten to know the man he was, gotten to know him so well that she could finish his sentences and often know his thoughts and he could do the same for her. She had never thought he could change; he was always so much the same—but now? Elise herself was a stranger to the woman she had been then, and she wondered if he would seem a stranger to her as well. She wanted to see him so badly, to touch him, to hear his voice, to know for herself that he was healthy and alive; she could even deal with it if he had been unfaithful in that time—but he had to return to her still Janson. He had to be still the man he had been.

She moved closer to the train, her hands clenched into fists at her sides with the tension inside of her. Her stomach was nervous, as it had been all morning. Her eyes first scanned the windows of the train, and then searched the faces of the men in uniform who stepped down to the platform. A cold nudge of fear creeped into her. She could not make herself move; she could only stand rooted to the spot, wondering if it had all been a mistake and that he was not coming home at all.

Then she saw him, stepping down onto the platform, leaning heavily on a walking cane, a young sailor coming down just behind him and reaching out to offer help, a look of pity on the younger man's face. Janson seemed shorter, bent slightly as he leaned on the cane, his green eyes showing a moment's obvious pain as he shook his head and then turned to look at Elise.

Janson—for a moment Elise stopped where she was, her eyes meeting his for the first time in almost a year. He did not smile. He just stared at her, what seemed an awful patience there on his face. He did not move toward her, but only seemed to be waiting.

Janson—Elise thought her heart would burst as she stared at him, unable to break the spell that held her there and make herself move in his direction. Then she rushed forward and into his arms, knocking the cane away accidentally in her need to reach him. He almost collapsed against her, then he was holding her and she herself was keeping him on his feet—he was home. At last, he was home.

～

The house had grown quiet, Henry and the girls in their beds already, and Elise checking the kitchen one last time. Janson sat on the edge of the bed he had shared with Elise before he left for the war, waiting for her, and wondering what it would be like to be with her now after all the months they had been apart—now, with the way his body was. He looked at the cane leaned against the iron headboard of the bed, then looked away again, feeling a touch of disgust with himself. It would hurt him if Elise herself turned away—but what would it be like now?

Coming home had been so different than he had imagined it might be. So many nights overseas he had lain in a hole and tried to imagine what it would be like the day the war was over and he could come home—but the war was still going on, and he had come home anyway to an Eason County that had changed, and a wife who had changed. He and Elise had come from the depot in the first taxicab ride he had ever taken in his life, had driven down a Main Street now bustling with people and activity in the midst of war. They had gone into the village, and it had seemed to Janson that almost every house had a flag hanging in a front window, so many of those now having gold stars on them. The mill itself seemed to be running all-out behind its high fence and gate. There had been men in uniform there, and Elise said they were helping now in the mill to get materials out for the war effort, but, other than those, there were few men of military age about.

Janson had seen quite a number of women on the street near the mill, and he had been surprised to note that some of them had been wearing slacks. Elise herself was wearing a dress, and Janson had stared openly at her legs on the taxicab ride home, for her calves were bare beneath the hem of her skirt, with white socks turned down at her ankles.

"It's impossible to even get stockings now," she told him, tugging self-consciously at the bottom edge of her dress as she noticed his stare. "I lost one out of the only good pair I had left down the drain while I was rinsing them out—"

So much seemed to have changed. There had been plenty of

vegetables at supper that night, but no meat—meat was hard to come by as well, Elise told him, or butter, or coffee, or so many other things. So much had been rationed, from sugar to shoes, to automobile tires, to gasoline, and what was not rationed there was usually a shortage of—so much he had forgotten while he was away. There had been rationing and shortages before he left, but that seemed ages ago now.

There had even been a truck on their street when they had gotten home. "Whip the Japs with your scrap," the sign on the side had read. Elise said they now saved everything, from bacon grease, to paper, to the tin-foil that came wrapped around chewing gum, anything that could be recycled and used in the war effort. Home was not the way he had remembered it at all.

His children seemed so much older, older than the passage of a year should have allowed them. Catherine, fifteen and looking so much like her mother, was not much younger than Elise had been when he married her. Elise had seemed a woman to him then, but Catherine was still his little girl. In some ways he could now under-stand why Elise's father had tried to kill him those many years before.

Judith, still his baby, just turning thirteen years old, all elbows and knees, but becoming a young woman. She had helped her mother prepare supper, and had set the table while Catherine spent the time talking about a picture show and some soon-to-be GI she thought looked like the singer, Frank Sinatra. Janson found himself admiring how much his youngest daughter had grown up, while at the same time wishing the GI shits on Sinatra's look-alike once he got overseas.

Both girls had fussed over him in their own ways, had worried about his wounds, and had been his little girls again even for just a time—but Henry seemed almost a man now. At sixteen and a half, he was almost as tall as his father, and his voice had deepened remarkably in the time Janson had been gone. He had shaken Janson's hand when he had gotten in from school, and had called him "sir" as if he were a stranger now in his own home. Catherine and Judith had each given him a hug and a kiss on the cheek, had called him "Pa," and had been obviously happy to have him home. Even Stan had put his one good arm around his shoulders and welcomed him back—but Henry had shook his hand.

"Hello, sir," his son had said.

Hello, sir—

That bothered him more than he was willing to say.

Elise had perhaps changed most of all. It was not just the bare legs beneath her skirt, or the knowledge that she had been working in the mill for the Easons, or even the thought of the time they had been apart—it was the way she had met everyone's eyes at the depot, the way she had told the man in the taxicab to drive them home, something in her very bearing.

She came into the bedroom and closed the door, then turned back to look at him, color rising to her cheeks a moment after she met his eyes—it had been so long since they had been alone together, at night, here in this room. It struck him suddenly that this was what he had thought of on so many nights overseas, what he had wanted to come home to: Elise, and this bed, and a night when the rest of the world could go away.

She hesitated at the door, then crossed the room to sit beside him on the bed, reaching out to take his hand in hers and intertwine her fingers with his. "I'm afraid you'll disappear if I close my eyes," she said. "I'm afraid I'll wake up and find out it's all a dream and you'll still be gone—"

"I'm not goin' anywhere," he said, smiling at her. He reached up and brushed the hair back from her eyes, then leaned to kiss her, but she seemed to hesitate and so he stopped and looked at her for a moment. Her blue eyes were moving over his as if she were looking for something.

"Janson, I have to know. You were gone so long—it won't matter, but I have to know."

"Know what?" he asked, wanting to touch her, but feeling almost as awkward as the first time they had been together those years before.

"I know how you are, and I can accept it if you did, but I have to know. While you were gone, did you—" for a moment she hesitated, "were you—" She seemed unable to finish.

For a moment he did not understand, then comprehension suddenly hit him. He looked at her with surprise, not wanting to believe she had even asked. The color rose to her cheeks again, but she did not look away. "You think I had another woman while I was gone?" he demanded, releasing her hand and moving away from her slightly where they sat on the bed. His hip hurt, but he did not care.

"Did you?" she asked, her eyes never leaving his.

Anger filled him. How could she not trust him after all the years they had been together? How could she think he would be with another woman just because she wasn't there? He had known GI's who had gone with women overseas, women who had no idea there was a wife and a family back home, but he never had. There had been buddies who had tried to introduce him to women, buddies who had told him his wife would never know—and he had never once been tempted.

"Were you with another man while I was gone?" he asked her, and then watched the rage immediately fill her.

"How dare you—you know I would never—" He thought for a moment she would slap him, but he sat still and waited until she took a breath.

"What's th' difference in me askin' you an' you askin' me?" he demanded. "You think I'm more likely t' cheat on you than you on me? I ain't been with nobody but you in all these years, not since th' day I first saw you; you ought t' know that just as good as I know you ain't never been with no other man but me. I cain't believe you'd even ask me, that all th' time I've been gone you ain't trusted me."

"It's not that. It's—"

"What?" he demanded.

"I'm sorry," she said after a moment, and then lowered her eyes. "It's just been so long. I know you haven't. I just wanted to hear you say it."

"I may not be much, but, whatever I am, it belongs t' you," he said after a moment. "I ain't never give you no reason t' doubt that."

She nodded her head, still not raising her eyes. "It's just—I've just missed you so much, and it's been so long. I—"

"I've missed bein' with you, too." He looked at her for a long moment. At last she raised her eyes to meet his, then after a time looked down again, her hand reaching out to touch his thigh lightly.

"Is it bad?" she asked, her eyes coming to his again. "Does it hurt?"

"It aches. It don't really hurt too much no more." He watched her for a moment, her hair moving down to cover her face partially as she looked to where her hand moved along his thigh and up to his side. "Does it matter to you?" he asked her.

"What?" She looked up, brushing her hair back from her eyes.

"This," he said, nodding with his head down toward his body, and then again toward the cane that rested against the iron headboard of the bed. "That I came home to you like this?"

"You came home to me. That's what matters."

"But, like this—"

"No." She moved closer, then stretched up to kiss him, her hand moving up a moment later to touch his face as she looked at him.

"But, you don't know yet how you'll feel."

"About what?"

"About having a cripple for a husband—I don't know if I'll have to use the cane for the rest of my life, but—"

"No—" Her fingers came to rest over his lips, silencing his words, and then moved away again. "That doesn't matter." She was touching him now, not lightly, and not in pity. "I want to be with you—is that okay; I mean, can we? Are you healed well enough yet?"

He didn't have to answer. She knew. After a moment he reached out to turn off the light, but she stopped him, her hand coming to rest on his arm.

"No, leave it on," she said, and, after a time, Janson felt that he had truly come home.

～

He awoke hours later in the midst of a dream, the images following him up from sleep and making him think for a moment that he was back there again, back lying in a hole with half of a world between him and where his life should be.

Then he felt Elise against him, and heard her voice, almost a whisper, breathed against his shoulder. "Janson, are you all right?"

"Yeah. Just a bad dream," he said quietly in the chilled room.

He felt her nod in the darkness, then felt her hand on his chest, her lips touch the skin just below his right ear. "Promise you won't leave me again," she said very softly, as she tugged the quilts closer against them.

He lay thinking of the nights he had lain in darkness and dreamed her there, of her breath on his skin.

Of being home.

If this was a dream now, he hoped never to wake up.

"I'm not goin' anywhere," he said, his lips against her hair. "I'll be here 'til th' day I die."

# II

THE WAS A PAINFUL SIL-
ence between them the next morning as Elise dressed for work. Henry
and the girls were still asleep, though breakfast waited for them warm
in the kitchen so they could eat before school, and Stan was working
the second part of a double. Janson and Elise were alone in the front
room, Elise standing only the space of half the floor away as she ironed
the cotton dress she would wear to the mill, but Janson felt distanced
from her. They had not been apart since he had gotten home, for he
had followed her to the kitchen when she prepared breakfast, and
even asked her to help him down the steps that led from the rear porch
and into the yard when he had to go to the outhouse, but now
morning had come and she would be leaving for her shift in the mill.
Janson would be alone in the house once the children left for school,
alone and staying here, for his wounds and the need for the walking
cane made both the front and rear steps seem an impossibility to him.

They had spent the night touching, talking. They had slept at last
only for him to wake this morning to find her staring at him in the
darkness. They had talked about how the children had changed, how
Henry would soon be a man, and Catherine too interested in this boy
she liked, and Judith becoming quite a young lady. They had talked
of the years they had spent together, the struggle, during the Depression and even before, and the dreams. They talked of the months they
had been apart, the loneliness, the worry—she had not asked about
the fighting, about what it had been like over there, or even of the

night he had been wounded, and he had found that he was glad.

He would tell her one day, but not yet. Now he just wanted to be home.

They had talked about how the town had changed, the people, about the privations on the homefront of a people at war—and most of all they had talked of what they would do after the war.

She dealt him a shock when she told him she had put their money in the bank—all that hope, all that work, all those dreams, and she had put it in a bank just as if that was not the very way they lost it back in 1930. The banks might be open again now, might have been open since not long after FDR took office back in '33, and there might not have been any talk of them going under since that time, but Janson Sanders would never trust a bank again. One had locked its doors and never given him what was rightfully his—he would never let that happen again.

"Did you forget what happened before?" he had asked her, having been for a moment almost too surprised to speak. "We lost everythin' when th' bank collapsed back then!"

"The banks aren't going to fail again, Janson."

"You don't know that! Elise, you could 'a lost everythin'!"

But she had only lifted her chin and stared at him directly in the darkness. "Do you think I'd take a chance if I thought that could happen again? Someone could have stolen the money with it here in the house. Having it in the bank is safer than leaving it here where someone could come in while we're gone and take it—besides, it's insured by the government, and if FDR says it's safe, then you know it's safe."

"But—" he had begun, but had realized that he could not argue with her. The money had been in the bank for months now, and she said that it was still there—he would just feel safer if it was where he could see it, could count it. Besides, he was home now and he could take it out any time he wanted and put it some place safer until the war was over, and then they could do what they had planned to do for so long—it was so much money, more than they had ever saved before.

He had been surprised when she showed him the numbers in the bankbook, Elise getting up during the night and turning on the electric lights so she could fetch it from a drawer across the room. He stared at the numbers for a long time, then got her to say them over to him again just in case he was wrong—it was a fortune in his eyes, and it would buy for them something that was worth more than any amount of money he could ever own. It would buy his land. It would buy a dream, and the life he had promised Elise for so long.

Janson sat on the side of the bed, watching as Elise unbuttoned the dress and slipped it on, knowing it had to be still warm to her skin from the iron. The savings had grown in the time he had been gone. He knew very well how much had been there when he left, and, though Elise had only told him that she had managed to stay out of it in the months he had been away, he knew she had added to it as well. Somehow that did not seem right, Elise's money, money she had worked for, Elise Whitley working in a cotton mill—what have I brought you to? he thought, staring at her as she buttoned the dress. He had intended to make her quit the mill the minute he got home, had fully well intended to make her do it when he had first gotten in the day before, but now he could not make himself bring up the subject.

She had told him she was glad to be doing something in the war effort, that it felt good knowing that something she was doing could help to win the war, just as her victory garden and her collecting scrap and her cup of bacon grease by the stove was helping—there was nothing he could do now, he had thought. He had no scrap to collect or bacon grease to keep by, and gardening was beyond him for the moment. The mill had no use for him now, no use for a man who was part cripple, he had told himself, returning "war hero" or not, as Judith had called him. No one needed him—not even Elise.

He had come home, but he had come home only to be one more person for Elise to have to look after and fret over. Her working had been bad enough. Her working for the Easons, supporting him now, pulling a shift down running a drawing machine, and him unable to do the work instead and make her stay home—he wished he had not seen this day.

He kept thinking about how she had been when he first met her: petted, spoiled, sixteen years old and living in her father's grand house, a girl with fancy clothes and motor cars and all the money in the world—and she was going today to work in a cotton mill, working to bring home money to support a husband trapped in the three rooms of a mill house, a man unsure as to whether he could even manage the front steps to reach the yard without falling.

He clenched his hand over the crook of the walking cane as it rested against his thigh, clenched it until the veins bulged out on the back of his hand and his knuckles turned white—he had never wanted her to work. It was not a woman's place to work, not if she had a man to look after her—but he could not look after her. He could not even look after his own children. He could sit home and make baskets, or bottom chairs, and get Henry to peddle them door-to-door—but it would be Elise who would make the wage that would put food on their table.

She was sitting in a chair before the dresser now, a drawer open beside her which she was looking through as if she were searching for something. She was talking as she moved things about in the drawer, but he could not make himself listen to her. He pushed himself to his feet instead, leaning heavily on the walking stick because of the ache in his hip, until he had straightened fully, then he made his way to the dresser, the sound the cane made on the floor loud to his ears. The dull ache in his hip became pain as he crossed the room.

He stood behind her, placing his free hand on her shoulder as he looked down at her reflection in the mirror. Elise smiled as her eyes rose to meet his in the glass, then she reached up to place her hand over his.

"I'm glad you're home," she said, still smiling, her hand squeezing his.

Her skin was warm where it touched him, her shoulder rounded beneath his hand, bringing back memories of the night—then his eyes caught the reflection of his own body behind her, of how he stood now with his weight all on one leg, of the cane gripped tightly in his hand, the cane he leaned on even now heavily for support.

Janson turned his eyes away, not returning her smile. She squeezed his hand again, but said nothing more. Janson moved away to slowly cross the room until he stood with his back to her, his eyes on the photograph of himself she had on the table by the bed. After a moment her voice resumed, talking of the children, but Janson found himself unable to listen. He stared down at his image, knowing she was talking just to fill the minutes until the time came when she would have to leave. He kept telling himself that it would only be like this until he could go back to work, kept telling himself that it would not be that long, kept telling himself that soon he would be rid of the cane and back to the mill and Elise could come home.

He turned and looked at her, her back to him as she opened another drawer—she was not so far away, he told himself. A baby could walk that distance, and he could certainly do it without the cane. The Army doctors had told him to take it easy, not to push his recovery, and that he might re-injure the hip, but it was not so great a distance. A few steps today, a few more tomorrow, and he would be back to the mill sooner than anyone expected. All he would have to do was work at it, to make himself take those steps each day, and to do it without the security of the cane that was supporting him even now.

Janson moved closer to the table to brace his hand against it, then leaned the walking stick against the wall alongside the headboard of the bed. For a moment he stood unsure, but then he looked again at Elise still sitting with her back to him, and he knew he could do it. So few steps and he would be able to touch her; so few steps and she would be in his arms.

She was talking lightly of the children, telling him how the girls had learned to cook over the past year. Catherine had almost set the kitchen ablaze four different times with a grease fire, until Henry had sworn he would never allow his sister near a stove again, but Janson was barely listening to her—only a few steps, he told himself. Only a few steps and he could stand beside her. A baby not even a year old could walk that distance. Only a few steps.

He turned loose of the table, gritting his teeth at the pain that shot through his hip and leg—the cane had been safety, assurance that he would not fall, something to counter-balance his weight so that it would not hurt so much to stand.

He kept his eyes fixed on Elise and took a step, then another—it was not so bad. It hurt, but he was walking, standing on his own two feet again. He had been a fool not to have tried it before.

Another step, and it was nowhere near as hard as he had thought. It felt as if one leg might be shorter than the other now, and he was certain it was caused from using the cane—I'll get used to it, he told himself.

Another step. She was looking in another drawer now. She had not seen him coming to her yet, but she would. She would smile and he would take her in his arms—the damn doctors; they did not know what they were saying. Telling him to take it easy, to be careful and not re-injure the hip; he wished they could see him now.

Elise would be happy and surprised. He would be back in the mill in a week or two, and he would have her quit her job the minute he was back to work, war effort or no war effort. She was just giving that as a reason so he would not feel so bad. She would come home and be a wife again, sew if she wanted, and could feel like a woman. He would be a husband she could be proud of. He would again be able to take care of her and the kids, provide for them—and once the war was over, there would be the land. Elise would have the home he had promised her for so long. She and the girls could hang curtains in the windows and plant flowers in the yard and they could know the house would be theirs year after year. He and Henry, and Stan if he wanted, would work the land. They would have crops that were all their own, crops that would see them through each winter, crops that would get them from one year and to the next. Only a few steps—

Janson had almost reached Elise when she lifted her eyes and saw his reflection in the mirror. Her eyes took in the pain on his face, and then moved beyond him to the cane where it leaned against the wall alongside the bed. She turned in the chair and started to rise to her feet and he reached out to take her into his arms—suddenly his leg gave way. A sharp pain shot through his hip and he fell against her, feeling her catch him, her hands going beneath his arms as she braced him with strength he had not known she possessed.

He grabbed for the edge of the nearby dresser and pulled away from her, gritting his teeth against the pain in his hip—he would have fallen if she had not caught him. For a moment he could not meet her eyes. He had wanted to show her that he was still a man.

Elise reached out to touch him but he moved away, bracing against the surface of the dresser for support as the leg threatened to give way again—he was not a man anymore, he told himself. He was not a man.

He was not anything.

~

A few days later, Henry Sanders stood in the open rear door that led into the kitchen in their half of the mill house, watching his father in the back yard. He knew that Janson did not know he was being watched that afternoon, and that was how Henry wanted it.

Janson made his way slowly from the rear porch, walking carefully over the uneven ground as he leaned heavily on his walking stick. When he reached the woodpile, he hooked the cane over his arm, braced his right knee carefully against a stack of large logs, and bent to pick up several sticks of firewood, only enough to carry on one arm, then cautiously made his way back to the rear porch. He had made the trip several times already, and, on each return trip to the porch, Henry had ducked inside and closed the door almost shut so that he would not be seen.

The stack of firewood at the edge of the porch was pitiably small, growing only by a few sticks on each trip as Henry watched. He knew that when his father was at last satisfied with the amount he had brought to the porch, he would repeat the entire process over again in taking the wood in to the woodbox in the kitchen. Henry could have reduced the entire process to one trip, could have had it over and done, but he knew better than to offer.

Henry could see the pain in Janson's movements, in the set expression on his face each time he turned back for the return trip to the porch, but Henry also knew that he was the last person from whom his father would accept help. A silent set of rules had come to exist between them in the few days his father had been home—Henry did not offer help. He did not fuss over his father or try to wait on him as his mother, Judith, and sometimes even Catherine did. Janson might tolerate it from the girls, greet it with silence from his wife, but he would not accept it in the slightest from his son.

At first Henry had wondered if he had done something to anger his father, but it had not taken long before he understood—his father was angry with himself. Janson was angry with how he had been wounded, and most especially with the fact that he could not work now or get about as he used to. The womenfolk could get away with trying to take care of him, but not Henry. Henry was only months short of his seventeenth birthday; he was tall and strong, and had two good arms; he knew that he could be of more help than the girls, his mother, or his Uncle Stan—but his Uncle Stan had never once tried to help his father:

"Let him do it on his own," his uncle told him.

It had been much the same as Henry had gotten from Janson—"I can get it," "I can do it for myself," or "I don't need any help"—but still Henry watched.

"I don't see how he can expect me to just stand there and not offer to help him," Henry had told his friend, Isaac Betts, earlier that afternoon. He had gone by Isaac's house immediately after school, had been waiting for him on his front steps when Isaac had gotten in from the school he attended there in the colored part of town.

Isaac's stepmother, Esther, had tried to get them to come inside, but Henry had declined—Isaac's little brother, Andrew, was four years old now, just old enough to be a bother, and he had a new baby sister, Clarice, who cried most of the time. After Olivia, Isaac was his best friend, the one person he knew he could always talk to, for Henry found that at times even Olivia could not understand the things going on inside his mind: Isaac was black, and Henry Sanders was part Cherokee. There was a common ground between them that Olivia could never touch. Neither Henry nor Isaac had ever fit in with the world around them.

Isaac had taken the time to read a letter waiting for him from his cousin, Wilson Jakes, who was overseas. Wilson had gotten his father's permission and tried to enlist in the Navy, but the Navy did not want black recruits, so he enlisted in the Army instead, going into a segregated division of black soldiers under the command of white officers. Isaac said even the Red Cross blood banks for the military were being kept segregated, which made no sense to Henry—blood was red. It wasn't black or white.

After Isaac finished Wilson's letter, Henry told Isaac about his father.

"I don't see how there's anything wrong with offering to help him," Isaac said, but Isaac's father spoke up from the open doorway behind them.

"Your daddy's a proud man, Henry," Nathan Betts said. He stood drying his hands on a mended dishtowel, his hair now more white than black, thinning at both sides just above his temples. "He ain't gonna take no help from nobody."

Henry thought about that now as he stood in the rear door, watching his father take up another armload of wood. After a moment Janson started back and Henry ducked inside, then, hearing him start up the steps at last, he closed the door quietly and moved to the half-closed doorway between the middle room and the kitchen, waiting for his father to bring the wood inside. He stood quietly, listening for the sound of a fall—he would go to help if his father fell, whether Janson wanted him to or not.

~

Janson was pushing himself for things to be as they had been before the war; Henry knew that. As the days passed, Janson seemed driven to walk about the house and the yard, until pain showed clearly on his face at the end of each day, and Henry began to worry, as he knew his mother did, that his father was doing too much.

On the second Sunday after Janson had gotten home, Henry paused in the rear doorway coming into the kitchen with a bucket of water from the tap outside, hearing his parents' voices.

"Janson, it's not that important," his mother said. "It doesn't matter which one of us is working, as long as we're getting by. With the war and—"

"It matters t' me." His father's voice was almost angry, and for a moment Henry was certain they were arguing. He had rarely heard them argue in all his life.

"If you keep pushing yourself so hard, you'll only end up hurting your hip all over again and it'll be even longer before—"

"I ain't gonna have you supportin' me any longer'n I have t'!" His father shouted the words.

"You'll only make it worse! You can't keep pushing yourself like this!"

"Maybe I ain't pushin' myself hard enough! I'm still usin' this cane, ain't I?" Henry had opened the door enough to look inside. His father was holding the cane out toward his mother, staring at her. She stared back, then touched his hand, at last taking the cane to prop it against his thigh. "I ain't gonna hurt myself," he said, more quietly.

His mother moved closer to his father and touched his face a moment before Henry closed the door. "You better not," Henry heard her say, then for a time he heard nothing more from either of them. He waited, then made a deliberate noise this time before he opened the door. His pa was still sitting sideways at the kitchen table, with his old, water-marked Bible open on his knee, his mother a few steps away at the stove.

"Here's the water you wanted, Mama," Henry said and set the bucket down on the old wooden eating table. His father looked at the bucket, then closed his Bible.

"You'll need more water than that t' do th' breakfast dishes," he said, pushing himself to his feet with one hand against the table, then reaching for his cane.

"No, Janson, this is enough," his mother said.

"I'll get some more." Henry took up an empty bucket from the floor by the stove, but his father took it from his hands.

"I'll do it," Janson said. When the door closed behind him, Henry turned to look at his mother, but she did not meet his eyes. She was staring at the closed rear door with worry on her face.

Nothing any of them did deterred his father. Each day Janson pushed himself harder, drove himself further, until at last he was able to walk the house without his cane, then to make his way down the steps and into the yard. Three or four times daily he made the venture, walking until pain showed clearly on his face and he had to stop. Each day he went farther, coming home limping badly but never seeming satisfied with what he had done. Henry's mother could not stop him. Henry could not stop him. Henry's sisters could not have stopped him, even if they tried. All that any of them could do was walk along with him in the times he would allow it. All Henry or his mother either one could do was prepare to try to catch him if he stumbled—and he often stumbled.

The first time Henry saw him fall in the yard, he immediately started to go to him, but his mother took hold of his arm.

"Leave him alone, Henry. He's got to do it on his own," she said, staring out through the screen door to where Janson lay in the yard. Her grip on his arm did not diminish, but she never once looked at her son.

"But, he'll need help getting up—"

"No, leave him be."

Henry turned away, unable to watch his father struggle to regain his feet. But his mother never turned away. Henry wondered how she could watch—then he saw the tears in her eyes. She watched until Janson was again on his feet, then she called to him, smiling, just as if she had seen nothing. "Dinner's almost ready, Janson."

He nodded and waved from where he stood in the yard, and Elise turned away, the unshed tears still visible in her eyes as she returned to the food cooking on the stove. Janson waited until he thought that neither of them was watching, but Henry saw—he made his way slowly back to the house, limping badly. When he entered the kitchen a few minutes later, the limp was barely noticeable, but pain still showed in his eyes.

Each day Janson worked harder, and each day he did more, until one day little more than a month after he had come home, he met Henry in the front room as soon as Henry got in from school.

"I'm gonna walk up t' th' mill. I thought you might want t' go." It was the closest his pa would come to asking Henry to do something for him, and Henry set his books down without a second thought, ready to go.

Janson did not use his cane. He walked beside his son, limping but unassisted. Once he almost stumbled and Henry started to reach out for him, but Janson caught himself against the trunk of a tree alongside the sidewalk, and, after a moment's rest, they walked on.

He was limping badly, each step bringing pain to his face by the time they reached the mill, but there was also satisfaction in his expression. "Why don't you wait out here," he said to his son. "I'm goin' in for a minute."

Henry watched him go up the steps and into the mill office, noticing with surprise that there was very little of the limp evident in his pa's walk as he entered the building.

A half hour later Janson came out of the office, causing Henry to rise from the step where he had spent the wait. There was again satisfaction on Janson Sanders's face as his eyes came to rest on his son. "Why don't you an' me re-bottom your ma's rocking chair tomorrow?" Janson said. "It'll be Saturday an' there won't be no school. It won't take too much time."

"Okay," Henry said, staring at him with surprise.

Janson looked down the street deeper into the village. "Won't be much time for doin' it next week or after," he said. "I'll be goin' back t' work Monday." He brought his eyes back to his son. "Lets go home, Henry," he said, placing a hand on Henry's shoulder. "I got a surprise for your ma."

They looked at each other, then they descended the steps before the mill office and started down the village street toward home.

~

Elise was the most damn-stubbornest woman Janson had ever known in his life. She would not quit the mill, not even with him back at work now, not even when she knew that was what he wanted: "When the war's over," she told him instead.

When the war's over . . .

There was so much talk about what would happen when the war was won. Some people worried that the Depression would return. A few hoped the fighting would continue because it had brought them good jobs. Everyone seemed to have victory lists of the things they would buy and do once the war was won. Janson himself planned for the day he would buy back his land, and the day he would at last see Elise quit the mill—all once the war was over. Until then it was not as bad as he had thought it would be. They walked to their shifts together in the mornings, and walked home together in the afternoons. He saw her at times in the mill during the day, and it was nice to know she was that close—not so bad as he had thought at all.

It was a spring morning in 1945 that Janson and Elise walked together to the mill. Elise was fretting over the boy Catherine was convinced for the moment she was in love with, and Janson had just about decided he would need to have a private talk with this young man, as he had the last, when Janson's cousin, Sissy, met them at the bottom of their hill. She had been crying, her eyes red and her face streaked with tears.

"Have you heard?" she asked and Elise took her arm. "FDR's dead—"

Sissy's words had been quiet, but they left Janson feeling as if he had been struck. FDR dead. The President—

"What happened?" was all he could ask, reaching out to take Elise's arm at the look of shock on her face.

"I don't know. They said it happened in Warm Springs, Georgia, late yesterday. I don't know—"

There was a numbness inside of Janson, and a sadness that he was surprised to feel over someone he had never met—FDR was dead. Words and phrases came back to him, all in that peculiar Northern accent that he had first heard so many years before—

"... the only thing we have to fear is fear itself ..."

"... I see one-third of a nation ill-housed, ill-clad, ill-nourished ..."

"... a new deal for the forgotten man ..."

"Yesterday, December 7th, 1941, a date which will live in infamy ..."

"... keep that faith constant, keep that faith high. . ."

"... to recommend the measures that a stricken nation in the midst of a stricken world may require ..."

"In this dedication of a Nation we humbly ask the blessing of God. May He protect each and every one of us. May He guide me in the days to come."

Franklin Delano Roosevelt had been a voice on the radio to Janson, a face in the few newsreels he had seen, a picture on the front of magazines Elise had brought home, but more than that. FDR had been President through the darkest years of the Depression. He had been with them through the attack at Pearl Harbor and the war— always there, since that day back in '33 when Janson had stood with others in that little country store outside Cedar Flatts and heard that voice over the radio for the first time. That had been twelve years ago. FDR had been elected to office four times; he had brought hope, drawn curses, had been damned and praised and reviled, and he had always had that ability to make people believe when it seemed they couldn't believe in anything anymore.

Janson himself had cursed Roosevelt with every breath when he had had to plow under part of his cotton in the early days of the New Deal, but he had come to think differently. If FDR had not been President, there would have been no relief for his family when they had needed it the most. If FDR had not been President, there would have been no WPA job to bring them out of sharecropping—and Janson could not imagine anyone else having led them in war.

And now the President was dead.

"His poor family—" Elise said quietly, tears moving down her face. But, somehow, Janson felt sorry for the whole family of Americans.

~

It seemed that Franklin Delano Roosevelt had been President forever, and it felt odd to say "President Truman" in his wake. The war was not yet over in Europe, but everyone was certain now that it was only a matter of time. Germany would soon be defeated, and then there would be Japan left to defeat. The war had to—certainly to God—be over soon, and the boys could come home, and people were beginning now to fret at what would happen when Victory was reached—would there be jobs for returning soldiers? Would people working lose out to those coming home from the war? How long would rationing continue? When would the shortages end? What would happen when the Allies reached Berlin and Hitler? Would the Japanese ever surrender?

Victory was coming. They could all feel it. The question was when. When would peace come?

As May came in, everyone was looking toward Germany. There were reports over the radio that the Allies were nearing Berlin, then the word finally came—Hitler was dead; the Germans had surrendered. The war in Europe was over at last.

But peace had come at a high price. Europe was a devastated land, bomb-pitted, fire-blackened, stained with the blood of its own young men and others. It was a people, a land, war-ravaged and in places desolate. Its treasures had been pillaged. Its homes burned. Its children frightened. The Allies had won, but the marks of the struggle would remain forever.

The war in the Pacific continued, and Elise began to wonder if it would ever end. The Japanese seemed almost inhuman, as if they would all rather die than be defeated. Sadness hung over the families of the boys returning from the battlefields—a face grown older, aged beyond his years, seen after years of worry and at times weeks with no word. Tears, hugs, joy, a rest, then to return, only to be retrained to be shipped out to the Pacific. People were whispering that there would be an invasion of Japan. Elise heard the whispers, and she could only feel relief that Janson was out of it now. If nothing else, he was out of it.

Summer wore on, hot and breathless. Many of the boys who had fought in Europe were now ready to ship out for the Pacific. Peace seemed as far away as ever, and Elise realized that her greatest worry was just beginning—if the war did not end with Japan, then Henry might have to go. He had turned seventeen already, and had begun to talk of wanting to enlist in the Navy. Elise felt sometimes as if her heart would stop with the very thought—Henry so far away from home, Henry on one of the ships the Japanese often sank. She and Janson both refused to give their consent, but still she worried— Henry could so easily pass for eighteen. All he would have to do would be to lie about his age. Even if he did not, in one year he would no longer need their consent. He could even be drafted—please, God, it had to end before that. She could not be worrying at every knock at the door that it was a telegram telling her that her son was gone—it had to end. It had to.

She and Janson were both working in the mill, both earning well, saving for that day after Victory when Janson's dream could at last come true—a Victory that she prayed for more fervently now than ever before. Perhaps Janson might understand now why she had had to go to work in the mill while he had been gone, why she had had to do her part in some way more than just conserving food and collecting scrap, why she had had to continue to work on her shift even after he had come home and had gone back to the mill. She could see it in his eyes now when he looked at Henry—they all had to do their part. They had to reach Victory before the war could take her only son.

They were leaving their shifts in the mill when word came that President Truman had ordered that an atom bomb be dropped on the Japanese city of Hiroshima. An atom bomb—Elise had never heard the phrase before, and at first she could only hope that it would bring an earlier end to the war.

Then she listened with horror to the radio reports of an entire city destroyed, uncountable people killed, more horribly burned, not just soldiers, but civilians, women and children, babies, old people who had a right to peace at last—and she realized for the first time in her life that she did not understand at all what her husband was feeling when Janson told her that the bomb was better than sending our boys in to be killed in an invasion.

"But, all those people, babies, little children—"

"More'n that'll die if we have t' invade."

Still she could not understand the thought—so many dead, so many hurt, so many—

Three days after the first bomb, a second, smaller one was dropped on the Japanese city of Nagasaki. The next day peace negotiations began at last, and four days later words came over the radio they had been waiting so long to hear—*"We have just received word that the Japanese have surrendered—"*

The war was over at last.

# 12

ELISE WAS LAID OFF FROM THE mill before Janson could make her quit. It happened almost as soon as word came of the Japanese surrender. Most of the women who had taken jobs after the war began received notice that they were no longer needed—*you've done a good job, girls, now go home and raise your children*. Janson was glad to have her home again, glad even when she put the sign in the window saying "Sewing Done," but he also found that he was angry—quitting should have been her choice, and his, not a decision made by Walter Eason.

The women in the mill village were not the only ones affected by the end of the war. For over a year everyone had been waiting, knowing that it was only a matter of time until it was over. But, even with all the talk that had gone on of reconversion to a civilian economy, of what people would do "after the war," or "when we reach Victory," no one seemed quite prepared for it when it came. The need for military goods was suddenly cut off. Stocks of supplies purchased to complete government contracts sat in factories. Finished products needed for the now non-existent war effort sat unneeded in warehouses the nation over. Women and blacks who had been taken on during the war effort all received notice that the plants, mills, and factories would no longer need their services. Even many of those who had taken jobs in retail stores were told they would have to vacate positions for returning servicemen.

War plants shut down, throwing thousands out of work with little or no notice. People were left stranded in big cities with no money on which to return to the towns where they had lived before the war—it had seemed such a boon, so much money after the long, desperate years of the Depression.

But there also arose a sudden, unbelievable demand for civilian goods, toasters, vacuums, automobiles, and other things that production had been halted on so that factories could produce the materials needed for the war. Shortages continued and even worsened. The war was over at last and it was time for the victory lists to be filled. They had all been planning for after the war, all dreaming of the things they would have, all the things they would do—and the day had finally come.

Janson had his own plans. They were not put away on a victory list or expected to be bought from a store shelf, but had been a part of him now for a very long time—he would soon have his land back. He had already gone to talk to the current owner of the land, and had even been taken on a walk through the house and out over the cotton fields—the man was willing to sell. It was only now a matter of time.

As he entered the lunchroom at the mill on a Thursday in mid-October, his mind was filled with plans of what he would do once the land was his again. He would clear more, plant more, than was in use now. There was a tenant in the house, and the land had been parceled out, but he knew that he and his family could be on the place well before the next spring. When their first crop came in the following fall, it would be all their own, without a share to go to a landowner, for Janson would be the owner of the land—there would be money to buy things for Elise, money to buy things for the girls and Henry; the life he had sworn to Elise so long before would be theirs at last. The house already had running water and electricity to it, luxuries the place had never known when he had been a boy—finally, all the things he had dreamed of for so long would be coming true.

His thoughts were so occupied that Janson paid little attention to anyone around him as he walked into the lunchroom, until he was drawn up short by the voice of Buddy Eason from not too far away.

"Yeah, I heard that the damned red-nigger was all crippled up—too bad the damn Kraut's bullet didn't kill him instead—"

Janson almost turned—but he knew that was what Buddy wanted. He sat down at a vacant table and opened the paper sack of food he had brought with him to the mill that morning—there had been too many fights between them over the years. Too many fights from the time they had been no older than Henry was now. He had almost killed Buddy Eason back then, and he wished he had. There would be at least one good man alive now if Buddy had died all those years before, for Buddy had been responsible for the death of the downtown grocer, Edgar Brown, and had almost allowed Janson to be lynched for Brown's murder, as well as for the burning of half of downtown, which Buddy had also caused.

"He's one ugly son-of-a-bitch, but he's got two girls who'd be worth having a go at. I bet even the youngest is old enough now, and the oldest has a pair of—"

Janson's hands tore his sandwich into pieces. He turned in his chair, rage filling him so completely that he could not hear the remainder of Buddy's words—he was going to kill Buddy Eason this time. He was certain of it. He was going to—

There was a look of satisfaction on Buddy's heavy face, pleasure at having gotten what he wanted as he stared now at Janson. He stood there in his expensive suit and tie, a man going rapidly to fat at the age of thirty-seven.

The men standing near Buddy moved away as Janson rose to his feet, as if distancing themselves from what Buddy said—but that did not matter. Janson knew the words had been meant for him, and for no one else. They had accomplished nothing more than what Buddy had intended.

"Do you think you can beat me now, Crip?" Buddy asked as Janson moved toward him, a smile on his heavily jowled face. "Do you think you can beat me?—I'm going to kill you this time, you crippled-up red nigger. I'm going to—"

"That's enough!" The voice came from just within the entrance of the lunchroom, and Janson turned to find Walter Eason standing there, his eyes on Janson and his grandson. The old man leaned heavily on his walking cane, but he came forward anyway, stopping only when he had reached a point between where Janson stood and where Buddy remained nearer to the doorway. "Go back to the card room, Janson," Eason said, but his eyes were set now on his grandson. "Go back to the card room—now," he repeated, his voice rising after a moment when Janson did not move.

Janson looked back to Buddy, and a look of hatred passed between them. Then Janson turned to leave.

"This is the end of it between you two—" he heard Walter Eason say to Buddy behind him.

No, it's not—Janson thought. It would not be over until only one of them was alive.

The mid-century mark was only five years away, and at last the modern world had come to the mill village. Elise stood in her open front door, looking out on the usually quiet street. There were men passing to-and-fro, trucks with carpentry supplies and pipes, shovels, bricks, and mortar. The sound of work could be heard from several streets away. At last, it was beginning.

She had walked to Dorrie's house earlier in the day, had seen the work going on in the streets, yards, and houses. Trenches were being dug to run water pipes into the houses. For all the years Elise had lived in the village, water had been supplied to the mill villagers through faucets in the yards between every other structure, each faucet supplying water for two houses, and each mill house had an outhouse in its back yard. Now rooms were being boxed in on rear porches for lavatory facilities. Toilets and claw-foot bathtubs were being installed, as well as running water in the kitchens. Houses were being underpinned, so that they no longer sat on stacks of rock—it was quickly becoming a village far different from the one she had first seen when she had come here eighteen years before.

It had taken the village so long to gain the comforts of the world she had lived in as a girl. Electricity, running water, a bathroom—a bathroom again, at last—they were things she had taken so little notice of as a girl. She had never once given thought to the fact that so much of the South around her might not have such niceties. Eighteen years ago—and now they seemed fantastic luxuries, until she found herself longing for the workmen to reach her street, her house, as she had once longed for Christmas mornings as a girl.

Elise turned from the view outside the screen door and went back to her sewing. The war was over, the days of work in the mill, the seemingly endless shifts, and now it was odd to be home during the days. She had never thought she would miss working in the mill, miss seeing the people, and having some place to go, but she did. She had the house to tend to, Janson, Henry, and the girls, and sewing to do, but still the days passed slowly while the children were in school and Janson on his shift in the mill.

The demand for her sewing had not decreased during the war, had in fact increased with the extra money in the town and village, but eight-hour shifts in the mill had left little time for sewing. She had the time now, and she turned her energies back to the sewing machine where she had spent so many hours for so many years. Janson had not objected to her returning to the work, had in fact surprised her with a new hand-lettered sign that read "Sewing Done." It now hung in the front window of the mill house. Perhaps they both had done a lot of growing up over those eighteen years.

Men were returning from the military. Families were being united after years apart, the dead cried over again, lives resumed. The county's population swelled as not only soldiers came home, but also many of those who'd left years before for war jobs in the big plants and factories, war jobs that had now ended. There seemed to be a great demand for everything, and people were buying as never before—houses, refrigerators, electric stoves, toasters, vacuum cleaners, all the things they had not been able to afford during the Depression and had not been able to get during the war. Stores could not keep up with the demand, nor could the factories, newly converted from war production.

Even Janson talked of all the things he would buy her once they were on their own place, but she knew it would take every cent they had just to get started—a few more months, he had said only that morning. Just a few more months.

Even as he showed her outward optimism, Elise knew he had to be worried. They had been so close before; they had saved for so long, saved and lost only to save again, dreamed and hoped and prayed. It seemed almost as if fate's hand would have to step in again as it had before to stop them.

Janson had driven her by the land a few days before in the old jalopy that Henry, he, and Stan had recently managed to piece together from an old frame and numerous car parts, an ugly vehicle that ran surprisingly well to be a concoction of several junk automobiles. They sat on a rise for a long time, just looking out over that red earth to the white house where he had been born, to the barn where he had played as a boy, the fields he had worked—only a few more months. The place was tenanted out now and the present owner had told Janson he would sell—by January it could be theirs.

The farm was priced higher than Janson had expected, and there would be a mortgage, but they had always known there would be one, no matter how much they had scrimped and saved. It was the size of the mortgage that worried Elise, as it did Janson. He had lost the land nineteen years ago when he was unable to meet the payments on it. She knew it would kill him if he were to lose it again.

But it was not just a mortgage that worried Elise, it was Janson himself. His hip seemed to be improving every day, and sometimes she could almost forget that he had been wounded in the war—but then she would see the scars, see him limp as he walked, or catch a glimpse of pain on his face. He refused to let the injury hold him back in the mill, at home, even with her when they were alone, but it was still there. The limp persisted, at times worse than at others, and they had both come to realize that he would likely have it the remainder of his life. He had not touched the walking cane again since the day he returned to work in the mill, but it still stood in one corner of the front room, as if he kept it as a reminder of the struggle—of all the struggles—he had been through.

His hip was better, but farming was far more strenuous than anything he was doing now, the little garden patch in their back yard nothing compared to the acres of fields he would have to work if they were on their own land—but it would do no good to speak to him about it. He was too stubborn, too determined, too close again to the dream, and no amount of worry or fretting on her part would stop or even delay him. He would have his land. He would plant a crop on it the coming spring. And he would drag himself to the fields each day if he had to.

The room had grown chilly and she got up to pull on a sweater, but stopped with her arm half-way into a sleeve when a thought occurred to her—what would the Easons do when Janson left the mill village to return to his own land? She remembered all too well the stories he had told her of what had happened twenty years before—the broken windows, the slaughtered animals, the fire set near the front of the house, and the second that had taken his father's life. Henry Sanders had refused to sell his cotton in Eason County at the prices the Easons were paying, and that refusal had cost him his life. Janson himself had told her that.

He had also told her he would do exactly the same.

～

Walter Eason sat behind his massive oak desk that afternoon, his fingers interlaced tightly on its polished top. His hands had acquired a tremble in the past year, at times worse than at others, but he refused to acknowledge even that slight sign of weakness and old age, choosing to clench his hands uselessly rather than let anyone else see the tremor—he was not that old yet, he kept telling himself. There were still things he had to accomplish, and he worried that he would not get everything done before his time ran out.

He sat staring at the closed, heavily varnished door that led into his office, waiting. Only a year before no one would have kept him waiting. Only a year before, Bickham would have been in his office almost before Walter's order could go out—I'm not that old, no matter what they think. I'm not so old that I can't break a man, any man, if I choose to, Walter told himself—but he had broken so many things that he now felt he should make right.

Eason County—his county—was not the same anymore, and neither was the South or for that matter the country. People had left for the cities. Men had fought in distant lands. Women had worked who had never worked before. The war had changed so many people, and now they were coming home, and so many of them did not want to stay in the village. They wanted homes of their own that were not rented or shared with another family. For days now a memory had lurked in the back of his mind about that very thing. Someone years ago had defied him by saying that a man had a right to something his own, something no one could take from him, *something he could work for and that would be his own that he could pass on to his children.*

Walter had set about having the mill houses piped for running water, having bathrooms boxed in on back porches, taking bids on bathroom fixtures and kitchen sinks, all while the thought continued to gnaw at him. He had made arrangements with his lawyers for selling off the mill houses, to give the people living in them a chance to buy them at a fair price and to have deducted from their wages payments on *something that would be their own.* Buddy would never keep the mill houses up once Walter was dead, and Walter knew it. Buddy would run the rents up so high the millhands couldn't afford them. It was better to get things arranged now, better to take care of his people, as Walter believed he had been doing all his life. The hands would never be able to buy houses on their own, he told himself. They needed him—they had always needed him. And this would give them *something of their own.* Each house would be offered to a family now living in it. Where two families shared a home, it would be offered to the one that had lived there the longest.

One vacant house in particular he set aside, had piped and the facilities put in, had it freshly painted and newly underpinned with brick. It had always been a duplex but he had connecting doors cut through the dividing wall, dispelling the ghosts, converting it into a single-family dwelling. Walter was going to offer that house to Janson Sanders, and that very morning, as he inspected the empty house, he finally remembered that it had been Janson's father, Henry, who spoke the quietly defiant words that had been haunting Walter for days. It had been Henry who told Walter that a man had a right to *something that was his own, something that he could work for and put into and pass on to his children.*

Walter realized that in preparing this house to offer Janson Sanders, he was trying to put right a debt. Walter had not thought twice when he cut off Henry Sanders's credit in 1926. Then Henry had died and the boy had lost his land and Walter had known he was to blame. He told himself the land would have been lost even if he had not interfered—so many lost their land in those hard years. But perhaps then Janson Sanders would not have held him to blame, in both his father's death and in a fire God himself had caused. But Janson did blame him, and Walter knew the blame was just—*I could have had Henry's credit extended,* he had told himself so many times; *I could have kept the foreclosure from taking place. The boy might still have his land, and Henry might still be alive—but he should have done as the other county farmers did and sold his cotton in Eason County.* All Walter had wanted was the continuation of the custom that had gone on in the county for so many years. He had not appreciated that Henry's cotton and land had been all his own, something no one could ever take from him. *Something he could work for and put into and pass on to his children.*

But Henry Sanders had died. And Walter Eason was to blame. And now he was too old for his own credit to be extended.

He stared at the door, waiting for the house boss. The house Walter had set aside would go to Janson Sanders for a fraction of what it was worth; Janson would never know, but Walter would, and at the moment that was all that seemed to matter.

There was a tap at the door and the balding house boss entered. Walter stared hard at him before ordering, "Tell the overseer of the card room to send Janson Sanders to see me when his shift's over, and I want you here as well. There are some things I need to get taken care of."

~

Janson Sanders would have back his land.

Walter sat staring at the closed office door long after Janson Sanders and the house boss had gone out it. Sanders did not want the mill house Walter had picked out and fixed for him. Sanders would farm again and have something that would belong to him. And he had done it with no help from anyone. Walter was surprised that he felt proud for Sanders, and felt as if a burden had been lifted from him— let Sanders farm his land, he told himself. Let him feed his family, see his children grow, play with his grandchildren.

Let him also get too old to care.

It was over, and somehow no one had lost. It had been a dying system that Walter had been trying to hold together twenty years before when where the Sanders cotton was to be sold had meant so much to him. Walter could see that now. The modern world had outgrown it. The independence brought on by two great wars, with the Depression in between, had only served to cover its demise. This was not his county anymore. It had not been his county for a very long time. It had only been the people's loyalty to the old ways and their respect for him, and for his father before him, that had kept those ways alive. It all seemed so simple now.

~

But nothing was simple where Buddy was concerned.

"I won't have him on that land," Buddy raged when he found out, coming to Walter's office that afternoon to pace back and forth.

"I won't have you interfering with—"

"Fuck you, old man!" Buddy roared, stopping in front of Walter's desk, a fist raised between them. "I don't give a damn what you 'won't have'!"

Walter rose slowly to his feet, placing his fingers spread on the desktop before him. "I'm tired of your smart mouth. I'm not too old to—"

Buddy laughed, which took Walter by surprise. No man had ever dared to laugh at him.

"You're too old to even jerk off anymore—and if you're too damn stupid and weak to put a stop to that red nigger, then I'm not."

"You're not going to—"

"I put a stop to his father, didn't I?" The words were spoken quietly, and for a moment Walter could do nothing but stare at him. "I made sure that son-of-a-bitch lost his land—you were too weak even back then to do anything, but I wasn't. I set fire to their fields and saw old man Sanders die and I knew that meant they'd lose the land— and I'll do it again. I'll see that red nigger's whole family dead before I'll see them on that land."

"You won't go anywhere near them!" Walter shouted.

"Go to hell," Buddy said, slamming the door as he left.

Walter stood for a long time, staring at the door, his hands shaking where his fingers were pressed to the desktop, staggered by the revelation that Buddy had been responsible for Henry Sanders's death. Buddy had set the fire in the fields, burned the cotton. Buddy had done what Walter had always believed had been an act of God— but God had no part in Buddy Eason. Walter had not known, but he now realized he was responsible and that he had to stop Buddy.

He rubbed his aching left shoulder but the pain worsened, moving down his arm and across his chest, making it difficult to breathe. It felt as if someone were squeezing him. He sat back into his chair, rubbing his arm, reaching up to loosen his tie. The pain was growing and he clutched at his chest—*not now*, he told himself. *Not now; I'm not ready yet.* He had to stop Buddy. He had to make certain Janson Sanders and his boy got their land. He had to see the twins taken away from

Buddy and Cassandra before they could grow up to be like either parent. He had to—

There was a great weight on his chest, crushing him down, forcing the life from him. He tried to pray but no prayers would come, only the halting words of a child:

*"Now I lay me down . . . I pray the Lord my soul to keep . . . Now I . . . if I should die before I wake . . . God forgive me . . . I pray the Lord my soul to take . . ."*

# 13

WALTER EASON WAS DEAD
and Janson found that he was sorry. After twenty years of holding the
old man responsible for both his father's death and for the loss of the
land, after all that time, and all that had taken place between them,
Janson Sanders was sorry. He had respected the old man, and he knew
somehow the old man had respected him. But now Walter Eason was
dead and Eason County was Buddy's county. It was Buddy's town
and village. Buddy's cotton mill.

Janson quit his job on the spot, walking out of his shift that
October morning just as soon as he learned that Walter Eason had
died. The mill had not shut down out of respect for the deceased, as
it had when other members of the Eason family passed away. Buddy
had countermanded the orders that went out from the mill office,
saying he had no intention of losing money by shutting down the
cotton mill.

Everyone was shocked, and much quiet whispering was going on
even though mill workers knew that to be overheard and reported to
the office would very likely cost them their jobs and the homes they
had been living in for many years.

"Did you hear? Old Mr. Eason died, and Buddy—I mean Mr.
Eason—won't shut the mill down. At first they said we were shutting
down, but Mr. Eason stopped it—"

"Haven't you heard—"

"Would you believe—"

"Poor old man, a heart attack right there in his office. You know he should have retired years ago—did you hear we're not shutting down even for the funeral?"

Janson had not whispered. He had gone directly to the overseer of the card room. "I ain't workin' for Buddy Eason," he said, and walked out of the mill.

On his way home he walked past men digging a trench in a yard, running pipe to one of the mill houses, several brick masons at work underpinning a house on the next street, the sound of carpentry work going on a block away—soon the houses would be modernized, with bathroom facilities and running water, underpinned and ready for sale to the mill workers, that is unless Buddy Eason decided to keep them, which Janson doubted that he would. Buddy would be think-ing only of the money he might make from the sale of the houses, the savings from not having to keep them up.

It would be a different life in the village with the mill workers owning their houses. Walter Eason had told Janson all about it the day before when he offered him a nice house on a corner lot, with a place in back for a garden. Janson had turned him down, and he was doubly glad now that he had done so—even if it had not been for his land, he would not have been able to live in Buddy Eason's mill village, for it would be no less than that now, no matter who owned the homes.

They would have to move now out of the mill house they had been living in for six years, and they would have to do it before Buddy Eason could have them thrown out. Janson had planned on quitting soon, but he would not have been ready for at least a few more months. There was a tenant on his land, and the man would have the place until his cotton was picked and sold—besides, the deal had not been closed, and it would be several months before they would be able to move into the house. They would have to rent a place for the time being. He would need work to keep them from having to live off their savings, Elise's sewing, or Stan's charity—that is, if Buddy Eason did not fire Stan immediately for his connection to the Sanders family.

Stan had been contributing to the savings, and planned to move with them to the farm—but, even if Stan managed to keep his job in the mill for the time being, Janson would not turn to his brother-in-law for help. Elise, Henry, and the girls were his responsibility, and he would take care of them.

The hardest thing now would be telling Elise—I quit my job. I quit my job, and we won't have a place to live.

She was waiting for him when he came into the yard, seated on a rocker on their half of the front porch. She watched him as he walked up the board steps. "Stan told me that Mr. Eason died," she said. "I knew you would quit. How long before we have to move?"

Janson stared at her in amazement. How could she know him so well? "Th' sooner we're outta th' mill house, th' better."

She nodded and rose to go into the house, but he stopped her. "It won't be for long. A couple 'a months, maybe a little more, an' we can move out onto our own place. I'll find work 'til then, an' a place we can rent. I just couldn't work for Buddy."

She smiled and touched his cheek, halting his words. "I knew you couldn't work for him. You didn't have any other choice but to quit." The note of worry in her voice made him think again of something he had been considering earlier—not only was it Buddy's village and mill, but so much of the remainder of the county belonged to Buddy now. Janson might quit his job in the mill; they might leave the mill village and town, but the land still was located in Eason County.

And Eason County was Buddy's county now.

⁓

Buddy sat on the front pew of Pine's First Methodist Church there on Main Street, frowning at his grandfather's face where the old man now lay in the flower-covered casket at the front of the church— damned old bastard, Buddy thought. The old coot had been an inconvenience when he was alive, and he was an even bigger inconvenience dead. He even looked as if he was still breathing, laying there, his face as ruddy as ever, framed by all that white hair, his eyebrows bristling out and meeting across the bridge of his nose. The damned old bastard had always been spouting his religion, so holier-than-thou—Buddy dearly hoped that he was burning in the hottest pit of hell at the moment, though he really doubted that hell existed at all.

He was glad the old man was finally out of the way, but there were other things he would rather be doing this afternoon than sitting here in a church pretending that he was sorry the old bastard had finally kicked off. This was the first time he had been in a church since the day he married Cassandra, and he hoped it would be the last time until the day came when he would have the pleasure of attending Cassandra's funeral—she was sitting beside him now, pretending to cry into a lacy handkerchief. How dearly he would love to tell the entire congregation of mourners behind him what a hypocrite she was now with her faked grief—the first thing she had wanted to know was how much money they would inherit now that the old man was dead.

He took out his watch and looked at it, wishing the damned Bible-thumper in the pulpit would get it over with. There were things he had to do. Most importantly there was Janson Sanders still to be dealt with—but taking care of Sanders would be a pleasure, a long-waited-for pleasure, if only the goddamn Holy Joe would just hurry up so they could get the old bastard in the ground. It had been damned inconvenient for the old coot to have died when he had. It was none too soon, and it had done nothing more than delay Buddy's plans—but at least the old man was out of the way now, and Buddy had the county in a way his father never had.

He lifted his gaze from the watch face and looked to the casket again, a smile slowly spreading across his face. He was aware that the preacher began to stare at him reprovingly, and Cassandra as well, but he did not care—they were nothing anyway.

He stared at the casket and continued to smile—with the old bastard out of the way, no one could stop him now. No one at all.

There was no man alive with power over Buddy Eason.

Buddy stood near the large front windows of what had been his grandfather's home the next morning, staring out—today was the day. The world would be different now. It was his, all of it: the mill, the village, the town, the county, the people. All his.

And he could do whatever he wanted.

This would be the first day when there would be no one looking over his shoulder, disapproving, trying to keep him in control. Never again—he was in charge now, as he should have been all along.

Most importantly, this was the beginning of the destruction of the Sanders family—they would crawl when he was through with them.

He had known this day would come for so long, for twenty-one years, since the day he had come upon Janson Sanders with his sister when he and Janson had been no more than seventeen or eighteen years old. It had not been the fact that Sanders was with her, for Buddy knew many men in the county who had had a turn at Lecia Mae by then—it had been the fact that Sanders had fought him and had whipped him. Buddy could remember so clearly the pleasure when he drove a knife into Janson Sanders's shoulder, and the fear, only moments later, when Sanders held that same knife to Buddy's throat—Buddy had pissed himself, pissed himself out of fear, and he could remember so clearly that look of disgust and loathing that had set on Janson Sanders's face when Sanders let him go.

Buddy had hated him since that day, sworn he would see him die—but he would hurt him first. He would hurt him and watch him bleed. He would hurt him in the way that could hurt Janson Sanders the most.

Buddy stood staring out the window as a car pulled up the circular drive, a shiny, well-kept Chrysler with a burly man in a dark suit behind the wheel, another big man in a matching suit beside him. The man who stepped from the back seat seemed out of place with the other two, ill-at-ease as he stared up at the large house before him. He looked to be just what he was, an old man from the country, a farmer, though of better means than most who farmed in Eason County. Inge Harper wore clean work pants and had heavy brogans on his feet, and wore a coat that had seen heavy use. The old man held a well-worn hat in his hands as he was ushered into the house and to the room where Buddy waited for him.

"Mr. Eason, I was sure sorry to hear about your granddaddy," he said. "Fine man he was. We'll all—"

"I hear Janson Sanders is trying to buy land from you, a farm you bought a few years ago." Buddy had had the man brought here, and, now that he was here, he saw no need to waste time.

"Yes, sir. Used to belong to his daddy years back. He—"

"You haven't closed the deal with him yet?"

"No, sir. We talked and came to an understanding. I got a tenant on it now, so we've got to wait for him to get his crop picked and sold, and then—"

"Good." Buddy had paid little attention to the man's words beyond the confirmation that the land did not belong to Sanders yet—and it never would, he told himself as a smile came to his face. "I'll buy it instead, and pay you cash for it right now."

"I can't see how you can do that, Mr. Eason." The old farmer turned his hat before him. "I've already shook hands with Janson on it."

"Goddamn your handshake!" Buddy shouted, taking a step toward Harper—how dare the man think his handshake with that half-breed was more important than an offer made by Buddy Eason. "I said cash money, up front. Your tenant can get out now. I'll even buy what crop he has left in the fields. I want that land!"

The farmer just stared at him, not speaking—more money, that was what he wanted, Buddy told himself. Well, all right. He would have the land, and he would go back later and teach this old man some respect for the Eason name when he had the time. It would be worth the extra money anyway just to see the look on Sanders's face when Buddy burned the entire place to the ground and razed the trees and made certain the bastard would never get his hands on it again—a first step, and so many things more that he had planned for Janson Sanders and his family. When he was through with them—

"I'll pay you twice what he offered," Buddy said. "Double." The excitement was now apparent in his voice. The farmer's eyes widened—twice the price, you bet he's excited, Buddy thought. Only a matter of time now. "Now, you go on home and think about what you're going to do with all that money. I'll send my lawyers out to see you tomorrow with a check and with the papers for you to sign."

"Well, I—"

"Go on. The lawyers will see you tomorrow—boys, take him back."

"Yes, sir, Mr. Eason," the man who had been driving the car said, and the old farmer looked at him warily, the hat brim now crushed in his hands—at least the old bastard will be able to buy a new hat after tomorrow, Buddy thought.

He watched from the window again as the farmer got into the back seat of the Chrysler, the old man's eyes coming back to the house one last time before the car started down the drive—this was the first day, Buddy told himself. Before he was through, what was left of the Sanders family would beg for mercy.

Before he was through, he would watch every one of them bleed.

~

Janson was bent among cotton plants the next afternoon, the weight of a long pick sack dragging at his shoulder. His hip hurt like hell, but on this day even the pain could not touch him. He had sworn that he would never work another man's fields again when he left Stubblefield's, but that did not matter now. This was only temporary work to occupy his mind and his hands, and to give them the money they would need to live on. This would last only until his own land could be picked and was free for them to move onto.

His own land—not yet, but soon. Just as soon as those rows of cotton plants, whiter and taller than these, he was certain, were picked. The current tenant would then be moving on to work in the orange groves of Florida. Janson had found a rented place for them to live and work he could do, and he counted himself lucky. There were so many men coming back from the military or from work in the war plants in the big cities, and they were sometimes returning to find there were few houses to be had, and, at times, even fewer jobs. Old Mr. Webber, who attended the Holiness church Janson had attended as a boy, had a three-room house empty on his place and needed help picking his cotton. Janson had happened by at just the right time.

By the time he came home with the news, Elise had the family packed up and the mill house scrubbed down—it might belong to Buddy Eason now, but the new tenants would come upon it even cleaner than the day the Sanders had moved there. They moved out to Webber's place that next day, including Stan, who had been promptly fired from the mill by Buddy Eason the afternoon of his grandfather's funeral—so much for mill tradition and the old man's word, Janson thought, for the loss of Stan's arm in the card room should have guaranteed him a job in the mill for the remainder of his life.

Janson and Stan had been going to the cotton fields on Webber's place early each morning, and Stan picked a remarkable amount of cotton for a man with only one hand. Henry joined them in the evenings, as did Judith for a short time, though her sister had flatly refused for fear that someone she knew might see her; and Elise was sewing—they would make it until the land was free. Janson had made arrangements to start clearing new fields on his land in any time he might find free from Webber's fields—the land might not be his yet, but he did not want to waste any time when there was so much work to be done. There was land to clear, fields to get ready, work to do on the house and barn. He would plant a bigger crop of cotton on the land than it had ever seen before, and raise vegetables, not for their use alone, for they could sell those as well. He had dreamed and planned for so long, and it was so close now that he could not waste a moment.

He lifted his eyes and saw Elise coming across the field from the direction of the house. She looked so pretty, with the sun turning her hair copper and the wind whipping her skirt about her legs—nice legs, he thought, and smiled to himself.

"Mr. Harper called and left a message with Mr. Webber. He wants us to stop by and see him tomorrow sometime after church," she called, coming down a row of cotton to him.

Mr. Harper, the man who owned the land—it had to be good news. Maybe the tenant's crop would be picked sooner than they had expected. Maybe Harper knew when the deal could be closed. Janson grabbed Elise, ignoring the heavy cotton sack hanging by a strap across his chest and shoulder, ignoring the ache in his hip, and hugged her close. He kissed her and smiled down into her blue eyes. "I bet you they're gonna have that crop picked pretty quick."

"You think so?" She was smiling, pretty, as she looked up at him.

"It cain't be anythin' else," he said. "I'll go help him pick it myself if it'll get him hurried up, an' he won't even have t' pay me t' do it." She laughed and he hugged her again, then danced her a jig until they got tangled up in the pick sack and fell to the ground between the cotton rows. She looked at him, concern on her face, and he knew she was thinking about his hip, but he only laughed and kissed her again, lying there on the red earth with the cotton plants to either side of them—all their dreams were coming true, he told himself. No one could stop them now.

The parlor of Inge Harper's house was unbearably warm that next afternoon. Elise knew that it might be from the fire that burned in the hearth across the room, but she thought it was more from anger as she sat beside her husband there on the parlor sofa. She watched Janson's profile—he looked as if he could do murder. His left hand was a tight fist on his knee, his jaw set, a hardness in his expression she had seen there only in matters concerning Buddy Eason.

"Buddy Eason did what?" he asked in a quiet tone that sent a chill through her even before Mr. Harper could repeat what he had already told them.

"He sent a couple of men for me yesterday, brought me up to his place. He offered me twice what we agreed on for the land."

A muscle worked in Janson's jaw as he stared at the fireplace across the room. After a moment he brought his eyes back to Harper. "I don't have any more'n we talked about, but maybe I can borrow—"

"No, Janson."

No—the word made Elise feel as if her heart would break. The muscle worked again in Janson's jaw. After so much work. After so many years. Starting again and again, dreaming all that time, and now—

"I'll tell you like I told Mr. Eason's lawyers this morning," Harper said, but Elise did not want to hear him. She just wished they were away from here. She just wished she did not have to see what she could see on Janson's face even now. She just wished—

But Mr. Harper was saying something altogether different, and Elise dragged her attention back to him.

"That land is meant to be worked—I don't know what Mr. Eason wants with it, but it ain't to farm it. Besides, you and me had a understanding and we shook hands on it. I'm a man of my word, just like anybody in this county can tell you—that land's yours, 'cause that's what we agreed—" Elise felt such relief that she barely heard the remainder of the words. Something about having his lawyer go ahead and draw up the papers. The tenant would get his crop picked and then would move on—but none of that mattered.

As soon as they left Mr. Harper's house, Janson drove her in the old jalopy to the land and parked so they could look out over the fields of tall cotton waiting to be picked, to the white house where he had born and where his parents had died. His home. It had always been his home, even when he had been far away from it. And soon it would be theirs.

"It's gonna be ours, Elise," was all he seemed to be able to say. "It's really gonna be ours—"

There was nothing she could want more in that moment than the look on his face.

He had finally gotten what he had dreamed toward for so long.

~

Always Janson Sanders. Anytime things had gone wrong in Buddy Eason's life, it had always been due to Janson Sanders.

Buddy paced furiously over the rug in the living room of his home. His lawyer, old Porter, had come by no more than an hour before—that old bastard out in the country would not sell the land to him at any price. Buddy had even had Porter call back, doubling the price again—no, the land belonged to Janson Sanders, or would, once the formalities could take place.

Sanders—always Janson Sanders. For twenty-one years now he had done nothing but try to destroy Buddy's life.

There was a noise on the stairs, the sound of a child crying, the front door opening and then slamming shut. Cassandra had overheard his conversation with Porter, and she had laughed in his face that he had not been able to buy the land—he had slapped her hard just to shut her mouth.

She would go crying home to her mother and dragging the twins with her, but Buddy did not care. Old Helene would listen to her complain and then send her back. That was what she had done every other time.

Goddamn it!—Buddy jerked up the phone from the table nearby, yanked its cord from the wall, and slung it across the room to crash against the cold marble of the fireplace. Goddamn it!—he had sworn Sanders would not win! He had sworn it! Goddamn Sanders and his entire family. Goddamn—!

He stood there for a long time, staring across the room to where the telephone now lay on its side before the fireplace, its receiver skewed out from it but attached still by its cord. If he had been able to stop the sale of the land, it would have hurt Sanders, he told himself, but if he lost *after* he had gotten it back—

Buddy picked up the telephone and slowly wound the cord around one hand until it was taut and he could yank it free from the base—it came loose with a satisfying feeling of separation, allowing

Buddy to sling the base away. He smiled at the dangling bit of wire hanging from his hand—separation hurt so much worse once you were attached, he told himself.

Janson Sanders would still lose his land.

And then Buddy would make certain he would lose his life.

# 14

J ANSON HAD AT LAST COME
home. There were long hours of hard work during the first months
they were on the land—work clearing fields, breaking soil, plowing,
readying the earth to plant, putting the seed into the ground—long
hours that left the body tired but the soul satisfied. The days began
before light and ended often long after dark. They worsened the ache
in his hip, but they were good days, days that ended in a satisfying
supper, the quiet of the house in sleep, their soft bed, and time alone
with Elise.

Janson made a partial payment on an old tractor and a used truck,
then traded out work for the balance owed. The trade created
additional work, but the tractor and truck were beyond value on the
place and Janson took great pride in them. He marveled to see fields
broken up and laid ready in hours, when the same work would have
taken days with a mule and plow.

He was contented, at last having regained the land he had been
born to, what he had dreamed of for so long—at last having given
Elise what he had promised so many years before. But the feeling
would not leave him that the struggle had only just begun. He feared
that holding to the land could be more difficult than regaining it had
been. He had lost it before, had struggled years to get it back—he
would sooner die than lose it again.

Working with Henry in the fields brought Janson to realize what
his own father must have felt, why Henry Sanders had been willing to

fight, even to die, to hold onto the land. The girls would never stay on the farm; Janson already knew that. They dreamed of other and, perhaps to them, bigger and better things. But as the late spring of 1946 came, and Janson stood at an outdoor ceremony and saw his son receive a high school diploma, he knew he had not dreamed for twenty years to have accomplished nothing. Janson had barely been able to read or write when he married Elise, and to him the land had been the only way he could see to have his pride. But so much else was open to Henry. No man would ever own Janson Sanders's son. No man would ever work him into premature old age in a cotton mill or on a sharecropped farm. No man would ever determine who or what Henry Sanders would be—the high school diploma guaranteed him that. Henry, who was not quite eighteen, would not need the land to guarantee his pride. Yet Janson could tell it was in Henry's blood, as much a part of him as it had ever been a part of his father. Janson had seen him come to life over the past months on the place, and he had known—Henry Sanders was a farmer, and none short of God could ever change that.

When laying-by and the swelter of dog days came that first year on the land, the fields were lush with cotton—*his* fields, Janson kept reminding himself. A quiet peace settled over the place and Janson had time to work on the house or to tend the vegetable garden, to take Elise for a picnic, to go fishing with Henry and Stan, and, on occasion, to treat the family to the picture show.

But the nagging worry that had been within Janson for months grew. Trouble was coming; he could feel it. Buddy Eason had tried everything to keep the land from Janson, had offered Mr. Harper twice what it was worth, and still Janson had won. But Buddy would not give up while Janson remained alive and held the land.

There was no doubt within Janson of that.

Still, he told himself daily, *it's over. We have the land. It can't happen again.*

He only wished he could believe it.

~

On a quiet Saturday afternoon, Henry had driven his sisters into Pine to leave them at the picture show before going to spend his own afternoon with Olivia Morgan. The old house was filled with the sound of Elise's sewing machine, mounds of bridal white at her feet, the date for some young couple's wedding fast approaching. When Janson walked off the porch, Stan had been seated in its shade, a book in his hands, his mind so wrapped up in the story that he barely noticed when Janson crossed the yard toward the fields.

Janson walked the fields, impatient for the fat green bolls to open and the wispy white squares of cotton to appear. It seemed as if the weeks of lessened work would wear on forever. He had been in the vegetable garden all morning, had done some chores around the house, until there seemed nothing left for him to do. He did not like being idle and he had never liked waiting.

The late summer sun was hot on his face. There was the sound of birds, and the stir of a slight breeze down the rows of cotton plants, even of the sewing machine over the distance from the house. It was only a matter of time. The bolls would burst open and the fields would turn white. The work would resume. Then money would be coming to them from their effort, from their land, from the crop that belonged to them alone. They would have money to see them through the winter, money to reduce the mortgage, money that would guarantee the land would be theirs again the next year and the year after. There might even be enough to put aside for the expanded dream he had nowadays, of hoping, in the coming years, to buy the next farm over. There would be more fields to plant then, and a house to tenant out, or perhaps that house would be for Henry and Olivia, if they married, as Janson suspected would happen before long. He could be a grandfather in a few years. He was only thirty-nine, and Elise was only thirty-five, but he already thought how it would be when they had grandsons and granddaughters, could not help but dream about the world they would have, and all he would want for them. Perhaps one of his grandsons would also want the land, would also be quieted and contented by walking the fields.

Janson's reverie was interrupted by the sound of a car coming up the road, slowing as it came alongside the field where he stood among the rows. He looked in that direction, thinking it might be a neighboring farmer, or maybe Henry and the girls returning early from town—but his eyes came to rest on a large, dark car as it slowed, coming almost to a standstill as the window lowered. Janson stared at the vehicle, finding Buddy Eason staring back.

Their eyes met over the distance, and Janson knew the waiting was over. He knew that if he intended to keep the land for himself and for his son and for grandsons he hoped to someday know, he would have to fight harder than ever. He understood clearly the hold this place had held on his father and now on him—it was something inside that had been bred from generations of men who had lived out their lives working the fields of other men while knowing that a man had a right to *something that was his own.* A man had a right to his dreams, and to pride.

∾

Buddy Eason snubbed out his cigarette in an ashtray on the massive oak desk, then exhaled a cloud of smoke. The three other men in the room, sitting in chairs or leaning against the wall, were also smoking and Buddy would have found it amusing that they were smoking in his grandfather's office—except that it was no longer his grandfather's office. Buddy had taken it as his own, and doing things here that his grandfather would have disapproved of had long since lost their flavor.

The men with him were on the mill payroll, but they did little work for the mill. All three had been in prison before Buddy hired them. It had been amusing to bring them into the mill in the last year before the old man died; the old fool must have been slipping even then, or he would never have let Buddy hire any "peace keepers," as Buddy had called them in light of talk of unions in the mill.

Peace keepers had been right, but it was Buddy's peace.

Buddy was still pleased with his choice in each man. Keats had killed a man in a fight; Billings, with his Massachusetts accent, had done time for assaulting a teenage girl, and for almost killing the police officer who tried to arrest him; Mender had killed his wife's lover, and, after he was released from prison, his wife, though her body had never been found. All talk of unionizing had died immediately after the arrival of the three burly men in their double-breasted suits. There had been no trouble since in the mill, in the village, or in town.

People knew better. Buddy Eason was in charge now.

"I don't care what you have to do. I want him stopped," Buddy said, lighting another cigarette. "Do whatever you want. But, if you blow his head off, I want to be there to see it." He exhaled another cloud of smoke, staring at the three through the gray haze. "Sanders better not make it out of Eason County with a crop this year—or you better make sure I don't ever find any of you." He meant his words and tone to be threatening, but none of his thugs even blinked in response. "I want Sanders out of business, and I want him off that land and foreclosed on—and then he's mine," Buddy Eason said, and began to smile.

～

It started slowly.

Someone drove circles through one of the cotton fields late at night, leaving a path of destruction in his wake. Rocks were thrown through the front windows of the house. The windshield of the old jalopy was smashed.

Then a cow was found slaughtered and mutilated in the pasture, one of the hogs was shot through the head, and Judith's dog was poisoned. Elise was shocked by the deliberate brutality and senselessness of the acts, but she could see in Janson's eyes that it was no less than he had expected.

As the weeks passed, it worsened. Someone shot at the house one evening from the cover of the shed in the yard, but vanished before Janson could get to them, driving away in a black Chrysler that had been parked at the edge of their land. Henry smelled smoke one night and found a deliberately set fire on the back porch. The family returned from church the following Sunday morning to find the house ransacked, drawers dumped in the floor, mattresses and pillows ripped open, mirrors shattered, and red paint splashed over everything and inscribing profanities on the walls.

The sheriff had been called out after each occurrence, but there was no evidence, no witnesses, no proof other than dead animals, broken glass, or scrawled profanities—they were on their own in Eason County, Elise realized.

Catherine and Judith were packed up and sent to stay with kin. Henry refused to go—he would not be driven off by Buddy Eason or by anyone else, he said with as much pride and stubbornness as Elise had ever seen in his father. He was eighteen now and a man in his own right, looking so much like Janson that it sometimes made Elise catch her breath—but she worried over him as if he were still that stubborn two-year-old that she remembered so well.

Janson tried to make her leave with the girls, but she refused. She was not going be driven from her home any more than their son would, and she would not leave Janson. She feared she would never see him alive again if she did.

Suddenly the harassment stopped, and the very quiet worried Janson all the more. The cotton stood ready to be picked. Every cent they had was tied up in those once-green fields, now white with cotton. There was no money to hire pickers; they would have to do the work themselves in that terrible, quiet stillness that had settled over the place.

Elise woke the night before they would begin to pick the cotton, finding the bed empty beside her. She got up without turning on a light and tied her wrap about her waist, then crossed the hall to the dark front room where Janson sat in a straight chair before the front windows.

She placed a hand on his shoulder, then felt his hand cover hers, though he did not look up at her.

"You couldn't sleep?" she asked, softly.

"It's too quiet." His eyes never moved from the view outside that window.

"Maybe he's given up." But she could not believe it, any more than he could, so she fell silent.

"He won't give up."

The darkness hung between them. "It'll be all right. It has to be." After all they had been through for him to regain this place and have it for the children—it had to be all right. He did not speak but she felt his hand tighten over hers.

A few nights later she lay awake beside him long into the night, knowing that he was also awake. She stared into the darkness, listening to his breathing, wondering and worrying with him, and also tired with him, from having shared the work, as they had shared everything over the years.

When Janson, Henry, and Stan, had begun to pick the cotton, Elise had gone to join them. Janson stopped for a moment and looked at her when she entered the fields, had reached out and touched her hand, then returned to his work. He had not wanted her in the fields and had promised himself, though she had never asked it, that he would not have her picking cotton again once they were on their own land.

Now he had the land, the dream, and to hold onto it she was picking cotton. But it was no longer Janson's dream alone. It was hers, and it strengthened within her when she saw Henry working with Janson, knowing the dream was alive within her son as well.

Henry was so much like the man she had met and fallen in love with nineteen-and-a-half years ago, the man who worked each day picking cotton a few rows from her, the man she loved more than even her own life. Elise had thought that many times before, but in the last months she had begun to know the full truth in those words—she knew she would lay her life down for him if that choice ever came.

There was the sound of a car coming along the road, slowing as it drew near the house. Janson was suddenly out of bed, holding the curtains back in one hand as he knelt before the window, the other hand closing over a shotgun that had been leaned into the nearby corner. The car passed slowly then sped up, going on, but he stared out for a time, then took his hand from the shotgun and allowed the curtain to drop back into place.

He turned to look at her, and rejoined her in bed without a word having passed between them. He drew her close and she rested her head on his chest. Neither spoke.

They only held each other, listened, waited, and prayed for the waiting to be over.

~

The waiting ended the evening Henry did not come home from a late trip into Pine. He had driven the old jalopy into town, and, when the hours passed and he did not return, Elise became worried. Darkness had come and it had begun to rain heavily—there could have been an accident, she kept telling herself. The car could have broken down— but Henry would have caught a ride, would have gotten word to them, would have walked the miles home if need be, and Elise knew it.

Janson took the truck and went looking for him, leaving Stan with Elise. She fretted, pacing across the bare wooden floor in the front room, her wrap tied securely over her nightgown, her eyes going to the blinding downpour beyond the screen door and the open front windows. She tried to shut out the deafening sound of the rain on the tin roof.

"Henry's off somewhere, parked in that car with Olivia," she said to Stan, trying to bring a fussing note into her voice. She felt chilled and rubbed her hands together and hugged herself for warmth. Stan watched her from the rocker near the fireplace. Elise wished he would just say something, but the silence stretched out between them.

"They've probably been drinking," she said, a desperate tone in her voice that surprised her. She stared out at the driving rain, then turned away, pacing the room again. "That's what some girls would do, get a boy drunk and get him to do something, then she'd be pregnant and Henry would have to marry her." She knew she was rambling now, but she could no longer stop herself. "You know how girls that age can be if they're not happy at home. You know—"

Light flashed across the front windows, and the sound of an engine became audible over the rain on the tin roof. Elise pushed the screen door open, then tightened her hand on the hook until the sharp end of it dug into the flesh of her thumb as their old truck rolled to a stop before the house. She stepped onto the front porch and let the spring on the door slam it shut behind her as Janson got out of the truck and started around to its other side.

The truck's passenger side door opened as Janson reached it, and Elise felt relief flood over her as she realized it was Henry stepping down from the cab. He and Janson started toward the house, and Janson's arm went around him. Henry's head was down, his feet dragging, his steps weaving drunkenly. He stumbled as he reached the bottom of the steps, though his father held him up, and Elise felt righteous indignation well up inside of her—he *had* been drinking. He had stayed out late, had gotten drunk, had worried them all to death. Why, she would—

Then they came into the light from the open front door and the windows behind her. Henry's clothes were ripped and muddy, his hair was matted, and his shirt was torn, mud-spattered, and stained with blood. Elise's heart leapt into her throat. She was suddenly at the edge of the slippery porch, reaching toward her son—dear God!

Henry, feeling her presence, lifted his chin and tried to stand on his own, to pull away from his father's supporting arm. "It's not really that bad, Mama," he said, his lip bleeding, the rain washing blood down his face, one eye swelled shut. "I'm okay. Don't worry—" But his knees buckled and Janson caught him in his arms, and together he and Stan, who was suddenly down into the yard, picked him up and carried him into the house to his bed.

Elise followed, gripping the iron footboard for support. She stood rooted uselessly to the floor as she watched her husband and her brother lay her only son on the dark blue counterpane. For an instant time folded back upon itself, back nineteen years to the night she had entered Mattie Ruth and Titus Coats's house to see Janson lying in a bed, having been beaten so badly by her father.

Not again—she found herself thinking—but this was her child, beaten, bloody. She made herself move to the side of the bed to brush the mud-streaked black hair back from Henry's forehead—*goddamn you, Buddy Eason*, she told herself, the hatred that flowed through her slowly bringing strength back to her legs. *Goddamn you*—

Henry had been on his way home from Olivia's when a large, dark car had driven up behind the jalopy at a high rate of speed and run the old car off the road and into a ditch. Before Henry's senses had cleared, the door of the old jalopy had been yanked open and he had been dragged from the car, then beaten by two men as a third stood by. Henry had been left lying in the mud listening to the sound of glass shattering, loud pounding—all the windows of the old jalopy had been broken out, the headlamps shattered, the seats ripped apart and tires flattened, and huge dents pounded into the already dented and rusting body.

Janson had found Henry lying in the mud at the edge of a field not far from the ditch where he found the old car. He had been beaten bloody and then left as a message—*give up and get out. You're finished.*

But they were not finished. Elise had never seen Janson as angry as when he walked out of Henry's bedroom. She followed him into the hallway and toward the front of the house, then stood in the open door of their bedroom as Janson took up the shotgun, broke it open and checked to make certain it was loaded, then snapped it shut. His eyes met Elise's, then he was out of the room and into the hallway before she could do more than touch him, her fingers barely brushing the wet fabric of his shirt sleeve before he moved beyond her reach— this time Buddy Eason had gone too far.

"Janson—you can't. It's what he wants," Elise said, trying to step between him and the front door. "Janson, no—"

"You stay here with th' boy."

"You can't—"

He pushed her hands away. The calm that had settled about him was far worse than the anger of moments before. He would not be stopped. He would kill Buddy Eason tonight, or be killed.

Then from behind them, "I'm not a kid anymore, Pa. You don't have to defend me."

Henry stood in the doorway to his bedroom, and Elise could see he was trying to cover up the pain of the aching ribs, the bruises, as he walked out into the hall, as much pride in his bearing as she had ever seen in Janson.

"He'll kill you," Henry said, walking slowly toward them, one arm pressed against his ribs. Elise knew he was trying not to show the pain, but it was evident in his voice, and his mother's heart hurt for him. "That's why Buddy Eason had this done, so you would come after him—all he wants is an excuse and he'll kill you. That's all he wants."

Henry's hand closed over the barrel of the shotgun. Elise knew the look that passed between him and Janson was not meant for her, but she also understood what it meant—this fight would not be over as long as both a Sanders and an Eason lived in Eason County.

But the end would not come tonight.

The father and son—the two men, for Elise knew her son would never be a child again—stared into each other's face, and Janson allowed Henry to take the shotgun from his hands. Elise shivered, hugging herself again as she watched the two men. They were so much alike—with that same pride, that same determination.

And, now, the same hatred in Henry's eyes that she had so long seen in Janson's where Buddy Eason was concerned.

~

Elise sat at the worn kitchen table with the family on a Sunday evening near the end of picking the cotton, her mind occupied with the scent and taste of the buttered chunks of potato on her plate. It seemed odd to worry over potatoes now, when she had been worried over so many other things for so many months, and she found herself dwelling on having something so trivial as scorched potatoes to occupy her mind. The day had been too good, the family together for most of the day, Catherine and Judith home from right after church until late in the afternoon when Henry had driven them back to Pine. The family had enjoyed dinner together after services, and the day had passed in peace, and now Elise had nothing to worry about but scorched potatoes for supper, not enough of a problem to ruin any family's evening. There had been no trouble on the place now in days.

She nudged a chunk of potato with her fork, pushed it about a bit, then cut it into two pieces and brought half to her mouth for another taste—definitely scorched. She was perfectly aware that she had never become more than a passable cook even after all these years, and that everyone in her family knew it. She had learned well enough how to feed them, and most of the time it was at least edible, but cooking was just not part of her make-up, no matter how hard she tried.

She saw Henry wrinkle his nose at the scorched smell of the potatoes on his fork even before they reached his mouth, but still he ate them. Stan had not tried after the first bite, but she saw that he had helped himself to more butterbeans, and that he was making good headway on her biscuits and fried chicken. At least that was something she had managed to learn from Janson's gran'ma through the many burned meals and fingers she had endured in the first months of her marriage. She could fry chicken and she could make biscuits as good as any Deborah Sanders had ever made—well, almost. Janson proved that by asking for fried chicken and biscuits more often than for any other foods she cooked. Whether that was because they were his favorites, or because they were one of the few things she could prepare with mostly consistent results, she did not know, or really even care.

She glanced at him as he sat at the head of the table, wondering if he had tried the scorched potatoes, and found him staring at her, in his eyes a surprising sadness, longing, a terrible need. He held her gaze, then stood without a word, stepped around his chair, and came down the length of the table to her. He took her hand and drew her to her feet. Then he led her from the room.

His hands were gentle, but insistent, the bedroom door closed behind them. Elise found she was trembling, and she could not understand why. They had been together so many times over their nineteen years as lovers, but this time there was something in his eyes that made her want to cry. Then she was crying, but with pleasure.

Hours later, after the house was quiet and Janson was certain Stan and Henry were in their rooms and likely asleep, he put on his overalls and brought back a plate of biscuits and cold fried chicken from the icebox. They ate by the light of the bedside lamp, naked, facing each other, enjoying a comfortable familiarity built from years together. He would not take his eyes from her, and, as she watched him, she knew how completely she loved him, how completely she would always love him.

"Have you ever regretted marryin' me?" he asked, surprising her at how different the question was from what she had been thinking.

"No, of course not. Have you ever regretted marrying me?"

"No," without a moment's hesitation. "You just gave up s' much when you married me, an' it seems like I ain't never give you nothin' but trouble for it."

Elise was startled that he could feel that way. "You've never given me trouble."

"Hard times. Worry—whatever you want t' call it."

"You didn't cause the Depression, or the War either, you know." Elise smiled, and she saw him half-heartedly return the smile.

"Would you do it again?" he asked, his face sobering.

"Do what?"

"Marry me, if you had t' do it over, even knowin' all that's come after."

"Yes, I would." She smiled, knowing she meant it. "I never wanted anyone but you. I could never even imagine myself going to bed with anyone but you. Even before you kissed me the first time, I used to wonder what it would be like to be that close to you, to have you touch me—"

"You shouldn't 'a been thinkin' things like that back then." There was a teasing note in his voice as he looked at her. His smile was genuine now, his eyes leaving her face to move down her body. Elise felt herself blush, then saw his smile broaden as his eyes returned to her face to see the color that stained her cheeks.

Then his expression changed. Suddenly there was a longing and a sadness that did not belong between them. He noticed Elise shiver.

"Are you cold?" he asked, moving the nearly empty plate from between them.

"I guess a little."

"Come here." He lifted the blanket, then laid back and drew her into his arms, pulling the blanket up over them both. She lay for a time with her head on his shoulder, one hand resting on the familiar warmth of his chest. He was silent, and Elise felt unease slip over her.

"Remember I'll always love you," he said, and she caught her breath.

She felt as if he had said good-bye.

# 15

LATER IN THE NIGHT, ELISE drowsed. She dreamed of the land, of the years Janson had worked to buy it back, of the days spent picking cotton in the fields, and the nights alone with him here in this bed. The bins in the barn were full, as were the two vacant sharecropper shacks, and Janson planned to board in the front and back porches of the house to store even more cotton. Then they would take the crop out of the county to be sold, as Janson and his father had done all those years before, and it would be over, at least until next year.

There was a sound that roused her from the edge of sleep. Elise lay for a moment and listened, almost certain it had been nothing—then again, and she sat up, holding the blanket to cover her breasts. She waited, hearing nothing but Janson's quiet breathing. Then she smelled smoke. Something was on fire.

She shoved the blanket back with one hand as she shook Janson with the other. "Something's burning—Janson, wake up!"

He stumbled from the bed, almost falling over the blanket, not fully awake. "What—are you okay?"

"Smoke. Something's burning—" She was struggling into the dress he had tossed aside earlier, and the panic in her manner found its way through the last remnants of his sleep, for he seemed suddenly to understand. He snatched up his overalls and began to pull them on as she ran out into the hall. She shouted for Henry and Stan, throwing open Henry's door to rouse him from sleep, pounding on her brother's door to make certain he was awake—Janson was already at the end of the hall and going out onto the porch, and she could see the glow of fire beyond.

From the back porch Elise saw one of the sharecropper shacks engulfed in flames, and she thanked God in one breathless instant that the ground around the shack had been cleared so that the fire would not move into the unpicked fields nearby. Janson was running toward the barn, a pronounced limp in his gait, and Elise followed, feeling her heart leap into her throat as she saw the double doors of the barn flung open and fire eating upward into one of the rough wooden doors, and spreading inward toward the bins of cotton.

Elise ran down the rear steps, almost falling as she reached the ground, quickly outdistanced by Stan and Henry as they jumped from the edge of the porch and ran toward the barn.

The reek of gasoline was in the yard. Janson was snatching burning burlap sacks from a pile just within the barn, throwing them out into the swept yard. The fire was deliberately set, empty sacks thrown on a pile of hay, then doused with gasoline before setting the stack alight—but why here? Why set hay in the doorway ablaze and not the cotton inside?

Then Elise drew herself up short, realizing that what had wakened her from sleep was the sound of breaking glass. She turned back toward the house and heard herself cry out. Fire was lighting the windows of the separate kitchen that was attached by a covered walkway to the side of the house. Not the house. Not her house!

She ran back up onto the porch, through the rear door and down the hall to the bedroom. She flung books and odds-and-ends from the cedar chest at the foot of the bed, snatched the lid open, and dragged out a quilt, knowing they could lose everything tonight—the cotton, the land, the roof over their heads. She ran back down the hall, out onto the porch, and over the walkway to the kitchen, smelling the mixture of smoke and gasoline. She snatched the door open, letting in a gust of air to feed the flames, then slammed the door, closing herself in with the fire.

The curtains over the nearby window were burning, and she yanked them from the wall, gagging as she slung them down into the fire spreading across the floor. Air was coming through a broken window, and there was glass on the floor beneath, the smell of gasoline even stronger within the room, and Elise felt anger as hot and enraged as the fire eating its way into her home at the thought that Buddy Eason had done this—he was going to burn the cotton and take Janson's land, destroy their home, take what they had worked so long to have.

She beat at the flames with the quilt. Sweat poured into her eyes, the fire hot on her face, and she gagged again, choking, unable to breathe—she would die here. No—her fury rose as she slung the quilt to the floor, smothering the flames, then beating at the edges with her hands where the fire still burned. A piece of jagged glass stabbed into her palm, but she did not care—she was winning against the fire. She was winning.

At last she stood on shaking legs, coughing, her hands and wrists smarting from burns—but the fire was out.

She dashed her hair out of her burning eyes, wiping the sweat away, then started out the door and onto the covered walkway, not certain if her legs were steady enough to get her down into the yard. She could see that the men were beating back the fire in the barn. The door was ablaze, but it looked as if the cotton was safe.

Then movement alongside the shed at the edge of the yard caught her attention. She stopped, wiping the sweat from her stinging eyes again, hatred and rage erasing all feeling of fatigue.

It was Buddy Eason, watching the blaze.

In the firelight, she could see the pleasure on his face.

~

Buddy Eason was happy.

He had waited for this night for so long. He had waited—and the time had come. Tonight he would take a man's life, and he would do it deliberately.

He had killed before—once indirectly, as the result of a fire set in these same fields of cotton; again through accident in the process of setting a fire; most recently, his own father in a heat of rage—but he had never committed premeditated murder before. This time it was with twenty-one years worth of premeditated thought that he would take a man's life. Premeditated since he had fought Janson Sanders all those years before.

He stood watching Sanders from the protection of the unpainted shed at the rear of the house, watching as Sanders, with his son and brother-in-law beside him, furiously fought the fire Buddy had set in the barn. He felt something very close to a sexual thrill in watching the flames and the man who would die in so short a time. Buddy had discovered tonight something he had never known before.

Murder was not that different from sex.

Both were best when they took a very long time.

The hired thug Mender shifted restlessly behind him in the darkness. Buddy knew the man was ready to have events finished for the night, ready to get away before they could be caught—but Buddy was not worried about being caught.

He was Buddy Eason, after all.

Mender shifted again, and Buddy realized he was not looking toward the fire, or even the men fighting it, though Buddy himself could hardly pull his eyes away—it was such a beautiful thing, so much power, something over which no one held any control.

"Mr. Eason, you ought t' take him now. There won't be no better time," Mender said, and suddenly something moved into Buddy's field of vision, Mender holding a rifle with the barrel pointing up to the sky. Buddy slowly brought his eyes to the gun, even though it threw the fire out of focus beyond, and then his hands were closing around the cold metal of the barrel, drawing the length of it back to his chest, until the wooden stock was pressed into his belly and the cold barrel nuzzled against his cheek—yes, it was time. After all these years—it was time.

The door of the barn was burning well, flames eating into the wood—Sanders would die as fire burned beyond him, just as Sanders's father had died. The flames would take the cotton—Buddy and Mender would make certain of that, for they would torch the other shack as well—and Sanders's wife and her family would lose the land. Sanders would be a rotting corpse by then, the climax of a hatred undimmed through so many years.

Buddy brought the stock of the rifle to his shoulder, then pressed his cheek to the cool wood, leaning his body against the side of the shack to steady himself as the excitement grew. He closed one eye, taking careful aim, feeling his body react as his finger closed against the trigger, that thrill that he was taking Janson Sanders's life at last. That—

There was a sound from near the house, and instantly something impacted the corner of the shack nearest his cheek, exploding it outward, sending splinters of wood into the side of his face. Buddy shrieked, the rifle jerking sideways, his shot going wildly into the yard as one hand flew up to cover the side of his face. He looked toward the house, and could not believe what he was seeing. Sanders's wife was in the yard, a shotgun to her shoulder, and the bitch was taking aim at him again.

Elise's second shot grazed the meat at the bottom of his ear before it exploded into the wood, sending tiny slivers into the side of his neck. Buddy screamed, a sound as high-pitched and terrified as any woman's, and then he was running before he could even think, throwing the rifle away, hearing Mender swearing just behind—the woman had tried to kill him.

He ran between two rows of cotton as he reached the unpicked field, headed toward the burning shack at the far end and the car they had left beyond it. Dry plants snatched at his trouser legs, gouging him as he tried to run, his belly jouncing up and down, his breath coming in hard, labored gasps through his open mouth.

He caught his foot on the uneven ground and fell, his arms pinwheeling out in a desperate attempt to catch himself, and then he hit hard on his face and belly there between the rows, the breath going out of him in a rush. He was wheezing hard, desperately fighting for air. He forced himself to his knees, then to his feet, took a step, and almost fell again—she was yelling at him from the edge of the cotton field, but he would not let himself look back, setting his eyes instead on the remains of the burning shack, and on Mender ahead of him crashing through the last rows of cotton to the car.

Buddy forced himself forward, trying to run, realizing suddenly that he was silhouetted against the burning shack, giving her an easier target. He could feel sweat greasing the insides of his thighs against his trousers as he ran—then he saw the Chrysler moving, turning around, and he knew he was being left behind.

He fell against the car door as he reached its side, but Mender barely slowed. Buddy yanked the rear door open, and suddenly he was inside—he landed with a jolt on his stomach in the backseat, his belly mashed into the seat cushion, one large thigh splayed out and a bruised knee against the floorboard, the stench of his own fear filling his nostrils.

⌇

Elise stared after the car long after it left her sight, a dark shape going down the dirt track that cut across their land, toward the road that would take it into town. She told herself that she should go help fight the fire in the barn, but she could not make herself move, no matter how hard she tried—she had never thought that she might be capable of killing another human being.

Tonight she had done all she could to kill Buddy Eason.

Her only regret was that she had failed.

A light touch on her shoulder made her cry out in alarm, almost dropping the shotgun before she realized the person behind her was Janson. He stared at her in the darkness, his eyes taking in what she knew must be an insane appearance, her hair disheveled and singed, her blue-print dress now gray with soot, and blisters beginning to raise on her hands and arms. She knew she reeked of sweat and smoke. She was coughing again as she watched him turn his eyes toward the disappearing car, and then back toward the house. At last he brought his eyes back to her and took the shotgun from her hands.

"The kitchen was on fire," she said matter-of-factly, wiping at her face with the back of one hand. "It's okay now. I put it out before I came out to help with the barn; that's when I saw Buddy."

"Th' cotton's safe. Th' fire's almost out. Henry's drawin' water t' douse what's still smolderin'." He bent to lay the shotgun on the ground at their feet, then took both her hands in his, examining the burns in the now-fading firelight. His eyes came back to her face, though he still held her hands in his, and she felt stupidly self-conscious at how she knew she must look, with her hair wild about her head and smut darkening her face. He looked again in the direction Buddy Eason's car had gone. "You was tryin' t' kill him, wasn't you?" he asked.

Elise looked away. "He was going to shoot you, or Henry, or maybe all three of you—I couldn't just stand there and—" Somehow she was afraid that he would not understand.

"Sh—" he said, and he drew her hands up to his lips to kiss them in the places where there were no burns.

Elise was surprised to see him smile.

"You never could shoot worth a crap—" he said.

And Elise surprised herself with the sound of her own laugh. He drew her close against him and picked up the shotgun again to hold it under one arm. "I need t' get you back t' th' house s' I can see about them hands," he said.

After a few steps in that direction, Elise stopped and looked up at him. "Janson, he'll come back again. I scared him tonight, but he'll—"

"No," he said, shaking his head. "I'm gonna make sure 'a that after I tend t' them burns."

Elise stared at him, both of her hands curled into one of his, his free hand in the small of her back guiding her toward the house.

She knew that this time he would go after Buddy.

And she knew that he had to. There were no choices left. Buddy

Eason had come here tonight with the intent to do murder. The Eason County law would do nothing to him. Nothing had ever been done to him, no matter what he had done to them or to anyone else in Eason County. Buddy had intended to kill Janson tonight, and perhaps Henry, Elise, and Stan. This time it had to end.

"Be careful," Elise said, afraid of what might happen to him tonight when he left the land. She could not see his features now because of the shack burning at a distance behind him, but she did not have to see the black hair only recently showing touches of gray, or the green eyes, to have him clearly in her mind.

Janson nodded and Elise understood.

She had just agreed he might have to kill a man.

～

When Buddy Eason woke in the pre-dawn the next morning, it was to the realization that a man stood beside his bed and that there was a gun pressed into his forehead.

Janson Sanders watched Buddy's eyes widen with fear in the sparse light from the nearby window, and he remembered that expression from two decades before when he had held a knife to Buddy's throat.

"Wh—what do you want?" Buddy croaked. The bandage on his left cheek made Janson think Elise might have grazed him with at least one shot. Buddy moved his hands slightly on top of the blanket at either side of his round belly, causing Janson to press the gun that had once belonged to Elise's father more firmly into his forehead. Janson wanted to make certain Buddy was awake, wanted to know beyond doubt that Buddy Eason knew this was no dream.

The ticking clock on the mantel across the room marked the seconds, witness to the time passing between the men—they were alone in the room. Janson had not been surprised to find that Cassandra Eason did not sleep beside her husband; he could not imagine that any woman would willingly lay down with Buddy Eason.

He had come here as soon as he had nursed the burns on Elise's hands, and after he made certain no danger remained of fire to the house or to the cotton stored in the barn or in the second shack. They had lost the one shack and the cotton stored in it, but most of the crop had been saved. There would be enough left to meet the mortgage on the land, if not be much beyond that. They would face a hard winter, but they would survive.

They had survived hell already.

There would be another crop in the spring. And there would be no problem with Buddy Eason to plague them in the new year—Janson was about to see to that.

He stared at the jowly face in the semi-darkness, pressing the gun muzzle into the broad expanse of pasty forehead, marking it. Sweat glistened over Buddy's upper lip, and the smell of fear was strong in the room—Buddy was afraid, and Janson knew he had every reason to be.

He also knew that he had never wanted anything so much as he wanted to pull the trigger.

"Aren't you going to answer me!" Buddy's voice rose, then fell again as Janson's hand on the gun to his forehead forced his head back into the pillow. Buddy's open-mouthed breathing was harsh and quick now, panicky in the otherwise silent room. There was a sound from down the hallway, a child speaking in her sleep, but still Janson said nothing until he could feel the fear stoke within Buddy as the silence stretched out.

When Janson did speak, his voice was so quiet that he knew Buddy had to strain to hear it.

"You come on my land again, an' I'll personally put a bullet in your brain," he said, then watched Buddy's eyes widen further. "You come near anybody in my family, an' I'll blow your goddamn head right off—you better not mess with me again. I killed men when I was in th' Army for no other reason than that they was shootin' at me— what'd you think I'd do t' somebody that comes on my land an' threatens my family? What d' you think I'd do t' somebody that sets fire t' my house an' my crop?—you don't want t' mess with us again after this."

Buddy closed his mouth and swallowed hard, his nose making a whistling sound.

"Th' rifle you left behind's bein' took to th' state police right now, an' it's got your initials carved right in th' stock. They'll be askin' why you was on my land t'night when somebody set fire t' my kitchen an' burnt part 'a my cotton, an' they'll be lookin' t' you if anything happens t' any 'a us after this—an' you better pray that you kill me next time if you come after us again. If you don't, you better hope th' law gets you before I do, 'cause what I can do t' you'll be a whole lot worse than anythin' they could do, believe me, a whole lot worse."

Buddy was shaking now, sweat beading across his forehead and the exposed cheek, until the open end of the gun barrel slipped slightly against the wet skin.

Janson lifted the gun barrel from Buddy's forehead and stepped back, knowing that if he stood there any longer he would kill the man. And he wanted to, certain that the world would be better off without Eason, that the county would be better off, and even Buddy's own children.

Shaking now enveloped Buddy's body completely. Great, gasping sobs made the round belly hitch and jerk. He was scrambling away across the bed, moving up onto his hands and knees, dragging the blanket with him, until he stood, clothed in nothing but his drawers, backed against the wall. His paunch continued to hitch with the almost-silent sobs, the blanket held against his mouth, the great, sagging mounds of flesh at either side of the material looking like malformed breasts in the sparse light.

Janson had finished what he came for. Buddy had always been a coward. Only fear and anger, and the power of the Eason name, had ever made him appear to be a man.

Janson left the room, going softly down the stairs to the first floor and out Buddy Eason's front door, leaving it standing open behind him.

He knew that Buddy Eason was nothing at all, and that he was done with him.

~

When Cassandra Price Eason's bedroom door opened, she did not open her eyes. She did, however, slide one hand underneath her pillow to the pistol she had kept hidden there since the last time Buddy had beaten her—and that was the last time, she told herself. She would kill him if he tried it again. Besides, soon he would not even have the opportunity—she would be leaving the county within days, leaving with a salesman she had been bedding for months.

Douglas Kirby would leave a wife and children behind when they left together, just as Cassandra would leave the twins—she was not cut out for being a mother, she told herself, even though she was pregnant again anyway. Douglas hoped they would have a son, and that was what Cassandra was almost certain she would have—at least she hoped it would be a boy, and she was almost certain it was his. She had slept a few times with the pimply teenager who delivered their groceries, and one afternoon she had spent with a man who changed a flat tire on her car, though she had not taken the time to ask his name. At least there was no chance the baby growing in her was Buddy's. Buddy had not touched her in years, and only twice since the twins were born, though he hadn't kept it up either time long enough to do her any good.

She opened her eyes when she felt the bed sag, his great weight sinking down beside her. He had not said anything since entering the room, and the sight of him made her stomach churn, with the mounds of flesh on his chest and the fat dimpling his sides. She knew she would throw up if he put his hands on her.

His face was wet. There was a bandage on his cheek, and she noticed that he breathed through his open mouth as if his nose was full of snot—he was shaking, making the bed quake beneath her as he got under the blanket and pulled it over himself, his naked calf brushing her leg and making her move away. He curled up onto his side, and she realized suddenly that he had only come to her bed because he was afraid to be alone—

As if she were his wife in more than name and joint bank account only and might comfort him.

"You are a piece of shit," she said, surprised at the sound of her own voice in the room, and the fact that her words made him start beside her. "What are you—afraid of your own nightmares?"

She watched him for a long time.

He never said a word.

# PART THREE

~ 1986 ~

# 16

IN THE FIRST MOMENTS OF awareness each morning, it was difficult for Janson to know what year it was.

He smelled coffee and frying bacon. There was the sound of a woman's voice, and the slight creak of the old house as it settled about him. He lay in that in-between time and he listened, letting the day come slowly. There were other sounds now, the sound of running water and of a radio—or was it television—sounds that did not belong in a world that in sleep, and in the early moments of day, was very much the world he had always known.

He opened his eyes on that spring morning to sunlight that filtered between almost-closed curtains, and to awareness that the day was in the present and not in his memories. He rubbed one hand over the stubble on his chin, hearing the slight scratching sound his fingers made against the bristles, then he raised that hand to look at it, finding dark veins along the back, and knuckles swollen with the arthritis that lived there. He tried flexing his stiff fingers, bringing the other hand up in an attempt to do the same, watching both hands as they moved painfully in the first minutes of his morning. He remembered how old man's hands had looked to him when he was a boy, and these hands of his had truly been old man's hands for many years now. Older than his own father's had ever been.

He could distinctly hear the television now from where someone was watching it in the living room, carrying the sound of President Reagan's voice—another old man, Janson thought, remembering the actor Reagan from movies he had seen back in the thirties and forties. Even now, Janson thought, the man sounded as if he were acting in a picture show.

Running water shut off in the bathroom next to the bedroom. Janson pushed himself up to sit on the side of the bed, then reached for the walking stick he had needed in recent years, especially in the mornings before his joints had limbered up. He rose from the bed and slowly crossed the room toward the partly open bathroom door, the thumping of the stick on the wooden floor loud to his ears. He stood in the doorway watching as Elise set aside a towel and reached for her bathrobe. Her hair, more white now than the red-gold he remembered, was wet, but Janson knew she would have it fixed, just as she would have her makeup done, before anyone saw her outside this bedroom. He watched her, thinking that age had only made her look delicate.

A smile came to her lips when her eyes met his in the bathroom mirror as she knotted the belt of the robe. Janson smiled back, realizing she had seen him watching. After almost fifty-nine years of being together, he still could never get enough of looking at her.

Then her eyes sobered, and his smile faded. He crossed the room toward the front windows, leaning more heavily on the walking stick, until he stood with the curtain held back in his hand, looking out over the land. This had always been his favorite time of year. It had been springtime when he first met Elise in 1927. Since then, it had seemed to him every spring as if almost anything could be possible. Over recent winters, he had looked toward springtime more and more, waiting for the warm months to come—he was seventy-eight years old now. Such simple pleasures could often be more than enough.

He stared at Elise's azaleas, blooming in the yard as they had bloomed for so many years, at dogwoods flowering, at grass turning green, ready soon to be mowed. The edge of a field was just within sight, a field that for so many years was planted in cotton—though none had been planted on it recently. There was not much money to be made in cotton these days. There was no longer much money to be made in any farming.

He felt Elise's touch, her hand resting on the bend of his arm, standing close enough that he could feel the warmth of her. They had been together for so long that sometimes they did not need words. It was enough to know she was beside him, looking at the same thing he was looking at.

"We'll make it. We always have," she said after a time, mirroring what he had been trying to tell himself in the past days.

He turned to look at her, at the blue eyes he had known for so long, eyes that had always trusted him no matter what he had led her to— a mill village, sharecropping, more trouble than she should have known. What she was saying was right: they had always made it. But Janson knew that *always* did not necessarily mean *every time*. Things were not the same in the world nowadays. Cotton mills had fled overseas, and maybe cotton farmers as well. This fall there would not be an acre peppered with white in Eason County. There were few fields with anything but goddamn kudzu and pine trees.

In all the years they had been on the place they had never been out of debt. There was always equipment to buy, seed and fertilizer every year, and another mortgage when they had the first almost paid down. Catherine and Judith had married and left the county long ago. Catherine was living in LaGrange now, and Judith in Roanoke. But Henry had stayed on the land, bringing Olivia to live here after they married. There had been doctor bills as the grandchildren came along, but Janson and Elise had been in the house to watch them grow, three boys born to Henry and Olivia one right after the other. Janson was proud of his grandsons, but there was also disappointment, for not one of them had shown any interest in the land. Then a surprise had come to them, a little girl born when her youngest brother was already twelve years old, and when her parents had planned for no more children.

Joanna Elise Sanders had come into life almost two months early, and she had kicked and clawed her way through the world almost from that first breath. Janson was surprised when he realized his granddaughter felt exactly as he did about their land, and that she intended to work it—but then he would think of his own mother, and his grandmother, and even Elise. He had long ago realized a woman could do anything she set her mind to, even if he had not wanted to come to that realization.

Joanna would be coming home tonight with a degree in agronomy from Auburn University, and Janson hoped their land would be here for her; they had been in trouble on the place for years now, with missed payments, and an extension on the mortgage. It had gotten worse. He had been able to fight Buddy Eason when Buddy had tried to take the land from them in the forties. What he was facing now he could not fight. He could not make the world again as it had been when he was younger. There was little place in the modern agribusiness world for someone like him, or like Henry. He wondered if it could be different for Joanna.

He felt the gentle pressure of Elise's fingers on his arm as he turned to look out the window again. A breeze was moving the limbs of a dogwood in the yard, and he thought of the touches of blood that were said to stain each of the white blooms—Jesus's blood—forever marked because it was on the wood of its kind that Jesus died.

"We'll make it," Elise said again.

"We already have," Janson said.

~

Joanna Sanders Lee became a college graduate that afternoon, walking across the stage in the Beard-Eaves Memorial Coliseum, accepting the rolled sheet of paper that, for the duration of the ceremony, represented her diploma, shaking hands with Dr. Martin, receiving her degree from Auburn University—in that moment she knew she was holding a dream in her hands. She had worked so hard for that piece of paper, worked so hard to make it to this moment. She was the first college graduate in her family. It had taken four years of work, worry, scrimping, saving, and barely squeaking by, but she had made it. After today there would be no more sleepless nights trying to get through chemistry or economic entomology. After today she could go home to the land to do what she had planned to do for most of her life.

She looked up into the audience to where she knew her three-year-old daughter, Katie, was sitting with her parents, her grandparents, and two of her brothers. Joanna knew that no matter what she had done in the four years at Auburn, Katie was her best accomplishment. Joanna had given up a husband for the sake of that little girl, and the decision to divorce Dwight had been the best one she ever made—they had been married for three months when she discovered she was pregnant. She could remember so clearly the look on Dwight's face when she told him, and how bad his words hurt moments later when he said a baby would ruin both their chances to get an education. He asked her to have an abortion, but Joanna had done away with him instead, piling his possessions on the patio of their trailer, where he had found them in a rain storm the next time he came home. She had seen him rarely since, but knew he was now in the business of selling cars in Anniston—Auburn University had had little use for him after he went on academic probation.

When the ceremony was over, she looked for her family in the massive crowd of people just outside the Roosevelt Drive entrance to the Coliseum, wanting badly to get back to her trailer so she could change into a tee shirt and jeans, and out of the high heels and dress that were driving her crazy. She saw her daughter's bright hair, the same red-gold as Joanna's, amidst the throng before she saw anyone else in her family—Katie was holding her great-grandfather's sleeve, trying to pull him, walking stick and all, along as she tried to reach the spot where Joanna stood. Joanna smiled as she watched Katie enthusiastically tugging at his coat sleeve—the smile on Janson Sanders's face was as broad as the one on Katie's. He was still a handsome man, Joanna thought, with his hair now completely white, and she could see within him still the young man in photographs her grandmother had shown her that had been taken when they were young. Her grandpa meant a great deal to her; he was the one person who always believed she could do anything she wanted to do, if only she wanted it enough.

"JoJo—let me get your picture with mama and daddy, and with grandma and grandpa," said her brother, J. T.—Janson Thomas, the same name as their grandfather—when she reached them, but Katie refused to be moved when either photograph was taken, obviously seeing no reason she should not be included. She took possession of her mother's mortarboard cap and put it atop her own head, then waited for her uncle to press the button on his camera, positioning herself before her mother in both photographs, and stamping her foot impatiently when she felt her uncle J. T. was taking too long.

Joanna still held her daughter's hand as she waited for her grand-parents to descend the two wide sets of three steps each that led down toward Roosevelt Drive, which they would cross in going to the parking lot where their cars and her father's truck were parked. She watched as her grandma waited on each step, her hand on her grandpa's arm, as he slowly descended while he held to his cane. Joanna smiled; she had been watching them all her life, and she had hoped she had found in Dwight something of what they had—how they were with each other. She had been wrong, and had not had time in the years since to even consider another man, to think she might find it with someone else. But she had Katie, and that was enough.

She looked toward the large bulk of Jordan-Hare Stadium just across Roosevelt Drive toward the east, and she thought of all the years she had spent on the Auburn campus—studying, working, taking Katie to football games, trying to survive and to make it to this day, with only the rare trips home between quarters or on weekends when she had not been working. It was hard to imagine a life without all that stress, without all that worry, without all that work to reach a point that seemed always just out of reach.

"Come on, Mama. We got to go home and load the truck," Katie said, pulling at her hand, wanting to get back to the trailer they had already sold, so they could finish packing the remainder of their things for the move back to Eason County.

"Sure, Bug," she said, nodding her head. "Let's go home."

~

Henry Sanders watched as his daughter supervised the loading of the last of her furniture into the U-Haul truck, staying well out of the way, knowing that nothing her brothers did now as they loaded the furniture, even under her supervision, would suit her as well as if she had done it herself. She was wearing blue jeans and an Auburn tee shirt, with her shoulder-length hair pulled back into a ponytail that bobbed as she moved, and she stood with her hands behind her at the small of her back, the ends of her fingers stuffed down into the rear pockets of her jeans.

Katie stood alongside. Her longer hair, though the same red-gold, was curly where her mother's was straight, and it was also caught into a ponytail. She had changed into an oversized Auburn tee shirt that was haphazardly stuffed down into jeans, and she also stood with her hands in her rear pockets, a brown teddy bear caught beneath one arm, as she assisted in the supervising.

"Matt, you're going to break my mirror—Matt!" Joanna called out to the brother closest to her in age, stepping up onto the rear of the truck, as Henry had known she would.

He could hear her bickering with her brother, out of sight in the rear of the truck, then Matt's response, and J. T.'s voice as he tried to calm them. J. T. was one of the few people who could do anything with her, and they had grown closer while Joanna attended Auburn. J. T. lived in Opelika, no more than fifteen minutes away, and he and his wife, Laurie, took care of Katie for Joanna while she was in class, as she tended their three children whenever she was needed—but even J. T. could do little with her at times. Joanna always seemed to think she should be in control, but Henry knew there were things in the world his daughter could not control, even if she had never

believed it. Matt was one of those things—for his temper and his sheer
cussedness were a match to hers—and the situation the family was in
now was another.

Henry knew they were losing the land. No matter how many times
he told himself those words, they were never any easier to accept—
they were losing the land, the house he had lived in since before he
married, the farm they had worked so hard to sustain, the dream his
father had struggled for, and his grandfather before him, a grandfather who had died trying to protect that dream. He remembered so
well the fire they fought the first year they had been on the place, the
fire that had taken so much of their cotton, and his fear that night—
he felt the same now, angry and afraid, and, more than anything,
helpless.

The difference now was that he did not know who to blame. At
least then he had known that what happened had been done to them
by Buddy Eason.

Now farmers throughout the country were losing their land,
more, they said on television, than at any time since the Great
Depression. One farmer's place in the county had been auctioned off
just the month before. The Sanders had not reached that point yet,
but Henry knew it was a matter of time. It did not matter what anyone
said, Reagan's "trickle down" economic theory did not work where
farmers were concerned. Or if it did, Henry Sanders was tired of being
the one getting trickled on.

Matt had abandoned the rear of the truck, to stand smoking a
cigarette at the edge of the street. Henry heard a commotion in the
back of the U-Haul, and a few less-than-quiet words, before J. T.
joined his brother outside the vehicle. They stared into the back of the
truck at what had to be, from the sounds coming from within, Joanna
struggling alone with a piece of furniture.

There was a bump, the sound of something scraping long and hard
against metal, then his daughter's clearly audible voice, "Oh, crap—"
Then all grew silent again.

After a moment, Joanna stood atop the rear bumper of the U-

Haul, her fingers shoved again into the rear pockets of her jeans as she stared down at her brothers. For a moment, Henry thought she would ask for help, then thought the better of it as she continued to stare, before telling Matt, "You know, you ought not smoke around Katie."

Matt did not say anything, but he glanced at his niece where she stood watching the exchange from the edge of the yard, the teddy bear now piggy-back at her shoulders, each little hand holding firmly to a bear foot. He dropped the cigarette onto the street where he ground it out with one heel. As Joanna continuing to stare, he picked up the flattened butt to drop it into the City of Auburn trash can waiting at the street.

"You see I was right," he said, dropping the lid back into place and turning to look at Joanna. "It won't fit any other way than the way we had it."

"I'm not admitting anything," she said, but she did move to let Matt and J. T. back up onto the rear of the truck. She never gives in, Henry thought, listening to the argument flare back up then finally die away. Henry had not known of a thing in her life that Joanna had not tried to control. Even when she had had to kick Dwight Lee out of the trailer, that had been her choice as well. But what she would be facing soon she would have to accept. For once in her life, Joanna would have to listen to reason.

There was a job waiting for her in Tift County in Georgia. Joanna did not know the job offer had been made, but it was one that would bring her a future she would never have on Sanders land—not that it would be Sanders land much longer anyway, Henry told himself, hearing the sound of his father's voice behind him as Janson Sanders came out the front door of Joanna's mobile home.

Henry turned back to see his father step out into the afternoon sunshine, one hand braced on the doorknob of the flimsy trailer door, the other closed over the crook of his walking stick. Losing the land could very well kill his father, Henry told himself.

He would not have it be the end of his daughter.

~

Elise realized that Katie was asleep in the backseat of Joanna's car long before they crossed into Eason County. She sat in the front seat of Joanna's old Ford Galaxie, staring through the windshield at the faded sections of the car's hood as she listened to the silence that had fallen within the car. Joanna had been talking about her plans now that she was finished with college, the things she hoped to do on the farm, until Janson had grown silent beside Katie, and soon Joanna had fallen silent as well. Elise knew Janson was staring out the window at the newly turned fields they passed, the acres upon acres of red earth open to the sun, then finally at the Chevron station, the Winn-Dixie and Harco Drugs, and at last McDonald's as they drew closer to Pine.

"Why don't we drive down through town?" Joanna asked as they stopped at the red light where the highway met up with Main Street.

Janson said nothing. Elise said, "Sure, go ahead," though she had little desire to see Pine.

Main Street was quiet, with few cars parked along either side of the road as they reached downtown. The highway that had come in a few years back had skirted the town, dealing a death blow to the stores located along Main Street. A number of businesses had moved out to the new shopping centers along the bypass, and those seemed to be doing well, but the businesses that had remained with the safety and tradition of downtown were slowly dying, choked out by the chain stores with easier parking and a wider selection of merchandise.

The shops still open along Main Street looked little as they had when Elise had come as a young wife to this town, and she could see no evidence of the fire that had taken so much of the downtown section in 1930. The old brick, burned black then, was in many instances now covered with aluminum or taken out completely and replaced with plate glass. The movie theater had been boarded up, its marquee bearing the single word "closed," and the front door of the drugstore had a sign stating the date it opened and the date it had gone out of business more than sixty-seven years later.

The brick paving of Main Street was now blacktopped, the once-busy bus station was a car lot, and not one grocer was left in all of downtown. Big supermarkets out along the highway, a Winn-Dixie and a Piggly Wiggly, had replaced the quiet little grocery stores, stores with pot-bellied stoves for warmth, cracker and pickle barrels out on the sidewalk alongside where gossipy old men sat playing checkers and spitting, and fat storekeepers inside who ran a charge and always got your purchases up for you—God, it did not seem that long ago.

Joanna turned off Main Street and onto Dell, going toward the mill village. Elise stared toward the houses along the street as they left downtown, seeing ferns on porches, and rockers and porch swings. Crepe myrtles grew along the street, bushes put out by the WPA women so long ago, and azaleas and dogwoods bloomed in yards, reminding her of so many spring days she had seen in this town.

Joanna topped the railroad tracks, entering the village, slowing to avoid dragging the undercarriage of the car. Elise stared down those lengths of rail that still divided the town in half, finding them rusty and broken, overgrown with weeds and kudzu vines. At one time they had been a lifeline for the County.

The village streets were just as tree-shaded as they had always been, but there was asphalt beneath the wheels of Joanna's car, where once there had only been red clay. The houses in the mill village seemed almost closer together, but they looked very different from the way Elise first remembered them. They had been sold in the years after World War II, and many had passed from hand to hand in the time since—they were green and pink, white and brown. Decorative shutters had been added to some, rooms built onto others; porches had been screened in or boxed into rooms. A satellite dish sat in one back yard, a chain link fence surrounded another. Children played noisily, and not once did Elise see a "day sleeper" sign.

She saw these shaded streets in memory as they had been so long ago, lined with row-upon-row of identical, white, two-family houses, and life here as a young bride with no electricity, no running water, and no indoor bathroom. She remembered the ice wagon and the milk man, both making deliveries on these same streets where now a snow-cone truck was selling treats to children.

When they made the narrow turn onto Pearlman Street, Elise was surprised to see the short strip of village stores was still standing. The first was now a beauty parlor, and the second had a front window labeled "God's Word Church" in gold-leaf backed by full-length white curtains. The third, behind cracked and grimy windows, looked to be vacant, and the fourth was open to the sky, its roof having fallen in.

A little farther down the street, Pearlman Street Baptist looked much as it always had, behind a "For Sale" sign that had recently been added to its front yard—the congregation had moved on to a bigger sanctuary out on the highway, Elise knew. So many things had moved on to "bigger," to leave the town, and the town's people, behind.

The village school was still being used, although it held only the first through the third grades, with new classrooms and a modern lunchroom taking up space where the playground had once been. Uptown, a few blocks from Main Street, there was a new high school, with higher SAT scores and a lower drop-out rate than many in the state, and a new public library for them all.

The "colored" school that Henry's friend, Isaac Betts, had attended as a child was closed, and all the children of the town, no matter the color of their skin, attended school together. Elise turned in her seat to look at Janson, finding his eyes on the mill village school as they passed. His hands, showing their age, with obvious veins along the back and dark spots on skin that looked almost translucent across his knuckles, were folded atop the crook of his walking cane where it rested against his thigh. So many times in the years they had been together, she had seen him judged for nothing but the color of his skin, color he had inherited from his Cherokee mother. She was glad that he had lived to see this day, especially since she knew he had lived to see so many things that he had never wished to see.

Janson did not fit in this world nowadays when the land had

grown to mean so little, when poor people were ignored again as in the days before the New Deal, and when one man had the power to destroy the Earth and all of mankind. He did not belong in a time when no one cared to learn from the past, or when children went hungry and families were homeless, when embittered farmers still lost their land, and when multitudes still followed madmen as in the days of Hitler. She knew he could not understand why there were few fields of cotton, and less and less cultivated land every year, even in a time when people went hungry, or why it was that the wealthiest nation on Earth could not even make certain that a high school graduate could read and write.

Janson had not understood things such as Jonestown or American hostages, Watergate, or the Vietnam War. He could not understand why man had not grown to be somehow better in this last half of the century, or why men like John and Robert Kennedy and Dr. Martin Luther King, Jr., had had to die for their dreams—but Elise knew he had also seen dreams come true. He had witnessed man walking on the moon, and pictures sent back by the Voyager spacecraft, the success of Live Aid and the African Relief Drive and Hands Across America. And of civil rights as well.

It seemed, at least, that the world had learned something.

The car slowed as they drew within sight of the red brick of the huge, long-vacant cotton mill. A fire not long before it closed had taken much of the once-white office building out front. That smaller building stood a gutted-out shell, with blackened evidence of where the fire had licked its way up the graying walls above holes that had once been windows. Many of the blue-painted windows along the front of the mill itself had been broken out, and the tall chimneys that had once belched smoke throughout the village were crumbling and in ruin, now nothing but a home for nesting birds.

An air of decay and utter desertion hung about the place, and even its sign, having for so many years proudly announced "Eason Cotton Mill" to the world, was askew and faded. The fence around the perimeter of the property was rusty, and the gate hung loose from one hinge and open, the worth of the place now existing only in the value of the brick and timber in the mill itself, for which it had recently been sold, and for which it would soon be destroyed.

Katie awoke before they left the mill village, but she remained silent as they drove out of town. Elise had looked back to see the little girl take her great-grandfather's hand from the crook of his walking stick, and that she continued to hold it by the first two of his fingers where it rested on the seat between them.

Elise turned back to stare out the windshield long before the Peace Memorial Gardens cemetery came within view at one side of the road toward Cedar Flatts.

"Would you like to stop, Grandma?" Joanna asked as they drew nearer the cemetery, as she had done so many times before.

The sun was going down and the late afternoon was cool when they stepped out of the car. Joanna stayed with Katie, lifting the little girl up onto the hood of the car as they waited, letting Janson and Elise walk into the cemetery alone. Cemeteries were a place for old folks and memories, Elise knew, and they held little interest for a small girl or a young woman.

She held to Janson's arm as they walked over the closely clipped grass, afraid that he would fall even here on this smooth ground. She could not help but to think, as they made their way through the rows of flat markers, that one day in the future the two of them would come here together for the last time. She hoped that it would be her to go into the ground on that day. She did not want to be the one left alive when the other was gone.

They found the grave they were looking for, among the rows of identical stones that seemed so little mark to the passing of a life—Stanley Denham Whitley, her brother, 1913–1974. Somehow she could remember him best as a child, with the round lenses of his eyeglasses reflecting the sun, so full of questions and curiosity about the world, and forever with his nose in a book. It was harder to remember him in later years, working in the fields, picking cotton, losing his arm in the card room at the cotton mill—he had saved

Janson's life when they had all been young, and he had been beside them through so many years, seeming contented to share their lives.

"No woman would want to marry a man who only has one arm," he had told her so many times, seeming to have allowed that one moment in the mill to have set the direction of his life. "I have a family—you and Janson, and your kids—"

And that, for him, he had decided, was enough.

She knelt by the grave and ran her fingers over the letters that spelled her brother's name, realizing that she was crying again as she had rarely cried in the twelve years since he passed away. This place in this clay earth seemed such a long distance from where she and Stan had grown up, and from where her brother had been a child.

After a time she stood, feeling the pain of arthritis in her knees as she reached to take Janson's arm and steady herself. She looked at him, finding peace in the green eyes, in the laugh lines and wrinkles of his skin, the way time had written life into his face.

"Lets go home," she said, and he nodded.

They had reached the car before she realized that this time Janson had held her arm as they walked, making certain that she would not fall.

## 17

BUDDY EASON SAT ALONE IN the huge Eason house on Pine's Main Street. He was an old man now, caught in the liquid sound of his own breathing, the congestion in his chest, the sound that kept him company at night—he had slept little, propped up on pillows in the adjustable bed that elevated his head enough so that he could breathe. He had not laid down free of pain once in years. He could medicate himself enough to sleep if he wanted, bringing a brief escape from the pain, only to wake again in the early hours sitting up in bed with his head lolled down and drool escaping from the corner of his mouth, aware suddenly that he had been unconscious and that anyone could have done anything to him in those moments while he had been away.

He could hear the voices of the male nurses who tended him in the hallway that ran the depth of the house, and Buddy wondered if they were the ones who had bathed him and helped him to dress that morning—Buddy had been sobbing by the time they finished, whimpering from pain caused by the rough handling, and he could still feel the marks that one left on his upper arm from when they had maneuvered him into the device that lifted him into his wheelchair. He stared down at his body, toward the great, round curve of his belly, and the flaccid legs hidden by the blanket covering his lap—living was something that he found to be no longer pleasant, but it was something he had to do.

Not living meant death, and death meant no longer existing. And, more than anything else in this world, Buddy Eason did not want to cease to exist.

There was an extended blast from a car horn on the street in front of his house, but it was a noise quickly drowned out by the coughing fit that overtook him, bending him forward in the chair as he hawked into the room. Then he sat for a time, trying desperately to clear his throat and open an airway as he choked on the phlegm he had brought up from his own lungs.

At last he could breathe and he sat staring toward the distant windows through the dark glasses he wore now almost all the time, realizing that not one of the men he paid so well had come to even make certain he still lived, though he knew they would have heard him clearly in the other rooms of the house. None of them cared if he lived or died, and he knew it. One day they would sit in another room, drinking his coffee and listening to him, while he choked to death alone and afraid.

It was just a matter of time.

He was on his own, though he had the men who took care of him. Both his children were gone. Rachel had left the county when she was fifteen, and Wally the year after. Buddy had not seen either of his children since, though he knew his daughter had died in a car accident years later, along with her husband, and that they left a son behind. The boy, Stephen, had gone into the care of his father's family for a short while, until Buddy sent for him. He could still remember his first look at the child, when Stephen had been a sickly looking five-year-old—Buddy Eason had seen something in his grandson even then that reminded him very much of himself. Perhaps it was for that very reason Buddy sent the boy away to boarding school.

Stephen had grown up, had gotten his degree from the University of Alabama, had sat for and passed the CPA exam, and had begun work for one of the big accounting firms in Birmingham when Buddy at last sent for him to come home that past winter. Stephen had spent very little time in Eason County until then, but Buddy needed him now. Buddy had no one else, and perhaps Stephen had no one either, though he had brought a woman with him when he first came to live with his grandfather.

Andrea Greene and Stephen had been living together in Birmingham, but Buddy knew her intentions were to get her hooks permanently into his grandson—it had not taken a month before she packed her things to move back to Birmingham, and she had tried to make Stephen leave with her. She had not liked living in the huge old house with Stephen, his grandfather, and his grandfather's nurses, and had accused Buddy of watching her dress and undress in the bedroom she shared with Stephen—she was right, though Buddy never admitted as much to his grandson, and Stephen never asked.

He could still remember very clearly the day she left. She had packed her bags and put them in the downstairs hallway, had even called Buddy a "sick old pervert" to his face, which had sent Buddy into a fit of laughter, followed by a fit of coughing from which he had feared he would die.

When he had been able to breathe again, the girl was pleading with his grandson to leave with her.

"I can't do that," Stephen told her, though he would not meet her eyes.

"Yes, you can. You have to." Her voice was almost begging now. "If you stay here in this county, you'll end up just like him, a sick, twisted—"

"I think you'd better go."

"Stephen, please—" She was holding to his arm until Stephen shook her off.

When she took up her bags and started for the door a few moments later, Buddy could not stop himself from saying what he was thinking.

"You think what you've been doing for him is worth what he'd give up if he left here?—believe me, he can buy better. He can—"

"That's enough, Grandfather," Stephen said, but Buddy had already reduced the girl to tears. She ran from the house, carrying her bags, and Stephen watched her go without saying another word.

Buddy rented a house for his grandson shortly thereafter, moving Stephen out on his own. Stephen needed a place where he could indulge his pleasures—and his vices—without having an old man in the way. Buddy wanted to give him that, and Stephen would need it.

He was Buddy Eason's grandson, after all.

Now Buddy was alone, except for the nurses, and the daily visits he demanded from his grandson. He had been alone for many years, though he had married again after Cassandra left. It had amused him to bring Adele Rustin here into the house that had once belonged to his grandfather. He often thought about the time she and the old man had stood face to face, the day Cassandra had given birth to the twins, that same day Buddy had risen from a tub to touch himself before his grandfather, calling Adele to him to—

Buddy had married her, though he had never divorced Cassandra, or been able to find her to kill her, which he had thought about and dreamed over often through the years. Few people in Eason County knew he and Adele had actually married, though it was common knowledge that she lived in the huge house with him, and even that he had had Wally and Rachel call her "mother"—what a fit old Helene Price had pitched over that, striding back and forth in the wide hallway, calling Adele a whore, when her own daughter had been little better, telling Buddy what she "would not have." Buddy hit her at last to shut her mouth, slapping her hard enough to send her to the floor. He had not allowed her in the house again after that, or allowed her to see her grandchildren.

Adele had been sick by then, thought Buddy had not known it. She began to stumble, falling once down the main stairs in the house, which had broken her collar bone. Her walk developed a jerky movement. She lived in dark rooms, or slept through the days, saying sunlight hurt her eyes in a way that reminded Buddy of how his eyes now hurt in the daylight hours. She had taken at last to walking down Main Street at night wearing nothing but her step-ins, and he woke one morning to find her standing naked by the bed, a butcher knife in her hands and the blankets pulled back where she had already taken hold of his privates—Buddy sent her away to the mental hospital at Tuscaloosa after that. She died there shortly thereafter, and the doctors came to him, telling him she had untreated syphilis, asking if they had ever been intimate—Buddy broke a young doctor's nose because he had dared to say Buddy could have the same disease that had driven Adele insane—

And then years had passed and his own steps had begun to stumble, with shooting pains in his legs and back that finally put him in the wheelchair. Light hurt his eyes, and he had begun to lose his mind—

Had lost—

Buddy heard a car door slam, and he knew it was Stephen. His grandson walked into the room a few moments later, having let himself in the front door without knocking, and for once Buddy allowed himself to enjoy the look of the boy, to be reminded for a brief moment of how he had looked long years before, for the boy looked so much the same. Stephen Dawes had the same height and husky build, but at age twenty-four, as the boy was now, Buddy Eason had already begun to go to fat, while Stephen's bulk was from muscle alone.

The comparison brought realization to Buddy of the years that had passed since he had looked as his grandson did, of the pain in the recent years that had stabbed through his legs only to have settled in his gut, and of the hurting in his back and the unsteadiness of his step that had condemned him to the chair.

And of how he now found himself at the mercy of the men who tended him.

Buddy did not like thinking about the past, and he knew he would not be thinking about it now if not for a trip he had made in his van out to his grandson's house the previous day. He had been going past the cemetery when he caught sight of an old man and woman walking among the graves. He had his driver stop the van and circle back, at last making the man drive through the narrow lanes between sections of the cemetery, and Buddy had been overtaken by such a fit of hatred that he began to wheeze and gasp for air and had to be taken back to his house—it had been Janson and Elise Sanders.

They were old, as was he. He had seen them rarely in recent years, but he hated them as much as ever. The Sanders were the one unfinished thing in his life that he had to take care of before he died.

"Don't worry, Grandfather," Stephen said, bringing a touch of satisfaction to Buddy with his words: "I'm here to take care of things now."

~

An absolute silence filled the Sanders kitchen that morning, a silence so deep that Joanna could hear the trucks passing along the highway several miles away. She stared at her father across the kitchen table, the napkin that had been in her lap a few moments earlier now gripped tightly and knotted in her hands—no, she would not believe it could be true.

They had sat down to breakfast and she had been enjoying the biscuits she made that morning, as well as fried eggs and bacon her mother had prepared, and grits yellow with real butter—she had never eaten like this in Auburn. She could cook rather well, thanks to her mother, who thought the ability to cook was as important as the desire to eat, but in Auburn she had often had little time to prepare more than cereal and milk, juice, and the sausage links Katie loved. With having to get Katie up and dressed in the mornings, and herself ready for class, there had never seemed enough time in the mornings for the full-out Southern breakfast Joanna had grown up with.

Now there would be time for many things. Now there would be no more tests, no more nights spent studying while Katie slept, no more worrying over every single penny in order to get through school. College was over now, and there was nothing ahead but years of doing what she had planned all her life, and of doing it here in the place that she loved more than any other place on earth.

She gave only a brief moment's thought to the people she gradu-ated with, now likely all scattered to the four winds with dipomas in hand, and she told herself that there were at least a few with whom she might like to stay in touch—they were all going to their own worlds now, to dreams they had worked toward through the years at Auburn. Some, she knew, had never known what they wanted to do with their lives, and there were quite a few who were in college only because it was what to do after high school, as well as a decent contingent of girls who had attended Auburn with no further plans than landing a "Mrs." degree—but Joanna had always known what she would do. She had known she would return here, to the Sanders land, and that she would make this place successful in a way it had never been.

Katie had been holding a silent conversation with a Barbie doll as she ate. The doll was seated with her legs straight out in front of her, her back against an AlaGa Syrup jar on the kitchen table. Joanna watched her, seeing Katie offer a bite of a strawberry preserve-smeared buttered biscuit to Barbie, then tilt her head to one side as she listened to the doll's imaginary response, her eyes fixed on the wide-eyed stare. Joanna had noticed her father was talking little as she sat down to eat her own breakfast. He stared into his coffee cup, hunched over it where he was sitting at the other side of the table, the cup held with both his hands wrapped around its surface on the tabletop, looking almost as if he were reading his future there in what was left of his morning caffeine. Her grandfather was at the far end of the table, his eyes moving occasionally to Joanna's father, and then to Joanna as he ate, as if he were waiting for something to happen between them. Grandma sat to his right at that end of the table, and Katie to his left. Joanna's mother, who had been dieting for as long as Joanna could remember, though Joanna had never been able to tell if she ever lost or gained a pound, had quickly finished her Special K and two-percent milk, then nibbled at some eggs before she returned to the stove.

At last, when Katie finished what she would of her eggs, and had eaten a biscuit with a slice of Velveeta cheese melted in it, and a few bites from the one that had been smeared with strawberry preserves, she left the room to go watch cartoons on television, and Joanna's mother went with her. Joanna looked at her father where he sat still staring into his coffee cup, her eyes moving from the cup in his hands to the almost-untouched plate that he had pushed aside. She brought her eyes back to her own plate, to the eggs that now looked slimy, and grits that had hardened into lumps that she could lift with her fork, and she knew that something was wrong.

"I was thinking I would make a reservation for a couple of rooms in Tifton for tomorrow night," her father was saying, and Joanna wondered when it was that he had begun to speak the words, for she could not remember now how they had started. "You remember Isaac Betts, Reverend Betts's brother? He and one of his sons just bought a place over in Tift County, in Georgia, and he knows you just finished at Auburn. I believe he wants to talk to you about coming to work for him."

For a moment, Joanna could only stare at her father—yes, she knew Mr. Betts. He was one of her father's oldest friends, and his brother, Andrew, was the pastor of one of the churches in Pine, as well as the founder of a food program for the poor in Eason County, to which the Sanders had often donated fresh vegetables and other foods, as well as their time. She had seen Isaac and Andrew Betts a few months before when the Sanders family attended Nathan Betts's funeral, and had never been so touched by anything as she had been by Andrew Betts's eulogy for his father, and the rendition of "Amazing Grace" sung by Isaac Betts, as well as the sight of Isaac and Andrew standing at either side of their mother, Esther, supporting her to keep her on her feet as their father was laid to rest—but she could not believe what her father was suggesting. He knew that she intended to stay here. He knew she had always intended to stay here—she looked around the room, at her grandmother now staring down at her own, almost-untouched plate, at her grandfather, whose fading green eyes were set on her in return—they knew what she had planned. They all knew. She had made no secret throughout her life of what she intended, and she could not believe that any of them would think she would consider leaving this land.

She looked back to her father, to see him lift his eyes from his coffee cup at last to look at her. There was a determined expression on his face. And something also that seemed undeniably sad.

"Joanna, things haven't been good here for years now," he was saying, staring at her. His voice was kind, but his words were not—she did not want to hear this. "There was equipment we had to replace last year, and some the year before. Expenses have all been going up, and the money's just not coming in. We've been losing ground steady for several years—and it's not just us. Most every farmer in the county is in the same shape, or even worse. Malcolm Gates, from over the other side of Wiley, lost his place last month; the Brimleys are being auctioned next week, and Joe Cagle just got his foreclosure papers—"

"We haven't—" She gripped the napkin tightly in her lap beneath the table—not us; not here. Not the land she where she had grown up, the home she had lived in all her life, the place where she had hoped Katie would grow to be a woman. "We haven't—" She could not finish the sentence, could not even allow herself to consider the thought.

"Not yet."

"But, if we have a good year, we could—"

He shook his head. "We haven't had a year that good in a long time."

"We could cut expenses, and get an extension on—"

He was shaking his head again. "There won't be any more extensions, and we already owe more on this place than it's worth."

"But, there has to be something we can do. We can't just—"

"There's nothing we can do," her father said, his face resolved, and the silence had descended as Joanna's hands knotted the napkin in her lap.

Nothing—but she would not believe that. There had to be something. There had to be—she had thought about this place for too long, dreamed about it, planned—there had to be.

"I won't believe there is nothing we can do."

The sound of her own voice surprised her, for it was so calm, so assured, so far removed from the hands clenching the tortured napkin beneath the kitchen table.

"We can't just give up. We haven't been foreclosed on yet. Maybe—"

"Joanna, you can't live your life on maybe. You've got your degree, and you ought to put it to use. The Betts have a fine setup over there—"

"That's not what I want."

"You can't just stay here and hope things work out. He's not going to hold that job open for you. We'll still lose this place, and you won't have anyplace to go."

"How can you just give up?" she shouted, rising from her chair. "You've worked this place for forty years. Grandpa worked it, and so did his father. How can you just give up and let someone—"

Her father's fist slammed down on the table top, making the plates and cups jump on its surface, and sending her into silence.

"I haven't given up anything!" he yelled back. He rose, shoving his chair back, to stand glaring at her. "They'll carry me off this place when they come to—"

His words stopped as he stared at her. He was breathing heavily, his shoulders tensed and raised, and Joanna could see what he must have been like as a young man—he was filled with rage, and it seemed an emotion familiar to him.

He seemed slowly to regain control. His muscles visibly relaxed, his shoulders dropped. He stood with the fingertips of one hand resting on the table before him, his eyes still on her.

"You can't just hang on here, hoping it will work out. You've got your future ahead of you; you can't just throw it away."

"My future is here," she said. "I'm a Sanders, and this is my land."

Her father seemed unable to do anything but stare at her, then Joanna turned at last and crossed the room to go toward the door. The knotted cloth napkin was still clenched in her hands.

～

Janson stared at the door his granddaughter had gone through for a long time that morning. He could hear his son drag his chair forward before he sat down on it heavily. Then Henry shoved his coffee cup on its saucer away, making a rattling, scraping sound on the tabletop. Henry was grumbling just at the level of hearing, seeming to be afraid now that someone in another room of the house might hear what he had to say, when he had been shouting loud enough to be heard in the yard only a moment before.

"Damn stubborn girl—throwing her future away. She's got that child to think about. She can't stay here trying to hold onto a dream when it's already been lost. Damn stubborn—"

"Did you really think she'd go?" Janson asked.

Henry lifted his eyes to return Janson's stare.

"My folks risked everythin' t' have this place. Me an' your ma worked years t' get it back, an' you fought t' stay here—did you really think she'd just leave?" he asked again. "She's a Sanders, just like th' rest 'a us."

"Your pa died trying to hold onto this place," Henry said slowly. "Buddy Eason almost killed you, and he had me beaten almost to death trying to take this place away from us—"

"Joanna's a Sanders," Janson said, and he felt Elise's hand come to rest on his, though he did not turn to look at her. He knew she understood, whether their son did or not.

"Joanna's th' same as you or me," he said, never taking his eyes from their son. "She'd die before she gives up this land."

# 18

NEVER ONCE IN HER LIFE HAD
Joanna Sanders Lee given up on anything. Not even when she was a
child. Not even when she was wrong. Not even when she was wrong
and had known it. She was that stubborn and determined. That
"mule headed," her father called it. That much like him, her grandmother said. She had never given up on anything, but she had never
faced something like this.

She sat, swinging slowly in the front porch swing on a Thursday
afternoon, one foot tucked beneath her, the other pushing lightly at
the worn boards of the porch floor to keep the swing in motion. She
stared out across the yard, across patchy grass that looked as if it would
feel dry and brittle to the touch, grass she had not had to cut in weeks,
for it no longer seemed to grow.

The grass was dying. The farm was dying. The whole damn
Southeast seemed to be dying.

The weather had been hot and dry for months, and people were
starting to talk drought—drought could mean disaster, not just to the
Sanders, but to every other farm family in the region, but Joanna
would not allow herself even the thought that the weather was also
turning against her. She had been home for several months, and she
had not once let herself give in to the idea that they might lose the
land.

So far they were making it. There were late payments almost every
month, and the ledger was showing red as she now knew it had been

doing for years—but there were few farmers in the area who were not losing money year after year.

Another county farm had gone on the auction block a few weeks before, another family dispossessed. A group of farmers had tried to block the sale, but it had done little good. Deputies from the sheriff's office had arrived and the sale had gone ahead. When the gavel fell, land that had been in a family for generations had passed into the hands of an out-of-state corporation that cared little for Eason County, or for Alabama. Land that had been cultivated by generations in a family; a home that had sheltered great-grandparents, grandparents, parents, and children, all of the same blood; a farm that had grown cotton and corn and hay, and that had raised cattle and fed people in the county for most of a century, had, by the fall of that gavel, become merely a business asset. It was now no longer love and sweat and work, family tradition and a way of life that even Joanna had to acknowledge was slowly dying, that would decide what would happen to that earth. Now the future of that rich, red land, land so much like this she had loved all her life, would be decided by economic projections and business plans, as to whether it would ever be cultivated again, or be broken into tacky little lots where cheap housing could be built.

Joanna had stood with those trying to block the sale, but they could not stop the inevitable. She knew she might not be too many months from that same place—but no matter what she had to do, she could not allow that to happen.

Isaac Betts had telephoned to offer her the job on his place. She knew that her father was behind the call, and the offer, though Mr. Betts had not said a word to confirm her suspicions—she had watched her father turn away, shaking his head with obvious disgust as she politely declined the job. He could not understand why she would turn down what he saw as an assured and successful future, for the uncertainty of staying on this place—but it was in her blood; she knew that, though her father seemed to have forgotten it.

She knew as well as her father or anyone else in the family the old stories, the tales of the past and of the people whose blood flowed in her veins. She had been reared on those stories, had had them told to her on so many Sunday afternoons as her brothers hogged the television and she had to look for her entertainment elsewhere, only to find it in her grandma or her grandpa, and their stories. She had walked in words alongside them down long, curving rows of share-cropped cotton, and over the hard-packed clay streets of a mill village; she had lived with the noise, and coughed in the dust and lint of a cotton mill; she had experienced the rationing and worry and short-ages of a world war, and the horror that could come with a telegram, and that one moment between touching a page and not knowing if your world would end—those things she had lived in her grandpar-ents' words, in a time and a place that existed now only in memories, until she felt very much a part of that past, and even of what had come before it, in a time long before she had ever existed.

She knew the stories of the Whitleys, her grandma's people, and of the place where Elise Whitley Sanders had been born in Georgia. She knew of the great, white house on its hill beyond the curving drive, and the people of Whitley blood who had lived there long before the Civil War. They were people who had lost their money and done without, only to rebuild their fortunes on cotton and good business sense when the war ended, even in a time when other men had tried to profit from what they perceived to be the bones of the South.

She knew all about the Sanders, of ancestors of her great-great-grandfather Tom who had fled Ireland in the days of the Potato Famine, and ancestors of her great-great-grandmother Deborah who had survived the massacres of French non-Catholics centuries before. She knew that her great-grandfather Henry had been the first Sanders ever to walk his own earth, to own the land where he worked and sweated and lived and died—this land. He had been born the son of a sharecropper, the grandson of a sharecropper—and he had worked and fought and struggled to have this place and to pass it on to his son, her grandfather Janson.

There had been Henry's wife, Nell, a small, delicately beautiful woman who had mourned herself into death not long after he died, and who had been laid to rest at his side in that Holiness cemetery where generations of Sanders had gone once their struggles were over. Nell's people had been Cherokee, so many of whom had been driven from their land generations before her birth in a forced march to the west, a march during which a great-great-great-grandmother of Joanna's had died and been buried in an unmarked grave alongside what had become known as the Trail of Tears.

There was her grandpa Janson, the first Sanders born to his own land in that line of Irish tenant farmers, Southern sharecroppers, and dispossessed Cherokee. He had lost this place when he had been younger than Joanna was now, and he had struggled for years to regain it, leaving the county to earn the money he would need to buy back his land, but returning with Grandma instead. He and Grandma had almost nothing when they began their lives together. They worked and saved, and then lost everything again when the local bank failed in the early days of the Great Depression; they sharecropped and worked in the cotton mill and were separated only once when Grandpa served overseas during the Second World War—but they never gave up.

They had regained this land at last, and had to struggle against Buddy Eason to keep it—there was a hatred that existed between Joanna's grandpa and that massive old man in a wheelchair whom Joanna had seen about town on a handful of occasions, a hatred that had existed for more than sixty years. She had been reared on that hatred, had lived with it, had absorbed it into her skin and flesh and the blood that flowed in her veins—it was not something she had been taught; it simply *was*. An Eason had been been responsible for the fire that killed her great-grandfather Henry Sanders more than sixty years ago. Buddy Eason himself had tried to kill her grandfather Janson on more than one occasion. And that same Buddy Eason had her father beaten bloody when he was no more than eighteen years old, beaten bloody and then left as a message for her grandpa to find: *You're nothing in Eason County,* the message had been meant to convey. *Struggle and fight all you want, you're still nothing in Eason County.*

Well, this might be Eason County, Joanna thought, but this part of it was hers. This part was where her great-grandfather had first dreamed of owning his own earth. This part was where her grandfather and her father had struggled. She would fight to the last inch of her strength to hold onto it—she was a Sanders, after all, a Sanders in Eason County.

She had no fear of struggle.

It was what she had been doing all her life.

The chains of the porch swing made a rhythmic screaking where they were attached to the eye-bolts above as she kept the swing in motion. Through the open living room window, she could hear her Katie's voice talking her grandma into baking cookies, and her great-grandma into helping. Joanna's grandfather came out onto the front porch, his walking stick in his hand, and Joanna watched as he turned back to pull at the handle of the storm door after it had latched shut behind him, as she had seen him do each time he had come through that door since it was installed, as if he did not trust the spring-loaded device at the bottom to close it properly.

"Are you ready to go, Grandpa?" Joanna asked. She had been waiting on the porch to drive him into town to the Feed and Seed. He no longer drove himself, though he had never told her the reason—his eyesight was failing, Joanna's grandmother said, though he was too proud to tell even Grandma that it was going.

She braced her foot against the porch floor to stop the swing, then rose, hearing the chains rattle and then become still as she started for the steps that descended to the yard. Her grandfather came down slowly behind her, holding to the railing with one hand, his walking stick with the other, his eyes on each step of the descent as he made his way.

Joanna had reached her father's rusting old Ford truck in the drive at the side of the house before her grandfather made more than a few steps into the yard. She looked back to see him stop and study the sky, and she knew without his having to speak that he was checking for signs of rain, as they had all done innumerable times in recent weeks.

"I don't remember it ever bein' this dry this time 'a year," he said as he pulled shut the passenger-side door of the old truck. The door made a hollow sound as it closed, the loose window rattling in its frame. The windows on both sides had been down and the doors unlocked when they got in. There had been little chance recently of a rainfall wetting the interior of the truck, and there was little risk that someone would steal this truck with its one bald tire and leaking oil pan gasket.

Janson Sanders sat back and rested the walking stick against his thigh, his right hand remaining atop its crook.

"We sure could use some rain," Joanna said, starting the engine and putting the truck in gear. She rested her right arm on the seat back as she turned to look over her shoulder and through the truck's rear window as she backed the Ford down the drive. Red dust rose at the sides of the pickup, small pebbles bouncing in the truckbed, as she slowed alongside the mailbox before backing out into the road. She turned to start forward, the taste of red dust and Alabama clay now in her mouth, breathed in from the drought and the hot day and the lowered windows.

She knew there were a great many things they could use.

The traffic was heavy on the highway as they drew closer to Pine. Cars and trucks were pulling out of the Kmart parking lot, as well as the Winn-Dixie, and there was a line of vehicles stretching from one side of McDonald's all the way to the dark blue Suburban parked at the drive-through window on the opposite side. The traffic thinned noticeably as they turned onto Main Street. There was a knot of activity before the video rental store a block off the highway, and a number of cars were in the parking lots of the utility company and the library, but the closer they drew toward the strip of stores downtown, the less movement Joanna noted along the street. She passed through downtown without having to stop or even slow down to allow anyone to back out of a parking space. There were few spaces filled, she noticed, and that seemed odd even to her eyes. Joanna was only twenty-two, but even she could remember when this short strip of downtown bustled with people and vehicles.

There were two cars and a number of trucks parked along the street before Abernathy's Feed and Seed when they neared the edge of downtown. Joanna slowed and tried to find a place to park at the front of the store, concerned at the distance her grandpa might have to walk even before he had to climb the steps to the elevated sidewalk. There were no empty spaces, however, and she drove past, and then past the next vacant storefront, taking at last the first empty parking space she found.

Joanna waited at one side of the rusting tailgate for her grandpa to get out of the vehicle and join her. She would walk with him up the street, and then wait for him to go up the steps just ahead of her. She would not offer to take his arm for the walk, or for the climb up the steps. Her grandpa would never allow that. No one but her grandma could take his arm to steady his step, and Joanna knew that.

As they walked up the street, she noticed a small, expensive-looking red convertible parked in the space directly before the Feed and Seed, sitting against the retaining wall in a way that completely blocked the steps from street level to the sidewalk. As they drew near, her eyes took in the glossy finish that did not show even one speck of red dust or bird poop. As they drew alongside, she found herself hoping there would be bird poop on one of the nice leather seats, for the top was down—but what she saw instead surprised her. Spread out and almost falling from the passenger-side seat, a magazine lay open to the centerfold of a naked woman. Alongside it lay a crumpled sack, with what seemed an extravagant supply of Trojans spilling out—Joanna glanced quickly at her grandpa to make certain he had not seen.

She waited a few minutes as Janson Sanders ascended the next clear set of steps up from the street. She glanced back to the red car, her eyes settling on the license plate bolted to its rear—she had expected to see a vanity plate there, but was surprised to see a regular tag instead. It was a tag from another county, at least, as she could see from its leading two numbers, and that pleased her somewhat. She had doubted that someone from around here would leave something like that laying open for the world to see.

Janson Sanders had pulled his list from a loose trousers pocket before they reached the front of the Feed and Seed. She had heard him telephone just after breakfast that morning to check the prices of several items he intended to buy, both with the Feed and Seed and with Jenkins Hardware situated at the mid-point of downtown.

After he hung up, Joanna had asked if he wanted the number for the big hardware store that had recently opened out along the highway, but her grandfather declined.

"I reckon they got enough money," he had said. "They ain't got no need 'a mine."

The familiar smell of the Feed and Seed greeted Joanna as they entered the building that afternoon, that smell of chemicals combined with the various plants for sale just outside the open double doors, a scent unlike any other she had ever smelled but one she had found in every feed and seed she had ever entered. She could see both Mr. Abernathy and his widowed daughter-in-law busy with other customers, as was Thomas Jackson, the elderly black man who had worked in the store for more than sixty of his eighty-three years.

Seeing her grandfather immediately drawn into a conversation with another man at the front of the store, a conversation of which she heard enough to know it was about the dry weather, Joanna began to look around on her own. The Feed and Seed was a familiar place, one she had come to often with her father and her grandfather in her years of growing up. It had changed little. At least here in Abernathy's, just as at Jenkins Hardware, there remained a bit of stability in a town and a county that she was afraid were changing too rapidly.

The tall, scarred wooden counter at the front of Abernathy's, just inside the window painted with its green curve of letters that spelled out the company's name, had been in the Feed and Seed since the day it opened what was now probably a century before. The counter's surface was stained and marked with black lines and pencil marks, but she knew it was clean and scrubbed every morning as thoroughly as any counter in town.

On it sat an old cash register with a new calculator alongside, as well as various and sundry items for sale, from plant food spikes to small gardening tools. An IBM computer, along with its monitor and a wide-carriage printer, had been added in the past year, and it sat now on a small desk to the rear of the counter, looking oddly out of place in the ancient Feed and Seed. There was a display of harnesses, choke chains, tie-out chains, dog collars, and leashes near the front windows, beside tomato cages, watering cans, insecticide bottles, and a stack of coiled hoses. On one wall mid-way of the poorly lit store was a display of hoes, mattocks, sling blades, rakes, shovels, and long gardening forks. To one side of the main aisle that led back into the store, large jars and several bins held seeds: curly leaf mustard, seven-top or purple-top turnip greens, white field or yellow sweet corn, white velvet okra, Jackson Wonder or Henderson bunch beans, cucumber, tomato, eggplant, squash, and sweet pepper. Just beyond that she could see sacks and bins of fertilizer: ammonia, guano, and the more modern chemical mixes. There were racks of flower seeds, axe handles, and work gloves; counters with boxes and bottles of pesticides and herbicides; sacks of peat moss, potting soil, dog ration, chicken feed, and cat litter. There were clay, plastic, and ceramic flower pots; pink flamingos; white, wooden rose trellises; and metal feed bins in the dim back recesses of the store, as well as cement water fountains, weathervanes, lightning rods, and rolls of barbed wire and chicken wire.

Mr. Abernathy at last came to wait on Joanna's grandpa where he stood talking with the other man near the front windows, but Joanna paid little attention to what they were saying. She knew they would have to exchange pleasantries first. Those polite, unerringly nosy inquires always had to be gotten out of the way before any real business could take place in Eason County. That was how it was here in this place where everyone knew everyone else, or at least everyone knew of most everyone, and where if you talked to someone long enough you found you were either kin to them or at the least that your grandparents had been acquainted with theirs.

Joanna spent some time looking at the seeds in their glass jars and bins, knowing that her grandfather would let her know if he needed her. She heard voices raise to one side of the store, and her eyes moved in that direction. Old Mr. Jackson was struggling with something, at last hefting what looked to be a fifty-pound sack of dog ration from a stack there and up onto his shoulder. Joanna heard a sound escape from her and she moved in that direction—he was at least several years older than Joanna's grandpa, and he had looked just as hunched-over and old from the time she had been a child as he did right now. She thought that he staggered slightly under the weight, but then he struggled on, speaking back over his shoulder to a man who followed him.

Joanna felt a flush of anger that anyone would stand back to allow the elderly black man to carry such a burden. Mr. Jackson kept walking forward, seeming to her eyes almost compressed beneath the weight, his overalls sagging loose at his sides and down over his legs to his cracked and graying work shoes. His eyes within the wrinkled face met Joanna's as he drew nearer to her, and Joanna saw that he understood she had been about to offer to carry the sack herself.

"No, miss, I got it," he said, his voice showing a touch of strain.

Joanna started to protest, but then he was going past her and she moved out of the way lest she somehow knock him from his feet—then she was almost sent to the floor herself as the man trailing him ran directly into her instead. His hand closed around her upper arm, hurting her as his fingers dug into her flesh, but he kept her on her feet. Joanna looked up, finding gray eyes only barely touch on her before he released her and continued to follow the elderly man toward the front of the Feed and Seed.

Joanna rubbed at her upper arm, feeling the grip of the man's fingers still on her skin, and knowing there would be a bruise there by the morning. She watched the man as he followed Thomas Jackson and his burden through the store, thinking that he had not said: "Excuse me," or "I'm sorry," or "I didn't see you standing there"—then she told herself it was unreasonable to expect decent behavior from someone who would let an old man pick up and carry a burden so heavy.

And she knew that this had to be the driver of the red convertible blocking the steps outside, the red convertible with its open men's magazine and its several boxes of condoms in plain view on the front seat.

Joanna stared at the man as he watched old Mr. Jackson set the dog ration down on the wooden floor before the counter, noting muscular legs below khaki shorts, a tan that she knew did not come from work in the sun, and a neat Polo shirt tucked in at a leather belt that had probably cost more than Joanna Sanders Lee had ever spent for an item of clothing in all her life.

"Joanna—" she heard, but did not turn for a moment. "Joanna—" her grandfather said for the second time, and Joanna at last turned to find her grandfather's fading green eyes staring at her from only a few feet away.

"Yes, Grandpa?" she asked, bringing her mind back to the moment and to the reason she had come here to the Feed and Seed.

"Mr. Abernathy said you can move th' truck on around back t' load th' chicken feed."

Joanna nodded and started through the store, walking past the men at the front counter as the tall man shoved a thick wallet back into one rear pocket of his khaki shorts, then bent and easily hefted the fifty-pound sack of dog ration onto one shoulder.

She was just getting into the old Ford truck when she heard the blast of a car horn from up the street, followed by a derisive shout in a teenaged male voice.

Joanna looked back to see the driver's side door of the red convertible open out in the way of an old pickup that had already swerved to avoid it. A boy was hanging out the open passenger side window, the middle finger of his right hand raised at the tall man standing by the convertible. Joanna could see the look of anger on the man's face as he threw the sack of dog feed over onto the back seat and started to get into the vehicle—then he shot back up and half-out of the convertible with a curse as his bare legs came into contact with the leather seats that had been baking in the Alabama sun. Joanna laughed aloud, unable to stop herself.

The man heard her and was staring at her now, but Joanna did not care. She had little sympathy for someone who so obviously had more money than he had common decency, especially when that person had just gotten a little something of what the world usually gave so freely to everyone else.

The man was still staring a moment later when she glanced into the truck's side mirror before pulling out into traffic.

# 19

SATURDAY NIGHT WAS THE worst night for being alone. Joanna sat that following Saturday night in the living room, pushing the buttons on the remote control, watching channels flip by on the television, not pausing at any of them long enough to really have an idea as to what was playing.

Her parents had driven to Anniston for the evening, and Katie was asleep. The little girl had been curled on her side with her teddy bear dangling from one small hand off the edge of the bed when Joanna checked on her earlier. Joanna had rescued Teddy from the imminent fall, had snuggled him against Katie and placed the little girl's arms around him again where he would hopefully remain safe—Katie had not even moved in her sleep, causing her mother to stand and watch her for quite some time, wondering what it felt like to sleep so soundly, so peacefully, so without worry.

Joanna had done nothing herself but worry since she had moved back home.

She finally shut the television off and moved to the shelf of books across the room. She could hear the steady faint screaking of the porch swing through the open front windows, along with her grandparents' soft voices there on the porch, though she could not understand what they were saying. Neither had turned on the porch light when they went outside earlier, though it had been growing dark even then. They wanted to be alone, and being alone could sometimes be difficult here in this house where so many other people lived.

On the other hand, being alone was something Joanna herself could not seem to avoid, especially on Saturday nights.

She ran her hand over the spines of books on the shelf there at eye level—*Wuthering Heights, Jane Eyre, The Great Gatsby, Great Expectations,* so many others—she had read them all, quite a few several times, and could not bring herself tonight to choose one to begin again. People were in love in almost every book that her eyes touched on. Oh, they might destroy themselves and each other and a few other people in the bargain, but they were in love.

Even make-believe people did not have to be alone, she told herself, or at least they were not alone unless there were some defect in their character, some wrong choice taken that would destroy them in the end.

Like Heathcliff. Or Jay Gatsby. Or even Mr. Rochester before Jane had taken pity on him. At least it was usually men who were alone in books—but then she thought of Miss Haversham haunting her halls in her rotting wedding gown, and that brought to mind the bad choices that Joanna herself had made.

But without those bad choices, Katie would not be here now.

And being alone was far better than being with Dwight Lee.

She cleared her throat loudly and moved toward the front door, stopping to rattle the interior handle of the storm door deliberately before she unlatched it and pushed it open. Her grandparents were swinging slowly in the darkness when she stepped out on the porch, and Joanna wondered what it was that she had thought she would find them doing. They were both in their seventies now, she reminded herself, and had to be beyond all that.

"I thought I would drive into town. Would you mind listening for Katie? She's sound asleep," Joanna asked, sliding her hands back into the rear pockets of her jeans with her elbows canted outward as she stared across the porch to where they sat side-by-side. They were holding hands, their fingers intertwined and their hands resting against the light-colored fabric of her grandma's dress. It was cute, and it said so much, for them to have been married for well over half a century and to still hold hands in the darkness.

People didn't stay together like that anymore, Joanna told herself. The world was too hard a place for things to last nowadays.

"It's late t'—" her grandpa began, but Joanna could see Grandma press her elbow into his ribs, silencing his words and bringing his eyes to her as Grandma finished for him instead.

"You go on. We'll listen for Katie."

They were just getting up from the porch swing when she came back out of the house with the strap of her purse over her right shoulder and the keys to the old Ford truck in one hand. Her own car was almost out of gas, and the old truck had at least half a tank. Besides, the truck was blocking her car, and it made more sense to drive it than move it simply to get her own car out.

She watched as her grandpa took a step, and then another, clearly favoring his bad hip as he always did after having been still for a time, his right hand holding securely to the crook of his walking stick.

"I didn't mean to make you go in," she said.

"We was about t' come in anyway," Grandpa said.

Grandma opened the door for him and held it while Joanna went down off the porch and started across the yard toward the old truck.

"You be careful," Janson Sanders said.

Joanna smiled to herself. It was the same thing he said each time she left the house since the day she had first begun to drive alone at the age of sixteen.

∼

It was good to be away from the house, driving alone in the darkness with the windows down and the wind blowing her hair. Joanna knew it would be a mess to comb out when she got home later, but that did not matter to her for the moment. Just having the freedom and the familiar noise and rattle within the cab of the truck was all she wanted.

For once she was not worrying about the land. For once she was not thinking about what would happen if God did not bring them rain—and a miracle as well if He could spare one. Lights were on in

houses she passed, and once she heard loud rap music from a car
sitting in a drive—but mostly there was just the noise of the truck, the
force of the wind against the palm of her hand when she held it up
outside the window, and being alone for a time.

That feeling of solitude lessened as she reached the highway that
skirted town. Both the Kmart and Winn-Dixie were open, as well as
Harco Drugs, and cars and trucks were pulling in or out of each
parking lot that she passed. She waited at the red light where the
highway crossed Main Street, then made the turn to drive down
through the heart of downtown.

The volume of traffic thinned considerably as she left the highway.
There were a few vehicles moving down Main Street, teenagers
cruising on a Saturday night, but Joanna paid little attention to any of
them as she drove down through town and out to the small shopping
center just past the cluster of stores that were the dying heart of the
town. She pulled into the parking lot of Allstate and circled around
slowly, then drew back up to sit for a minute at the edge of the parking
area to watch the cars go by before pulling back out to start up Main
Street again.

After the loop through downtown, she came back to the bypass
and pulled into the parking lot of McDonald's. She shut off the lights
and killed the engine, then sat for a moment while she listened to the
motor cough and sputter before it at last understood that it was time
to die.

Lights washed over her from a car as it pulled into the lot and then
into a space near hers. She took up her purse and got out of the
truck—she was accomplishing nothing by just sitting there, she told
herself as she slammed the door. She felt as if she ought to be doing
something, although going into McDonald's seemed a little enough
accomplishment.

She started across the parking lot, not having bothered to roll up
either of the truck windows or to lock the doors, though she had at
least thought to take the key from the ignition. She was fishing in her
purse as she neared the sidewalk and the lighted windows of the

restaurant, wanting to make certain that she had at least some change, for she did not want to order a Coke only to find that she had no money with her—but the purse was suddenly gone from her shoulder, her hands missing it an instant before it hit the pavement of the parking lot and her checkbook and the truck keys spilling from it. She bent to pick it up, but felt a touch just below her sleeve, then fingers closing around her upper arm as she was drawn up short.

She started, fear changing to rage in an instant as the thought came to her that whoever had knocked her purse from her shoulder had to be a teenage boy who had mistaken her for some high school girl—but the eyes she looked up into were of a man who was vaguely familiar. For a moment she did not know how she knew him—and then she did, instantly jerking her arm free to take a step back and stare up at the man who had allowed old Mr. Jackson to carry a heavy sack in the Feed and Seed two days ago.

"Aren't you a little old to be knocking someone's purse from her shoulder to get her attention?" Joanna asked. She could see the red convertible now, parked nose-in one space from her pickup, and this man, in expensive blue jeans and a tee-shirt with a crimson curve of letters spelling out "Alabama" over one breast pocket. Cowboy boots that she could tell even in the darkness did not have one crease of character or one scuff over their surface completed the picture. He was trying to look like he belonged here, she told herself, trying to look like he was just anybody—next he would trade the red convertible in for an expensive pickup truck hoisted up on big mud tires. He probably had no idea even what the crimson "Alabama" on his shirt meant, any more than he would know what "War Eagle" in orange and blue stood for either, for they would be nothing but a fashion statement to someone like him.

This man belonged in Pine, Alabama, about as much as he belonged driving a dirty pickup truck hauling hay down a country road.

"I had no intention of knocking your purse from your shoulder," he said, seeming almost angry that she had spoken, although he had been the one who had stopped her, ostensibly to speak. She could only infer that—as lowly as she must be in the eyes of someone such as this—he did not think she should have been the first to speak. What else could she imagine of someone who would let an old man carry a sack of feed that had to weigh almost half as much as himself. The stranger stooped to retrieve her purse, checkbook, and keys, but she bent after them herself, moving to avoid having her head collide with his in the process. He had to be close to a foot taller than she, and she could just see herself being knocked to the pavement if their heads bumped, and she could not bear the thought of him trying to help her to her feet if it should happen.

He had retrieved her keys before she could stop him, and, after she stood and shoved her checkbook back into her purse, she found herself having to accept them from him as he held them out. She did not say "thank you"—but then he had not said "sorry" for knocking her purse from her shoulder, or even "excuse me" when he had bumped her in the Feed and Seed, either.

She found herself wiping the keys, ring and all, down along the leg of her Levis once she had them in her hand, until it occurred to her that the pavement would not have gotten them all that dirty.

Then she realized she was wiping them off because he had held them in his hand, and she made herself stop.

"Did you want something?" she asked, dropping the keys into her purse and zipping it with a quick and satisfying sound of finality.

He looked at her with dark eyes that she knew were gray from the brief encounter in the Feed and Seed, thick brown hair that waved uncontrollably from the most current men's hair style, broad shoulders and a build that made him look as if he worked out. He could have been a model for *GQ*, she thought. But *GQ* was not even the sort of magazine this man bought, she reminded herself, taking another step back from him and crossing her arms before her chest, safeguarding her purse strap in the opposite hand just within the crook of her arm.

"Well?" she asked.

"You laughed at me," he said at last, in a deep voice that sounded oddly petulant from this big man.

Joanna opened her mouth to respond, but was unable to think of anything to say. It was so childish and stupid a remark that there seemed no worded response within her. She laughed instead, then watched a look of absolute rage come to his face.

"I'm sure you've been laughed at before," she said, unable to stop herself.

"Not by someone like you."

That silenced her as assuredly as a slap. She stared back, rage filling her this time. "Is that why you stopped me, knocked my purse off my shoulder, just so you can insult me?"

"You laughed at me," he said again, as if that explained the entire confrontation, and why it was that she was standing here in the McDonald's parking lot on a Saturday night talking to a man she already knew without a doubt that she did not like.

Then he seemed to reform the statement, as if making it into the question he had intended to ask the entire time.

"Why did you laugh at me?"

"Why not?"

"You shouldn't laugh at other people."

"And you shouldn't allow old men to carry something that weighs almost as much as them, either."

He surprised her as he seemed almost to relax, as if that explained why she had laughed at him in the first place.

"I didn't 'allow' him to carry it. I said something, and then I couldn't stop him—" But he did not finish. He stared at her instead.

"You insulted Mr. Jackson, too, then," Joanna said, certain of it.

"Mr. Jackson?"

"The elderly man who carried your dog feed for you? The elderly man you followed through the store?—*someone like* him would have a name, you know, just like *someone like* me would." This man's absolute dismissal of the remainder of the world outside himself made her madder than anything else about him so far.

"So what is your name?"

She had not expected him to ask. "None of your business," she said, knowing it was childish even as she said the words. She turned away from him and started toward the restaurant, seeing the sidewalk just in time to step up to keep from falling over the curbing that fronted it. She forcefully regained her composure, realizing how close she had come to sprawling to her knees before this man right there on the sidewalk.

Joanna looked back to see him still standing there in the semi-darkness.

"What did you say to Mr. Jackson, anyway?" she asked, smoothing her hand over the front of her blouse.

There was a second's hesitation. "I said it looked like somebody would be taking care of him at his age, so that he wouldn't have to work."

There was even less hesitation from Joanna herself. "No—I bet what you said was that, at his age, somebody ought to take care of *someone like* him so that he wouldn't have to work," she said.

He only stared at her in response, and she knew that she was right.

"But, then again, what else could he expect from *someone like* you," she said, then turned without another word and crossed the remainder of the sidewalk to push at the glass door and enter McDonald's.

# 20

THE CAR HAD NOT MADE A sound, at least nothing beyond its normal, running wheeze before it simply died, coasted to a rolling stop alongside the road, and refused to start again.

Joanna sat that following Saturday morning staring through the windshield at the faded hood of the old Galaxie, then beyond it to the dry and patchy grass along the roadside where she had pulled off between Pine and Cedar Flatts, willing the car to start the next time she turned the key. Not today, she kept telling herself. Not this morning of all mornings. She turned the key again, holding her breath, afraid she would somehow keep the engine from turning if she made even a sound—but the engine did not turn, the damned car did not make a sound, and she released the key with a terrible sense of frustration. She had gotten a call at mid-week from Dwight, the ex-husband she had not heard from in more than two years. He had come to see Katie only twice since her birth, but he wanted to see her now—today in fact—and the thought of seeing Dwight after all this time had Joanna in a state of worry and panic.

She turned the key again—please, God, make it start. Please, God—start, car, start. Start—

She had gone into town to get Katie's asthma medicine filled, for the little girl had had an attack that morning, her first in close to a year, and Joanna was horrified now that Dwight might reach the house before she could get home. There was no way Katie would recognize him, even though she had seen his photographs; Dwight had never once even tried to talk to his daughter on the phone— Joanna leaned across the seat and yanked open the door to the glove box, fished inside for the screwdriver and pliers she usually kept there, then slammed the glove box shut as she reached to jerk on the door handle. She stepped out onto the edge of the pavement, feeling large pieces of gravel and broken blacktop beneath the soles of her tennis shoes. Several cars whizzed by, one honking its horn loudly in a sound that increased in pitch as it approached, and then deepened as it zoomed away.

She slammed shut the door and went around to the front of the car to raise the hood, then stood inspecting the greasy black mass topped by its covered air filter, smelling oil and gas as she stared at the thing in disgust. She set the screwdriver and pliers down on the edge of the rain gutter under the hood, then twisted one of the battery cable ends to see if it was tight—but she already knew it would do little good. The car was broken down more often than it was running, and it never had an ailment that was easily diagnosed, or easily fixed.

A vehicle was approaching from the direction of Cedar Flatts, headed toward town, and Joanna heard it slowing. She glanced back over her shoulder, squinting against the glare of the sun, as it drew almost alongside her, and saw that it was a truck, dirt caked over a finish that must have once been near to white, with lettering on the driver's door—but she did not have time to see more than that before she lifted her eyes to meet those of the man behind the wheel of the vehicle, and she immediately looked away. There was something slightly familiar in the face she had seen behind the slowly lowering driver's-side window, a familiarity that had sparked a faint sense of unease. That unease had increased at the thought that the man had been staring at her, and not at the obviously incapacitated car.

She heard the truck drive on past, then knew without looking that it made a u-turn and was headed back, this time on her side of the road.

When she looked from beneath the raised hood, it was to see the front of the truck move up slowly alongside where she stood, then the passenger-side of the windshield, and the passenger door, and she noticed with an odd sense of irony that the words stenciled crookedly on the door were "Goode Helpers Septic Service."

She knew she would rather clean out a septic tank herself than to accept a ride or any other help from the man who was now staring at her through the window that he was reaching across the seat to jerkily roll down.

When he sat back, he hooked his left arm over the steering wheel, and then reached with his right to take up a grimy Styrofoam cup that had been sitting on the dashboard—Joanna swallowed hard, knowing before the man said or did anything that the cup did not contain coffee or Coke or any other drink known to humankind. He spat into it, black goop from a jaw full of chewing tobacco, and then he grinned at her, displaying teeth stained brown and so disgusting that she had to turn her eyes away. The man could be no more than twenty-five, but with his dirty brown hair that straggled back from his forehead, and filthy overalls that had not seen washing in any recent time, he looked to her to be almost rotting alive. The smell that reached her from the open window confirmed her impression—tobacco and sweat, mixed with body odor, and worse.

"Car got a problem, sweetheart?" he asked, and Joanna knew that he had looked her up and down. She did not have to see the look to know that it had been there. It was just the kind of man this one was.

She made herself look at him at last, then forced herself not to gag as he grinned wider and she got a better look at his teeth, rotted as well as tobacco-stained. His eyes left hers immediately to move down to her chest, where they remained.

"I have it taken care of," she said, deliberately forcing her attention, and her gaze, back under the hood. She wiggled a battery cable, though she knew it would do the car little good.

"I'll give you a ride. Com' on," he said, and she heard a grunt just before she heard the click of the truck door unlatching.

She looked up to see him sit back up again from where he had leaned across to pull up the door lock on the passenger side.

"You can use th' phone at my house. I live just down th' way." His eyes were set on her chest again.

Her skin crawled at the thought of getting in the truck with him, and even more at the thought of what he most assuredly thought she would be willing to do if she went with him to his house. He must have noted her refusal coming, for she could hear the truck's emergency brake being engaged as the vehicle sat still running and blocking that lane of the road.

The driver's side door popped and made a groaning sound as it opened.

"I said I don't need any help," she said, louder this time. "Go on. My—my husband has gone to call someone and he'll be back any minute," she lied, afraid all the while that he knew she lied.

He came around the front of the truck, grinning at her again as she turned fully to look at him, his eyes moving down her body all the way to the scuffed toes of her tennis shoes, then back up again. He spat into the cup he had brought with him, and then reached to the side to place it on the hood of his vehicle.

"You don't remember me, do you, Joanna?" he asked, grinning again but for once keeping his eyes on her face and not her chest. "I wa'nt but a few years ahead 'a you in school. I heard you got divorced and that you got a little girl—you know, when we was in school, I always use t' wonder what it'd feel like t' have those long legs 'a yours wrapped around me. Why don't we—"

"Get out of here," she said, spitting the words at him with every bit of the disgust she felt. She turned her back on him and reached up to grab the hood with the intention of slamming it down—but it stuck, leaving her feeling helpless as she yanked at it again, stretched up to her tiptoes. She knew that he stepped closer, heard the crunch of gravel beneath his shoes, and she turned loose of the hood to reach instinctively for the screwdriver she had left sitting alongside the motor, glad that she had not managed to bring the hood down—she would drive the flat head right into his filthy hide if he tried to touch her. She would—

When she turned she found him so close that she had to back up against the front of the car. He was grinning, and the smell, along with the sight of those rotting, brown teeth at such close quarters, made her want to gag.

"You gonna poke me with that thing?" he asked, the grin in his voice as well as on his face. He stepped closer, and she felt his hand touch hers that held the screwdriver at the ready, his grin becoming nasty in a way that went far beyond his teeth—then his eyes moved away, angry disappointment coming to his face. His gaze narrowed and his mouth shut, and then he turned away just as Joanna heard why, the sound of a vehicle coming to a stop nose-in toward her own.

She stepped to the side, breathing what seemed like incredibly clean air after having been in such close quarters with the Goode Septic man. She looked past him to what appeared to be a new Dodge truck, its silver ram's head ornament at the front of its shining blue hood. The driver's door opened and Joanna saw Septic take a breath and she knew that he was about to tell whoever this was that they did not need any help.

"Hey, I got it—" he started even as Joanna moved past him and toward the blue truck, keeping her eyes on Goode Septic all the while—then his words stopped mid-sentence, his eyes narrowing further, set on the other truck. Joanna saw that his mouth remained open, and a trickle of tobacco juice escaped from the side—then he swallowed hard and started coughing, and Joanna knew he had either swallowed a mouthful of the mess or possibly the cud itself.

She hoped he would choke.

She turned her eyes toward the Ram pickup, hearing shoes now scrunch on gravel, and then she thought she would choke—it was the man from the Feed and Seed, the man who had accosted her outside McDonald's. He looked at her, then at the coughing man.

"You okay, man?" he asked.

Goode Septic nodded his head, still coughing, then started to move away, snatching up the Styrofoam cup from the hood of his truck and slopping out part of its contents before he made his way around its front end toward the other side. He got into the vehicle and slammed the door after himself, and after a moment it started away. Joanna could hear him still coughing.

She turned to the tall man beside the Ram truck again, finding he was staring at her.

"Is your car in running condition?" he asked.

Joanna shook her head, the irrational thought occurring to her that he did not even talk like a normal man. "No," she said simply, turning to look under the hood again. She realized suddenly that she felt exhausted. It seemed an eternity since the car died.

"Do you need a ride?"

She could never remember saying yes, but found herself a few minutes later sitting on the leather seat inside his Ram pickup, staring out the window as the truck started away. She kept her chin in her hand, her elbow resting on the door's padding alongside the window. Her other hand held the white sack containing Katie's medicine, both the hand and the medicine resting atop the purse in her lap as she felt the cool air wash over her from the truck's air conditioner.

"You forgot the mud tires," she said, almost without thought. She dug her chin into the palm of her hand, her eyes fixed out the window, remembering how she had told herself he would soon have to have a pickup in his effort to look like everyone else.

"They're installing them on Monday," he said, surprise and questioning in his tone.

She was too tired even to laugh at him this time.

The tall man was at least courteous in driving her home. He spoke little, and Joanna could not keep from glancing around within the cab of the truck while thinking of the things she had seen in his car the day she first met him in Pine.

He said his name was Stephen Dawes, and that he worked for his grandfather.

"But, what do you do?" Joanna had asked.

He seemed to shrug, for she had turned to look at him fully now. "Whatever he wants me to do."

Joanna found herself glancing at his left hand where it rested on the steering wheel, checking for a wedding ring, then she became angry with herself at even the thought that she had done it. She did not have time for a man, and most especially not for this one. He had at least one woman to keep him entertained—after all she could well remember the Trojans she had seen in his car.

And his magazines if he was ever alone.

She could do without that, as well.

"What do you do?" he asked her after she had at last told him her name.

"We have a farm."

"A farm?" He laughed, which surprised her—he stifled it almost immediately, but there was no doubt of what she had heard. He glanced down at her left hand where it held the pharmacy sack clenched in her lap. "Who's we?—you're not wearing a wedding ring."

She took her elbow from the leather padding of the door and covered her left hand with her right. "My family—my father and grandfather and I, if you must know." Her voice sounded angry, but she did not care. It was no business of his whether she was married or not.

"You're a farmer?" There was amusement in his voice so clear that she knew she was being laughed at.

"Is there something wrong with that?"

"Could explain why you're not married."

"I'm divorced," she said, then wished she had not answered.

*Could explain why you're divorced*—she could almost hear him say the words, though he never did.

"So, do you do anything—other than what your grandfather tells you to do?" she asked, wanting him to feel uncomfortable as well.

For a moment there was silence.

"No, I don't," he said at last, and Joanna thought she had never heard such finality in so few words. That was the last thing he said until they reached Sanders land.

∼

"Oh, damn," Joanna said as they drew within sight of the white house and could see a rather expensive-looking gray car with a padded landau roof in the driveway. It was a car that she would never have pictured Dwight Lee driving, and it looked oddly out of place behind her father's rusting Ford pickup truck.

"What's wrong?" the man sitting beside her asked.

"My husband's here already," Joanna said without thinking.

"Husband?"

"Ex-husband—whatever," she said irritatedly, scooting forward on the truck's leather seat, unease gripping her stomach muscles at the thought that she had not been there when Katie met Dwight—*met him,* because there was no way her daughter would remember him from the last time when she had been no more than six months old. "We weren't married long enough for me to get used to calling him my 'husband' then, and I haven't seen him since then enough times to get used to calling him my 'ex.' He wanted to see my daughter— our daughter—today. He's only seen her twice since she was born. She's three now. She won't even know who he was—is—wouldn't have—"

She realized she was babbling and made herself stop. When she looked at Stephen Dawes again as he turned the truck into the drive, she saw his eyes on the gray car, a frown on his face. She yanked the truck door open almost before he had brought the vehicle to a stop.

"Thanks for the ride," she said, not looking at him again, then she dismissed him immediately from her thoughts, slamming the truck door as she started for the front steps.

~

Dwight had come to see Katie only to annoy Joanna; she was certain of that later. He paid the child very little attention, and called her Kate each time he referred to her, as if he could not remember his own daughter's name, which made Joanna angry and Katie outright livid, even at the age of three.

"My—name—is—Katie. My—name—is—not—Kate," she told him at last, emphasizing each word with a noticeable pause, finishing with a stamp of her foot.

She stared up at him, hands on her hips, teddy bear hooked under one arm, and Dwight seemed suddenly at a loss for words. His blond hair was thinning noticeably at the top and receding at both temples, which pleased Joanna to no ends; he would probably be noticeably bald by the next time she saw him, if she ever saw him again. She remembered vividly his rude remarks years before about a balding professor at Auburn—"professor cue ball," and "old slick-as-a-boiled-egg." Perhaps he would even have a comb-over. She could well remember his remarks about those, too.

His first comment when entered the house that afternoon had been to ask who had been driving the truck she had gotten out of.

"Your boyfriend?" he asked.

Joanna had not dignified the question with an answer.

Dwight did not stay long, and did not mention visiting Katie again when he rose to leave.

"He don't know my name," Katie said after he left the house. She jumped up to sit on the couch beside her mother, sitting Teddy on her knee to stare at him thoughtfully.

"He knows your name," Joanna assured her, bringing a smile to her face when Katie looked up to her, all the while wanting to throttle Dwight Lee for being the man he was. Or, perhaps, for not being the man she had once thought him to be. She stared at her daughter's face, seeing something of both herself and Dwight there—Katie had

Joanna's coloring, and in many ways resembled the image Joanna had seen in photographs of her great-grandmother when Elise Whitley Sanders had been a small girl. Katie's features were more like Dwight's, however, especially in the shape of her eyes and nose. She was also the one good thing he had done in his life, though Joanna thought that he did not have enough sense to realize it.

"He don't remember it—and he smells like cigarette smoke," Katie said, dismissing him, wrinkling her nose with distaste, then turning her attentions back to the teddy bear.

# 21

THE FOLLOWING WEEK PAS-
sed with the normal worry over money that now plagued every day.
By the next Saturday, Katie's asthma was under control, and Joanna
let her ride along with her grandparents when they left to visit J. T.
and his family in Opelika.

With Katie gone for the day, Joanna spent the hours working, for
there was always plenty to do about the place. As afternoon came, she
went in to bathe and change, then got her purse and keys to drive to
the little country store only a few miles from the house. She had been
dying for a Coke all day, and they needed a loaf of bread.

The little store looked much as she remembered it when she was
a child, with its screen front door and several fading Coca-Cola signs
nailed to its exterior. There had never been a sign lettered with the
store's name, though it had changed hands and names twice in her
lifetime alone. It was Webb's Grocery now; it had been Linden's and
Jones's before that. Her grandpa sometimes called it Owens's Store,
for it had been owned by the Owen family from before his birth in
1907 until sometime late in the 1960s.

As Joanna pulled open the screen door that Saturday afternoon,
hearing the loud screak of the door spring as it stretched open, she
could not help thinking that her grandparents had shopped in this
same store when they first married, and her grandfather's parents had
shopped here, and his grandparents, as well. Tom and Deborah
Sanders had sharecropped land owned by the same Owen man who

had once owned this store. Something of this place was very much a part of her life, she thought as she looked around at the painted board walls, and at the ancient Coca-Cola cooler and glass-sided Tom's Peanut display alongside the front counter, both of which had sat in those same locations for uncountable years.

The person behind the counter was a part of her life, as well, Joanna thought as she met the woman's small eyes. An unwelcome part.

Vertie Webb sat on a high stool behind the counter, a stool with a seat obviously not wide enough for Vertie's ample backside. She hung over it, all the way round it, Joanna noticed as she stared at the navy polyester pants whose lower hems had ridden half-way up both Vertie's calves to expose knee highs where they had rolled themselves down to encircle Vertie's puffy ankles.

And she was Dwight's mother's sister, which made her Katie's great-aunt.

Vertie sat with hands folded neatly atop one chunky, blue thigh as she met Joanna's eyes, but Joanna had seen what had been in those hands up until the moment Vertie had noted her entering the store. Vertie had been reading a thick, historical romance novel when Joanna first stepped up onto the store porch. She had seen the book clearly enough through the screened door, for Vertie had seemed reluctant to tear her eyes from the page, much less to put it down. Vertie's mouth had been slack and open, her eyes riveted to the page, one pudgy hand clenched into a fist and pressed tight into the blue and white flowered fabric of her polyester blouse between two substantial breasts. There was no doubt that it was a historical romance she had been reading—a bodice-ripper. Its front cover, complete with half-clad man with rippling muscles and young woman in hoop skirts, with a bodice and sleeves trimmed with substantial quantities of lace—a young woman with one hand clenched into her own chest in a pose strikingly similar to the one Vertie had been affecting—left little doubt. The book had been put away beneath the counter the moment she entered the store, though Joanna knew that it would be taken out again the moment she left.

"Well—hello, there!" Vertie said, bringing a smile to her face.

As always, the smile was forced, as well as phony, and Joanna returned it in kind. Vertie was one of the worst gossips in Eason County; she had never approved of Dwight marrying Joanna, and had made her feelings known, though, of course, never to Joanna's face. Joanna had heard it second- and third-hand from various people throughout the county.

"Did you bring Katie with you?" Her eyes moved from Joanna out through the now-closed screen door.

"No; she went with Mama and Daddy to visit J. T. today."

"I want you to bring her to see me. I haven't seen her in months now. She won't even remember her Aunt Vertie."

*Oh—she'll remember you*, Joanna thought. Katie had left here the last time Joanna had brought her to visit, with a mouthful of bubble gum that her Aunt Vertie had given her over Joanna's protests. The wad of gum had gotten stuck into Katie's long reddish-gold hair behind one ear before they had gotten home. It had taken Joanna the remainder of that afternoon and the better part of the evening to get the mess out of her hair. The evening had ended with a screaming, red-faced three-year-old stating that Aunt Vertie had known that she wasn't supposed to have gum, and Joanna reminding that red-faced three-year-old that Katie, herself, had known as well.

"I have some new pictures," Joanna said, pulling her brag book out of her purse. She moved closer to the counter and handed the book across to the woman. Vertie took it and flipped through the photographs of Katie, but Joanna could tell she was paying them little attention.

The woman's eyes kept straying to Joanna instead as Joanna moved to a shelf holding a half-dozen loaves of bread. While she tested each by lightly squeezing the loaves through their wrappers so she could choose the softest, Vertie begin to make a clucking sound with her tongue against the roof of her mouth. When Joanna turned back the woman was still looking at her, and for a moment Joanna thought she was about to be reprimanded for squeezing the loaves of bread.

"You know, I heard about the problems you've been having at your place—is it really as bad as they're saying?" The brag book, face open on the counter, was forgotten now.

"What is it they're saying?" Joanna asked, though she knew. Here in Eason County, where everyone not only knew most everyone else, but where most people could also name several generations of your ancestors, and gossip about relatives of yours who died decades before your birth, people thought it their right to meddle in each other's affairs: business, personal, or otherwise. Joanna had little doubt that Vertie knew they were behind on their mortgage. She probably knew how many payments they were behind.

"Are you about to lose your place?—there are so many farms going under. Why, John Renfroe—" and she was off gossiping about someone else. Joanna knew Vertie had not forgotten her question, however. Joanna would not answer it, which Vertie well knew, for the Sanders did not talk their troubles outside their own family.

Vertie would not need an answer; she would happily supply one herself, and would likely tell it to most anyone who would listen to her, out of all the people who would visit in the store in the next week.

Vertie was staring at her when Joanna looked up from placing a can of Coke on the counter beside the loaf of bread.

"You know, I don't think you've gained an ounce since high school; have you?" Vertie asked, smiling.

Joanna shrugged, not certain what to say. She knew she had rounded out a bit, but she weighed much the same. It just was not like Vertie to mention such a thing.

"I remember you wearing that same blouse when you were in high school."

Vertie was still smiling, pulling the loaf of bread and the Coke closer on the counter so she could ring them up. She was leaning now off the front of the stool, her pudgy thighs and large bottom resting almost exclusively on the edge of the seat. Joanna watched, thinking the prop would skitter away and out from under her at any moment to send her crashing to the floor. She started to say something, but stopped herself.

"That's the good thing about being so small on top, isn't it?" Vertie continued. "Things still fit you like they did back when you were a child—"

Then she interrupted herself before Joanna could say anything in response, Vertie telling her how much she owed for her purchases. Joanna reached into her purse to pull out her wallet, willing herself not to answer. It would accomplish nothing.

Vertie accepted Joanna's money and made change, then pushed the loaf into a too-small paper sack, which only made the bread more difficult to carry. The edge of the sack did not even come up as far as the end of the loaf inside its plastic wrap, causing Joanna to have to cradle it on one arm to keep from either losing the sack or mashing the bread. Vertie had the brag book again and was staring at a photograph of Katie when Joanna looked up.

"She doesn't look at all like Dwight or any of the the Lees," Vertie said, studying the photograph for a moment, "or like the Mitchells."

Vertie had been a Mitchell before her her marriage, as had Dwight's mother.

"You know, she doesn't look like your family, either, does she?" Vertie said, her eyes fixing on Joanna, her tone making certain the insinuation was clear.

She snapped the brag book shut at last and handed it back to Joanna. Joanna clenched her teeth to keep from responding, knowing that anything she said would only make Vertie gossip all the more, and she was not about to have the woman gossiping about Katie, if she could help it. She accepted the small photo album and stuck it into her still-open purse, took up her can of Coke and started for the door.

"You bring Katie to see me, you hear?" Vertie called after her, but Joanna did not respond. She went on out the door and onto the porch, then down the board steps and out into the parking area before the store. She was so furious that she had squashed a section of the loaf bread even before she could reach the car, then accidentally ripped the side of the paper sack and dropped the wrapped loaf out onto the ground. She was cursing furiously under her breath by the time she was in the car and putting it into gear. She had to force herself not to shove down on the gas pedal, for to peel out of there would only give Vertie more to gossip about:

*"I just mentioned to her that that child of hers don't look like nobody in our family . . . Poor Dwight—you remember she just threw him out . . . Poor boy—he had to drop out of school after that . . . I wonder if he caught her with someone else . . ."*

Joanna could just imagine the gossip.

When she reached the turn that would take her back toward the house, she kept going straight instead—she had to calm down before she went home. Of all the nerve, for the woman to insinuate something like that about Katie, or about Joanna.

When the blue lights came on behind her car a short while later, Joanna could not help but to think—*of course, what else could happen. All the people in this county, and I'm the one to get a cop behind my car.*

The officer was all business.

"Where is it you were going in such a hurry, ma'am?"

"Home."

He studied her license. "You were going the wrong way to be going home, weren't you?"

"I was driving around—"

"Driving around?"

He sat in the patrol car watching as she put the car in gear and started away slowly, a speeding ticket now on the seat beside her.

She didn't start to cry until she was more than a mile down the road, when it hit her that speeding tickets cost money and money was one thing she didn't have—*of all the stupid things.*

She was crying so hard she knew she had to stop the car. There was an abandoned store on the opposite side of the road just ahead, so she slowed and pulled across the other lane and over into the potholed parking area out front. The brakes scrubbed slightly as she stopped the car and put it in park, and it occurred to her that she had been hearing that sound for more than a week now, doing her best to ignore the noise, for there was no money to have anything done to the brakes. By the time she had the money, they would have probably done additional damage which would cost only more. Dwight would not pay his child support, and had never paid it, more than an occasional check here or there when his conscience—if he had one—was bothering him. Joanna knew the talk that Katie might not be his might very well have started with him, in an attempt to save his own precious reputation here in Eason County where he had so many relatives— *Why should I pay for a child who might not even be mine?* she could almost hear him now, when he knew damn well that Katie was his. Even now, years after Joanna divorced him, he was the only man she had ever been with—*God, what a loser,* she told herself, though she did not mean Dwight in that moment. She had a college degree, but she was driving around in an eight-year-old car with a hundred and forty thousand miles on it. Her child wore hand-me-down clothes, and the blouse Joanna wore today truly was one she had worn in high school. There was no money for clothes. There was no money for anything. They were losing the land, and she was working for almost nothing—and what else could happen now? What else—?

There was a tap on the rolled-up window beside her. Joanna lifted her head from where she had rested it against her crossed hands at the top of the steering wheel, thinking it might be the cop again and that she might have done something else that would cost her more. But the man standing beside the car, knuckles tapping again on the closed window as she stupidly wiped at her wet cheeks with the back of one hand, was Stephen Dawes, with a frown on his face.

~

Elise Sanders stood at the front window in the living room that night, staring into the darkness beyond the lighted porch. She was still dressed from the day, as was Janson, who sat, silent, in the recliner across the room. He was leaning forward in the chair, tapping his walking stick steadily on the floor between his feet, waiting, as was she—Joanna had not come home all afternoon. Now, well into the evening, there had been no word from her.

Henry and Olivia were not home with with Katie yet, though Janson had called J. T.'s house to find they had left more than two hours ago. Janson had wanted to go looking for Joanna on his own and had gotten the keys to Henry's truck, but Elise had taken the keys and refused to give them back.

"I can see good enough t' drive!" he had yelled, though he had not driven a vehicle in years.

He had almost hit a child on a bicycle and of his own decision had not been behind the wheel since.

"I didn't see him 'til I was almost on him," Janson had told Elise that day, shaking still an hour after he reached the house. "I didn't see him—an' then it took s' long t' stop. I could'a hit him, Elise. I could'a hit him—" even as he wiped his face with one shaking hand.

But tonight he was determined to drive.

"I can see good enough—give me th' keys, Elise," he said, holding out one hand, as determined and as mad as she had ever seen him. "Joanna could be hurt. Th' car could'a broke down. She might be out walkin' in th' dark—give me th' damn truck keys, Elise!"

But Elise had refused to hand them over. She was just as worried as him, and if her own night vision were not so poor, she would have tried to drive herself.

Janson had retreated to the telephone, muttering all the way.

"I ain't that old . . . Taught her t' drive, but I wouldn't do it again if I had t' do it over. Damn woman. Damn—"

He had called J. T.'s house, and had tried to reach Matt, then had turned on the local radio station, hoping not to hear a report of an accident, or even something worse, in Eason County.

Elise kept telling herself that Henry and Olivia would be home soon and if Joanna was still not back then Henry could go look for her. Janson could ride along, for Elise knew very well that he would not stay home. Joanna had a good head on her shoulders; she knew how to take care of herself. She had probably just let the time get away from her—but the thought kept reoccurring to Elise of a night when Henry had not come home during their first year on this place. That was the night Janson found him beaten and bloody, and the old jalopy demolished, at the side of a road. Buddy Eason had been responsible for what happened that night—but Buddy Eason was an old man now. He had left them alone since Janson had made it clear that to bother them again would be a fatal mistake. Buddy would not have done anything.

But he could, and Elise knew it. Things happened in Eason County, things for which only Buddy Eason could be responsible. Now she could not get out of her mind the image of that huge, twisted old man in his wheel chair. Buddy Eason was nothing but a sickness on this county, a sickness that had grown progressively worse as the years passed and the sickness inside Buddy's own mind increased. He was capable of anything, and Elise knew it.

She looked at the clock on the nearby wall, feeling suddenly chilled even in the warm room. She rubbed her arms and looked out the window, hearing the steady tapping of Janson's cane.

Lights swept across the yard, and then turned in the drive. The tapping of Janson's cane stopped abruptly as Elise moved toward the front door, relief washing over her—she would give Joanna Sanders Lee a piece of her mind. Worrying them all so—

The thought went unfinished as she recognized Henry's Ford LTD and watched him get out and come up onto the porch with the sleeping Katie in his arms. Olivia was beside him.

"Joanna's gone; she's been gone since the middle of the day," she whispered, stepping out onto the porch to hold the door open for him so that he could carry Katie inside. "She said she was going to the store for some bread. Henry, you don't think—?" But she could not finish the sentence.

His eyes moved to where his father now stood in the open doorway. Janson moved aside as Henry entered, then waited while their son went to lay Katie in her bed. When Henry started back outside a few minutes later, he found his father already getting in the passenger side of the LTD. Olivia tried to follow, but Henry put a hand out to hold her back.

"No, stay here in case she comes back while we're gone."

"But, your mother will be here—"

"Stay here." His voice rose. She stood beside Elise and watched as he and Janson pulled away.

Elise had thought she would feel better once she knew someone was looking for her granddaughter, but she did not. She wished there was something she and Olivia could do, though she could think of nothing. Olivia sat in the white rocker near the front door to wait, and Elise joined her in the other rocker there on the front porch.

More than an hour later Henry and Janson returned. The two waiting women rose as one while Henry's car came to a rolling stop in the drive. Olivia descended the front steps as the car doors opened and Henry and Janson got out. Henry came toward the front steps, and then past Olivia and up onto the porch, talking back over his shoulder to his wife.

"We found Joanna's car," he said, snatching open the front door and starting inside. "It was locked and we could tell from looking in the windows that her keys weren't in it. We didn't find—" but the remainder of his words were lost as Olivia followed him inside and the storm door closed behind them. Elise stood at the top of the steps waiting for Janson as he made his slow climb to the front porch. He reached out and took her hand with his free one when he reached the porch, his other hand gripping the crook of his cane as he leaned on it for its support.

"We didn't see nothin' of Joanna," he said, staring at her, the whiteness of his hair vivid in the darkness. "There was a loaf 'a bread on th' passenger side in th' front seat, an' a can 'a Co'Cola beside it. Joanna's pocketbook wasn't there, an' neither was her keys." They started in the front door now, following Henry and Olivia. "There wasn't no flat tire, an' nothin' wrong with th' car that we could see.

Henry woke folks up in two houses near where we foun' th' car, but they said they didn't see—"

But Elise was no longer listening to him. Henry was at one side of the hallway, unlocking the gun cabinet with keys he kept in his pocket. Olivia was in the living room, talking to the police on the phone.

"Nothing on a young woman?" Elise could hear through the doorway. There was a pause, and then, "Twenty-three; she has reddish-blonde . . ."

Henry took ammunition from a locked drawer in the cabinet, and then started checking and loading a rifle.

"So help me, if someone's hurt her, I'll—" he began, but never had the opportunity to finish.

There was the sound of a car pulling in the drive before the house, and headlights hit the open front doorway. They all moved to the front door to see Joanna getting out of her car, obviously unharmed. She walked across the yard and up onto the porch, smiling as they stepped back and she came in the front door.

"Why are you all at the door?" she laughed, then stopped to hug her mother. "Is it that late?" she asked, then looked at her watch. "I had no idea. I'm sorry—"

"Where were you?" Henry demanded, furious. He had the rifle still in his hands, which Joanna seemed to notice for the first time. She laughed.

"What were you intending to do?" she asked, hugging her father now and trying to take the rifle.

"We found your car—where were you?" he demanded again, pushing her hands away.

"I went for a ride with someone; I forgot the time. Katie's asleep? Did she ask where I was?" She was looking down the hallway now toward her daughter's room.

"Who were you with?" Henry demanded. It seemed to be the only tone of voice he could use now, though Elise could not blame him. Joanna had scared them all.

"His name's Stephen; I just forgot the time—"

"That's no excuse."

"I know. I know. I won't do it again." She shook her head, still smiling. "Why don't we all go to bed. It's late—"

Henry was muttering under his breath, unloading the rifle as she walked past him and down the hall. Elise heard Janson mutter something as well, just before he shook his head and flipped a switch by the front door and shut off the porch light.

## 22

STEPHEN DAWES, OR STEPHEN
Eason, as his grandfather preferred that he be called, though he had
never gone through the legalities of a name change—sat in the living
room of the huge old Eason house on Pine's Main Street the next
afternoon, listening as his grandfather argued on the phone with one
of his liquor suppliers. Eason County was supposed to be a dry
county; Stephen knew that, just as he also knew that people were
going to drink, and they were going to buy liquor, no matter where it
was they lived. There was no reason why his grandfather should not
supply those demands, or any other, at a profit if he so chose, and the
law had little choice but to bend to Buddy Eason's will if and when he
chose to break it in matters such as this.

"I told you what I pay per case. Either you take it, or you won't be
selling liquor here or anywhere else ever again," Buddy Eason said,
then fell silent for a moment, listening to the voice at the other end of
the telephone. His voice was only harder when he spoke again. "You
know who I am—do you think I can't see to it that you'll never do any
business of any kind on this earth again?"

Buddy sat in a massive electric wheelchair pulled up behind an
antique cherry wood desk that appeared to be little more than a table
supported on long, spindly legs. He was a huge man now, with thick
lips in the middle of a jowly face, and a bulbous red nose below dark
glasses worn even in the house. His suit was expensively cut in a dark

blue material, but one lapel, as well as the white shirt that had been so exquisitely laundered and pressed that morning, and the dark blue tie, were liberally spotted with both food and drink. Buddy was an imposing presence in the room, from the stark white hair still full and thick above a face red from both liquor and disposition, to the wheelchair that creaked as he shifted his weight, though Stephen could not keep himself from staring at the stains on Buddy's clothing. Buddy listened for a moment to the voice at the other end of the phone, and then he nodded, as if satisfied.

"I knew you'd see it my way," Buddy said, into the receiver.

People usually saw it his grandfather's way, Stephen thought, himself included.

He could still remember how frightened he was of Buddy Eason the first time he saw him. Stephen had been no more than five years old, and small for his age, brought here to Eason County from some place he could dimly remember living for a short time with his paternal grandparents after his parents died. Buddy Eason had seemed so huge to him then, such a massive presence, towering over the small boy Stephen had been—and he still seemed that way to Stephen. Buddy was just as dominant, wheelchair notwithstanding, just as much in control—and he seemed still to wear that same slightly disappointed look concerning his grandson that he had worn the day Stephen met him.

"He doesn't look five years old," Buddy Eason had said, staring down at the small boy. "Is there something wrong with him?"

Stephen felt he had been doing nothing since that first day so much as trying to please his grandfather, as fascinated by the powerful man as he was fearful of him. Stephen had gone to the schools his grandfather chose for him, had studied the subjects his grandfather wanted him to study, had graduated Summa Cum Laude from the University of Alabama. But still he had never gotten the one thing he wanted most—his grandfather's approval, Buddy Eason's congratulations for a job well done. Sometimes Stephen thought that he would do almost anything to garner that approval from the old man.

As a child he had felt his grandfather hated him. He could remember lying awake night after night, wondering what he had done to make Buddy Eason feel toward him as he obviously did. Stephen had grown up in a series of boarding schools, and had concocted elaborate lies to explain to other children why he was never asked home for Christmas or on summer vacation. He had spent most holidays and school breaks with the families of a few close friends. He knew now that the parents of those boys had probably realized the truth. His grandfather just did not want him around.

But Buddy Eason had done good by his only grandson. Stephen had attended the best schools. He wore the most expensive clothes. He had had his choice of new car on the day he turned sixteen, and for every birth date since—but still Stephen did not have the one thing he was almost certain Buddy Eason would never give him.

He had been fascinated by the respect people had shown his grandfather in the few times he had been in Eason County in his years of growing up, as well as by the power he had seen Buddy Eason wield. Stephen had never realized the full extent of that power until he was called here by his grandfather a few months ago, and he still did not know the full extent of who Buddy Eason was. Stephen had not been made privy to all the business dealings, the private telephone conversations, the meetings, but he knew he would learn everything he needed to know when the time came. His grandfather had told him he intended for Stephen to take on more responsibility in the coming months, which pleased Stephen immensely. If he proved himself capable in his grandfather's eyes, he might at last gain the old man's respect. That was what Stephen wanted—and to be just like Buddy Eason.

He watched Buddy disconnect one call, only to immediately place another. The old man held the phone with one hand, the fingertips of the other resting against the wooden surface before him. Buddy alternately tented his fingers, lifting his palm from the desktop, holding it there for a moment, then slowly lowering it against the surface, over and over.

The habitual gesture reminded Stephen of a spider poised, ready to strike.

His grandfather was speaking into the phone now, checking up on another supplier, making certain of the control he held regarding so many things. That was the one thing that Stephen did not like, for that control was also exercised over him. He had hoped things would improve once he moved out into a place of his own, but if anything it had increased. Sometimes Stephen felt as if the old man considered him nothing more than a possession, little more than this massive house, or Buddy's three wheelchair lift-equipped vans, but in those times Stephen would remind himself that he owed the old man too much to complain. If not for Buddy Eason, there might have been no one willing to see to his welfare after his parents died. His paternal grandparents had given him up easily enough when Buddy sent for him and he had not heard from them since.

Stephen rarely allowed himself to think of the short while he had lived in their home, or before that when his parents were alive. He never spoke of those times—but he had spoken of them last night, to Joanna Lee, and for reasons he could not quite comprehend.

He had been on his way between his grandfather's house and the place his grandfather had rented for him when he came upon her car. He had assumed the vehicle was broken down again, considering its age, and that the girl was just sitting in it—but he had been surprised, when he tapped on her window and she lifted her head, to see that she was crying. Her face was tear-streaked and her eyes red, but she wiped at her cheeks with the back of one hand and rolled down the window.

"Are you okay? Is your daughter all right?" Stephen had asked, concerns passing through his mind, as well as the thought of the last time he had seen her. She had been on the way home then because her ex-husband was coming to see their daughter. "If your ex is trying to take her away from you—"

But she shook her head, clearing her throat lightly before she spoke. "No. No—it's nothing like that. It's—" She made a slight gesture with one hand and shook her head again, as if she could not

put the problem into words. "It's everything, I guess—I don't know."
She shook her head once more.

*That time of the month*, Stephen thought, though he did not put
the thought into words. "So, your car's in working order?" he asked.
"That's why I stopped, since it was broken down the last time—"

"It's working fine." She looked to one side of the steering wheel,
to the ignition switch and the key there in the off position. "Funny,
I don't remember shutting it off—" she said quietly, almost if she
were speaking to herself. She reached to take hold of the key and the
engine turned over several times before it at last caught and started.

"You know, you really should think about buying a new car." He
looked around the interior through the open window. The seats were
worn badly and the headliner was beginning to sag near the rear
window. When he looked back at her, she was smiling, the tears gone.

"I do good to buy gas for this one," She laughed. He thought that
he could more easily understand her crying than the lightness in her
tone—lightness but seriousness, too; he didn't know what to make of
it.

"I could more easily buy new tennis shoes and walk instead, but
there's not even money enough for those." Stephen looked down at
her feet on the floorboard of the old car, one on the brake pedal even
though the car was in park, the other turned slightly to its side. Her
tennis shoes *were* worn, their strings broken off, one frayed below
where it was knotted into a short bow. She self-consciously tucked
them back as far as possible against the bottom edge of the car seat,
almost out of his sight, and he lifted his eyes to meet hers again. She
smiled, a slight color raising to her cheeks, and wiped at her face one
last time with the back of one hand. A bit of gray smoke rose from the
tailpipe of her car, along with the smell of its exhaust, and Stephen felt
suddenly uncomfortable standing here beside her car.

"It's not catching, you know," she said, still smiling.

"What's not?"

"Not having money."

It was said so simply that he caught himself about to ask if she was poor. He shut his mouth so quickly that his teeth snapped together. He could not think of anything to say; he had the uncomfortable feeling that she had known exactly what he had almost given voice to. He remembered her having accused him, in their second meeting, of being insulting, and she was right. He realized that he did not consider how something he said might sound to someone else.

"I guess I had better be going," she said, reaching to put the car into gear.

He stepped back and she started to roll up the window. He realized suddenly that he did not want her to leave. "Is your daughter waiting for you?" he asked, putting one hand atop the partially rolled-up glass and leaning down to look in at her again.

"No, she went with my parents to visit my brother."

"Why do you have to go, then? I mean—why not do something else? We could go for a ride in my truck. You could show me the county; my grandfather's lived here all his life, and my mother grew up here, but I came here only a few times as a child."

She was looking back at him, obviously uncertain.

"I promise I'm not a crazed maniac prowling the county looking for my next victim."

She smiled, though he could see she was still unsure. He wondered if she might not think he was exactly what he claimed that he was not.

"Come on," Stephen said, giving her his most winning smile. "Take a chance."

He was almost certain she would not agree, and then she did, rolling her window up and shutting off the engine, and stepping out onto the cracked pavement beside him. They drove for a long time and she did show him the county, directing him to places he had never seen in Eason County: Blackskillet Ridge, which she said was the highest elevation in the county, then a place called Lightning Stump, where Blackskillet Road met up with the road to Rock Fill. Every place had a story, from the abandoned sharecropper shacks scattered about the countryside, to the downtown movie theater in Pine that she said had burned at least three times. She had him stop at Shoop's

Dairy Stop outside of Wells, where they bought the best burgers and fries Stephen ever tasted, and then they sat for hours talking with the truck parked in the deserted lot before the high school in Wells. At some point their conversation moved from this county where she had grown up to their own lives, and Stephen found himself telling her things he had never told anyone, the few memories he had of his parents, and of his life before he had come into his grandfather's care. Somehow, he would realize later, he never mentioned Buddy Eason's name. He didn't know why.

"Since then, I grew up mainly in boarding schools. Holidays and summers I spent with friends." Stephen said, finishing the subject as far as his life was concerned. He had not expected the look he saw come onto her face.

"I'm sorry," she said, sympathy evident in her expression. She reached out and placed a hand briefly on his arm.

He shrugged, for what had happened in the past did not matter to him, and never had. "Tell me about your daughter," he said, smiling now. "How old is she? Is she a lot like you?"

Her face brightened immediately at the thought of the child. She told him of her brief marriage, and of the husband she was happy to be living without, as well as stories about the little girl she had been raising alone for more than three years.

"We're home now, living with my parents and my father's parents since I finished at Auburn," she said. "We have a farm." She shot him a look as if she thought he would say something of which she might not approve. "It's what I've wanted to do all my life," she said, as if she were explaining. She shrugged slightly and looked away. "My father farmed the place, and my grandfather, and even my great-grandfather." Then she smiled. "I guess you could say it's in our blood."

Stephen smiled as well at the look in her eyes, the absolute assurance that she was doing in her life just exactly what she had been meant to do.

"You love it, don't you?" he asked, leaning forward so he could see her face better.

"Yes, I do." She looked up at him. Her smile broadened.

"I wish I felt like that about something," Stephen said.

"You don't? At least about something?"

He looked away, toward the growing darkness beyond the ram's head on the truck's hood. "No. I don't."

Her hand came to rest on his arm. "I'm sorry," she said, but Stephen shook the sentiment away.

"It doesn't matter," he said, dismissing the thought as she moved her hand back to her lap. "Do you plan to stay on the farm?" he asked, wanting to change the subject. "You'll probably marry again and leave your parents' house. You may even leave the county."

"I doubt that. I grew up here and I want Katie to grow up here—"

They talked for hours, and there was still more to say. Stephen had never felt as comfortable with a woman, and she seemed comfortable as well, except for a few brief minutes—

"Won't your wife or girlfriend be wondering where you are?" she asked, her eyes on his face. "We've been gone a long time."

"I don't have a wife. Or a girlfriend."

"Oh?" She was watching him still. "Girlfriends, then," she said, stressing the plural. "Playing the field and having a good time." It was a statement, not a question, Stephen noted. She had folded her hands together in her lap, distancing herself from him.

"No." Stephen was staring at her. "I was living with someone in Birmingham. She came here with me when I moved to Eason County; we talked about marrying, but it didn't work out." He did not say more, though he could have. Andrea had lived with him in his grandfather's house for barely three weeks. She moved out after she said she had found the old man staring at her through a partially opened door as she was dressing one day. She begged Stephen to return with her to Birmingham, but he refused.

Stephen had watched as she went down the front steps to her car the day she left. She was crying so badly that he did not know how she would see to drive to Birmingham.

"That's my boy," the old man had said, reaching up to take

Stephen's hand for the first time Stephen could remember. Buddy Eason had held his hand with what appeared to be close to affection, and Stephen watched, allowing the bloated, liver-spotted fingers to move over his own until Buddy released him at last. By then, Andrea had driven away.

He stared at Joanna now. He thought possibly that color had risen to her cheeks there in the semi-darkness. He could tell she did not believe him.

"You think I pick up every woman I meet, and take her for a ride to Blackskillet, Lightning Stump, and Wells, and then let her eat a burger and fries in my truck?" he asked, in a lighter tone.

"Not exactly." There was an extraordinary dryness to her words, which made Stephen laugh.

"I guess I'm behind schedule, then. Do you want to get undressed first, or shall I?" he asked her, then immediately regretted the words, thinking she would never see the joke behind them.

But she laughed, pushing reddish-gold hair back from her eyes.

"The direct method, huh?" she asked, and he smiled. "I guess that's why you carry such a supply of Trojans around with you."

Stephen looked blankly at her.

"The day we first met—well, I don't guess we actually met that day, but the day I saw you at the Feed and Seed, I happened to pass your red car out on the street. You had quite a supply in the car that day. They were spilling out all over the seat, along with a magazine that really ought not to have been out in the open."

"Oh, good God, my grandfather—" but then he stopped. She was damned direct, and nosy as well.

He did not know why he had been about to explain.

But then he did, anyway.

"It was a 'care package' from my grandfather. He said I should make sure to use them, that he didn't want any little 'problems' running around." Stephen shook his head. "The magazine came from him as well. He said wanted me to see what I was missing since Andrea moved out, that I was too young and healthy to be alone—yeah, I looked at it. I'm human. That day I just threw it in my car when I left his house." He realized he was angry. He did not know why he was explaining to her, but he found himself continuing. "I didn't know it was laying open until I went back to get in the car. I threw it over into the floorboard and sat down—that's when you laughed at me." He was pouting as he stared at her, and he knew it.

She laughed again. "You were such a funny sight, catapulting yourself out of the car. I thought you deserved it, for letting that old man—"

"Enough," he stated firmly. He intended to remain angry at her, but found that he could not. She was smiling, and it struck him for the first time how pretty she was. Her red-gold hair was like honey in the dim light, and he could not see the color of her eyes now but he knew they were a brilliant blue. Her smile made him feel comfortable as he sat back against his seat—and then he impulsively leaned toward her, put his hand to her hair at the back of her head and drew her forward. The kiss was nothing but an impulse to begin with—and then it continued and he felt her lean into him. When it ended at last she moved slightly from him, taking up the purse that had fallen into the floorboard and holding it tightly. The thought occurred to him that she might hit him with it if he tried anything else. He began to laugh as that image came into his mind, of being beaten about the head with a woman's purse for getting fresh in a truck in a school parking lot. He laughed harder.

When he took a breath at last, she said, "Maybe you'd better take me back to my car—" Which made him laugh all the more.

"I'm sorry," he said, calming down. "I just had this image of you beating me to death with your purse because I kissed you." He was smiling now.

She seemed to try to repress her return smile, but it came anyway. "'Man found beaten to death by purse in Wells High School parking lot; kiss turns deadly—film and story at ten'. . .?" she suggested, improvising for him the mock news bulletin, and her smile broadened even further.

It was hours later that he drove her back to her car.

"Can I take you to dinner tomorrow night?" he asked, after having gone around his truck to open her door, which he could never remember having done for a woman in his life. She stood now between her vehicle and his, her keys in hand.

"I can't. I should eat supper with Katie. She expects me to."

"Well, how about later, after she goes to sleep? We could go for a ride, maybe take in a late movie. There's no theater in Eason County, but we could drive to Anniston."

"Sure," she said, smiling. "I'd like that." He had not kissed her again after that first time, and he wondered now whether he should, but then she was getting in her car and it was too late. "I'll see you tomorrow night," she said, after shutting the door and rolling down her window. She smiled up at him. "Katie should be asleep by eight."

"I'll pick you up at eight, then."

He had watched the taillights of her car recede after she drove away.

The time since had dragged interminably.

He sat now in his grandfather's office, waiting for the old man to finish his call. Stephen just wanted to get this day over with, and for the remainder of the afternoon and early evening to pass so he could see her again. He had done little else but think about her from the moment she left last night, and it seemed now this damned meeting with his grandfather would never end.

"Boy—"

His grandfather said the word twice before Stephen even knew he was being spoken to. Buddy was staring at him when Stephen lifted his eyes, the telephone back in its cradle, disapproval on the old man's face.

"Did you say something to me, grandfather?" Stephen asked, regretting the almost awe-filled tone he could hear in his own voice— but he could not help it. His grandfather always made him feel as if he were still that frightened, small-for-his-age five-year-old the old man had so disapproved of.

"I didn't send for you so you could just sit in my office and daydream."

"I'm sorry, grandfather. I just—"

But the old man had already turned away to papers on the desk an arm's length away over the massive stomach, as if Stephen's excuses or explanations were of little consequence. Stephen watched him, knowing he would be spoken to again when the old man was ready, and knowing that what he had done truly was beyond excuse. He should never have allowed his attention wander in his grandfather's presence.

When Buddy Eason thought his grandson had been properly chastised, he lifted his gaze and looked at Stephen through the dark glasses.

"These reports the accountants made can't be right," Buddy said, shoving the papers in his hands across the desktop. "There's something wrong with them. Find it."

"Yes, Grandfather," Stephen said. He would find the error, whatever it was. If there was no error, he would simply make one up. He had done it before. Buddy Eason expected something to be found, and Stephen Dawes Eason would give his grandfather exactly whatever it was that he wanted.

# 23

S TEPHEN WAS RUNNING LATE by the time he reached Joanna's house that night. When he pulled into the drive, he found her out in the yard by her own car.

"My father—and my grandfather, especially—objected to my 'going off,' as they call it, with someone they don't know," she told him after she had gotten into his truck. He caught a quick glimpse of someone watching them from the front windows of her house, and he did not like it. "I reminded them both that I'm twenty-three," she continued, "that I've been married and divorced and that I haven't been a minor for a long time now, but that doesn't matter to either one of them."

He turned to look over his shoulder as he backed out into the road. "They didn't want you going out with me, huh?" A problem with the parents of a grown woman was one headache he did not need.

"Especially not after I told them you were taking me across the state line for a night of wild sex," she said.

He choked, and then started to cough so badly that he had to pull over to the side of the road to try to catch his breath. She was pounding him in the middle of his back so hard by the time he could breathe again that he was almost certain he would have a bruise there.

"You told them what?" he asked, his voice still a harsh, strangled whisper in the cab of the truck.

"I was kidding—" she said, looking embarrassed and trying not to laugh at the same time. "I didn't tell them anything, other than that I was old enough to look after myself."

He was clearing his throat now, trying to get his voice back. "Good God—I could just see your father following us tonight with a shotgun."

She laughed outright then and Stephen found himself smiling— she really was rather pretty.

"A night of wild sex, huh?" he asked, grinning now.

"Don't even think about it." But she was still smiling.

"Oh—I'll think about it," he assured her.

They did drive to Anniston to see a movie, the details of which Stephen could not remember later, and then took their time afterward driving back to Eason County. When they were within a few miles of her home, he pulled off into the parking area before the abandoned store where he had found her parked crying the day before. Joanna was smiling and looking at him quizzically when Stephen turned to her.

"I figured it would be safer to kiss you goodnight now instead of waiting until we reach your house. Your folks will be waiting up, won't they?" he asked, and her smile widened.

"Probably. Daddy might turn the lights out and watch from behind the curtains, but my grandpa does not believe in subtlety; he'll leave the lights on and probably come out on the porch if I don't come into the house within two minutes of the truck pulling into the drive."

Stephen laughed. In some ways she made him think of some other place and time. He reached to brush her hair back from her eyes, realizing that if she were any other woman, it would never have occurred to him to wonder if her parents and grandparents might be waiting up to make certain she got home. The thought had come to him tonight without any accompanying doubt, and he found that he did not really mind.

She came into his arms easily enough, and he kissed her, but when he tried to prolong the moment she gently held him away. Stephen returned the smile she gave him and released her.

"Not exactly wild sex—but it'll do," he said, then turned to put the truck back in gear.

When he pulled the truck into the drive, the lights were on. The curtains moved and he thought he saw the shape of a man inside looking out at them.

"They did wait up," Stephen said unnecessarily. She was opening her door, and Stephen realized suddenly that he should have put the truck in park, gotten out and gone around to open the door for her, but it was too late now.

"Can I see you tomorrow night again?" he asked, turning his eyes from the house to the girl getting out of his truck.

She stopped with the door open and turned to look at him.

"After your daughter is down for the night?" he qualified as he put the truck into park, knowing that was what she would say.

"Sure," she said, and nodded, smiling.

Though he had stopped the truck before they reached the house so he could kiss her goodnight, he did it again now without a conscious decision to do so. He leaned toward her and drew her into his arms. She seemed surprised but returned the kiss, her arms going around his neck. After a moment she gently pushed him away again and turned to get out of the truck. He could see the front door of the house open now, an old man in a white shirt and dark pants stepping through the doorway and out onto the lighted porch, a walking stick held in his hand—her grandfather, making certain her date behaved himself.

"Hey—" Stephen said, turning again to Joanna before she could close the truck door. "I don't have your phone number."

"It's in the book, under my maiden name, Sanders," she answered, smiling up at him, "It's actually in Grandpa's name, Janson Sanders—" just before she shut the door.

Sanders—grandpa's name—Janson Sanders.

Stephen looked toward the old man on the porch.

He had heard that name before.

～

Stephen Dawes had often heard the name Sanders in the months he
had been in Eason County—but he had heard it as well in his years
growing up. Almost every time he had visited his grandfather through
those years, the Sanders name had come up. His grandfather hated the
Sanders family.

And he hated Janson Sanders most of all.

There had been almost-incoherent stories of how Janson Sanders
and his father had tried to destroy the agricultural system that had
kept the county farmers afloat during the Great Depression. The
Sanders family had tried to drive the old Eason Cotton Mill out of
business. Janson Sanders had made attempt after attempt on Stephen's
grandfather's life.

Stephen remembered asking the old man, after one extended
tirade, "Why didn't you just put an end to him one of the times he
tried to kill you? It would have been self-defense—"

But his grandfather just rocked back and forth in the creaking
wheelchair, crooning, almost to himself: "You can't kill him—he
won't die—you can't kill him—he won't—"

Sanders's only son had also tried to kill him, according to Buddy
Eason.

That would be Henry Sanders, Joanna's father.

Joanna Lee was a Sanders.

And she did not know who he was.

Or did she?

But Stephen dismissed that thought immediately. The Sanders,
from all that Stephen knew from his grandfather, were not a subtle
people. Joanna had said herself last night that her grandfather did not
believe in subtlety.

As soon as morning came, Stephen went to see his grandfather. He
had paid less and less attention to the stories over the recent months.
His grandfather was always cursing and ranting about something—
but this was something Stephen had to know. He told himself that he
was only getting to know her, that he would not call her now, or see
her again—but he knew that was a lie. Knowing she was a Sanders

made him want to see her all the more. He wanted to know what had happened between their families that had caused her grandfather to try to kill his so many times.

And what would her family do now if they realized she was seeing an Eason, for Stephen was an Eason, whether he legally took the name or not.

And he might as well take the name.

He was his grandfather's only grandson, after all.

Stephen did little more than mention the Sanders name that morning to his grandfather before Buddy Eason began to shake so in the wheelchair that the arm of the device vibrated against the desk.

"That goddamn bastard. That goddamn—I'll see him dead yet. I'll see him—" There was a hatred in Buddy Eason's voice now that Stephen had heard but few times, and each of those times had been when his grandfather had spoken of Janson Sanders and the Sanders family. "That son-of-a-bitch—all of them—they tried to destroy me, but I'll destroy him. I'll destroy him and his family and wipe every goddamn one of them off the face of the earth. I'm not that old—all of them—every Sanders—"

Buddy Eason was staring now far beyond this room, unaware even that his grandson remained here, until Stephen spoke again.

"What did he do, Grandfather?"

Buddy's eyes turned to him, a cold dead blackness in them that startled Stephen. "What did he do!" Spittle flew from Buddy Eason's lips, his face red with rage. The massive man put his hands on the arms of the wheelchair and pressed down as if he were about to rise. He leaned forward, shoving down with his arms until he had elevated himself from the seat a few inches. He glared at his grandson with that dead hatred in his eyes, and Stephen stood and stumbled back, upsetting and almost falling over his chair. "Goddamn—he tried to kill me! He tried to kill me! Him and that boy—he tried to kill me!" For a moment the huge mountain of flesh trembled, then he collapsed back into the chair. "She—she tried to make a fool out of me—they— he tried to ruin me—to— Those goddamn bastards—those goddamn—" The words were now barely intelligible, spat out between gasps for air.

Stephen made himself move to the old man's side, but was pushed away as one of the male nurses reached Buddy first, pushing a needle into Buddy's arm even as the old man tried to fight him away. After a moment, the attack died away and the heavy eyelids lowered toward a drugged sleep, the massive chest rising more normally at last, the insane breathing becoming more regular where the old man sat twisted sideways now in the wheelchair.

Stephen collapsed into a couch. He felt drained, exhausted simply from having watched the fight for air. He saw the nurses roll the now unconscious man from the room, and knew they would put him to bed. He stared through the open doorway long after they had passed from his view and he was left alone. If the very mention of Janson Sanders's name had done this to his grandfather, Stephen had little doubt what it would do to the old man if he were to learn that Stephen had an interest in Sanders's granddaughter. He knew—for his grandfather's sake if for no other reason—that he should stay as far away from the girl as he possibly could.

But he could not stop himself.

He was late in calling her house that night, and, when he did, an old man answered the phone.

"May I speak to Joanna, please?" Stephen asked, clenching his teeth tightly together until his jaws ached, having to fight the urge to tell the man who he was, for he knew the man on the other end of the line had to be Janson Sanders.

"Hold on," and the phone was covered as the man called Joanna's name. *What am I doing?* Stephen asked himself.

Then he heard her voice.

And he knew he was only doing what he had to do.

〜

Summer had brought the worst drought within the memory of most everyone in Eason County. The red earth stood parched and dry, the corn stunted. The well was low, but Joanna knew they were better off than those dependent on city water in the surrounding towns. Most water systems were pitiably low, and water restrictions were in effect. Fines were being charged those caught washing cars or watering lawns or gardens. The local car washes bore signs on their aluminum fronts that said: "Will reopen when drought is over," or "Out of Water," or "No Wash, No Water." Gardens withered, lawns turned brown, and new cars sat dust-covered on car lots, but it was the county farmers who were suffering worst.

The combination of heat and no rain had left fields dry and crops dying. There was little grass in pastures for cattle to graze, and truck and train loads of hay were being sent south by Northern farmers who heard news reports of the drought that was plaguing the Southeast.

It was too little too late. Cattle were being sent to slaughter early to reduce the cost of feeding them, and market prices had dropped. Crop yields were non-existent. Farmers were hurting not just in Eason County, but all through the South.

Things had been bad on the Sanders place before, but the drought made them far worse. There had been late payments before, even missed payments, but they had managed to hold on. Now they had to buy feed for the cattle, and profit was drying up in the fields. They hauled water from the creek to the fields, until even the creek dried up. There was nothing that any man or woman could do when it seemed that God Himself had turned against them.

To Joanna, Stephen Dawes soon became a respite from her days. Daytime was work on the land, and fighting the drought, and worry over money—but late evenings, once Katie was down for the night, quickly became time she could spend with Stephen, time she could be nothing more than a woman interested in a man, without the worries of the day to intrude between them. When they were together she did not have to think; she could just simply be. She did not have to talk about her problems and worries, for she knew he did not want to know, and she knew as well that he would never understand. She had seen his truck; she had seen the expensive clothes, and his home.

Stephen had money. He could have anything he wanted. He would never understand what she was going through.

And she did not want to tell him.

She did invite him to supper with her family, for she felt it was something she should do, but was relieved when he declined—"I'm not good with people," he told her, and she accepted it as truth.

The honest fact was that she did not want him to see the little six-room house, the decades-old furniture, the bills lying on the hall table, bills that there was no money to pay. It was not that she was ashamed—she was not ashamed, she told herself—it was just that the life he had known was so different from her own.

He came to the house to pick her up the first few times they went out, and each of those times Joanna met him at his truck without even giving him an opportunity to open his door, to which both her parents and grandparents objected loudly. Later, after she had been to his house for a late dinner one night, she often met him there, or at a neutral location, when they were to go out. He suggested she bring Katie sometime for lunch, but she declined; she did not want her daughter becoming accustomed to him until Joanna knew where she stood with him. She was becoming very attracted to Stephen Dawes, and she knew it. She also knew there was very little chance of a future with him. Men like Stephen Dawes did not fall in love with women like her. There was also the knowledge that he had never really had a family from the time he was five years old. He did not know what having a family meant. She had made a horrible mistake in her choice of Dwight. She had no intention of making that kind of mistake in a man ever again.

Joanna drove to Stephen's house for a late supper one evening that fall. She had only picked politely at the meal she shared with Katie and the family, for Stephen had told her to come hungry that night.

"You're going to make me fat," she had told him on more than one occasion when they planned a late meal together to follow the one she would have with her daughter, "making me eat two suppers in one night."

"I think we can find a way for you burn it off," he would suggest each time, grinning down at her. He would stand with his arms looped around her waist, so tall that her head tucked neatly under his chin when he held her against him. "I'm still waiting for that night of wild sex."

"And you'll keep waiting, Mr. Dawes," she always told him, though the same thought was increasingly on her mind. She knew there had to be more to sex than what she had known with Dwight; the encounters with him had been more frustrating than anything else. She had an inkling that Stephen could be very different.

She sat in the den that night as he put the finishing touches on the supper they would eat together. He would no longer allow her into the kitchen, not after the first night when she tried to help, which had done nothing but create an argument between the two of them over the ingredients of corn bread.

"It's corn-*bread* not *cake*," she had instructed, aghast that he dumped sugar into the mixture.

"That's how you're supposed to make it."

"No, it's not supposed to be sweet—"

"Yes, it is—"

"You cook like a Yankee," she told him at last, shaking her head with disgust, which had only gotten her banished from the kitchen.

That suited her just as well. He usually had supper ready by the time she arrived, and, if he did not, she just spent the time setting the dining room table or looking through his collection of record albums. His taste in music was far different from hers, and it was amusing to listen to the things he apparently preferred to listen to, which were far different from anything she owned. Tonight she had exhausted her interest in the albums and was browsing through several shelves of books—horror novels by Stephen King, Dean Koontz, and Peter Straub, among others, also far different from her own tastes. Even the concept of some of the books made her skin crawl, and she had just sat back down on the couch with one of them when he entered the den from the kitchen.

"I don't see how you can sleep after reading these things," she told him, closing the book to set it on the coffeetable. She hugged her arms for warmth as she stared down at the cover. It was about a plague wiping out most of the population of the earth, which was not the most appealing reading material just before sitting down to supper.

"That's one of my favorites, actually," he told her, picking the book up as he sat down beside her. "It's about the struggle of good and evil. It has all these Biblical overtones, which really aren't my thing, but it's good." He put it into her hands. "Give it a chance; you'll like it."

"Well—" she looked at him speculatively, but accepted the book. "We'll see."

Supper went smoothly—although he had sugared the cornbread again. He made it almost every time they had supper together, just, she believed, to see if she would say something about it—which she didn't. She also didn't eat the cornbread after the first tentative, trial bite.

She helped him do the dishes later, during which he broke a glass, cutting his thumb in the process. He let her bandage it only after a fuss.

"You're worse than a three-year-old," she told him, making him hold still only by pinning the injured hand between her knees as she applied antiseptic and a Band-aid. He was looking at her in a way that did not remind her in the slightest of any child when she lifted her eyes to his a moment later. Then he slipped his hand to the back of her neck to loosen the clamp holding her hair back, running his fingers through it for a moment before drawing it down over her shoulders. When he kissed her, she leaned into him, and, when he drew her to her feet later to lead her toward the bedroom, she did not object in the slightest.

∾

Joanna lay in his arms afterward, amazed at the feel of his chest hair now beneath her fingers, for Dwight had had no chest hair at all—

Stephen was very different, she told herself, very different in many ways—

And, oh, yes, she had been missing a lot.

She kissed his chest, feeling his fingers now draw her hair back from her face so he could see her better when she looked up at him— she loved him, she realized. She started to say something, to tell him what she felt, but pressed her lips to his chest again instead.

"I could get used to this," he said, smiling at her when she brought her eyes to his again.

"So could I." She was smiling as well, thinking—yes, she could get used to a very many things, as she ran her fingers again over his chest.

But he was suddenly pressing her back, taking her by the shoulders, moving so that he leaned over her. There was a seriousness in his expression as he met her eyes.

"I need to tell you—" he began, but then he fell silent. He stared at her, and there seemed to be a struggle inside of him. She smiled and reached up to touch his cheek, telling herself that she understood—he loved her; she could see it in his eyes. He did not have to say anything.

"I love you," she said at last, though she had not known she would say the words until they passed her lips. He opened his mouth, but not a word came out. He stared at her, and then she drew his mouth to hers, in a kiss that lingered.

Later she slept in his arms, waking hours later in the middle of the night. "I've got to go," she told him, sitting up as she caught sight of the clock on the table beside the bed. It had been his hands that had awakened her, and he pressed her back now. "It's the middle of the night," she protested. "My folks would never understand—"

"To hell with your folks," he told her, just before he drew her mouth to his. She started to protest again, but the insistence of his lips, and the warmth of his body, drove the words from her mind.

# 24

ON AN AFTERNOON SEV-
eral weeks later, Stephen sat, feeling useless, in the bank president's office as he listened to his grandfather and the bank president discuss business. His grandfather sat beside him in his wheelchair, wearing an expensively tailored suit and a sour look as he gave the banker hell, asking questions, probing, unbelieving of anything that was told him—as usual.

Stephen had no idea why he had been ordered here. The driver and male nurse who had ridden along were waiting in the van outside, but Stephen felt he was of little more use in this meeting than the driver would have been. He was mostly being ignored as the two men talked, and had begun to toy with an antique-looking paperweight from the desktop, which seemed to annoy the banker, though that did not make Stephen put the paperweight down. He wondered if he were here simply to be displayed—the next Eason in the line, Buddy Eason's prize possession—but there were other matters on his mind today beyond his grandfather's current motives. There was Joanna.

He had known that he would have to tell her sooner or later that his grandfather was Buddy Eason, but there had never been a time that seemed right. He had thought it might be easier if they became lovers, for that would be something of a commitment between them. And he knew now that she was in love with him—but that had made it only worse. Now he knew he had remained silent too long. He was almost certain now that she would turn away when she learned the truth—she was a Sanders. That knowledge still did not sit well with him, but he loved her anyway. He had not been able to speak those three words to her, had never spoken them to any woman, and he could not imagine himself saying them to Joanna—but he did love her, and he was afraid now that he would lose her. He had to tell her about his grandfather, and he had to tell her tonight. He had come to that decision in the sleepless hours after she had left him the previous night to return to her home and her Sanders land.

Stephen listened for a moment to the banker discussing some tax shelter plan, to his grandfather interrupting rudely again and again. He tried to follow what they were saying, not to think about—

Last night had started out as many of their evenings together started. He had dinner ready for them—fried chicken breasts, rolls, and potato wedges from the Super Chick in Pine, which he knew she loved, though he had yet to understand what charmed her so about the greasy mess.

He intended that night to suggest again that she bring her daughter along early some afternoon, so they could grill out on the back deck and maybe watch a movie in the den, and the notion of that homey time with the three of them together had him thinking about what it could be like if he and Joanna could have a future together—but Joanna was silent and distant as they ate, and later, after they dimmed the living room lights and while he was holding her, he could tell she was thinking of something far different from where she was and what he was doing.

"What's wrong?" he asked.

They had never talked of troubles or problems in their hours together, for those hours were so few and far between they seemed suitable only for happy things, so he was surprised when she said, "We've lost our farm. We got a foreclosure notice a few days ago," she said, sitting back against the sofa cushions, now out of his arms.

"Foreclosure? Why didn't you tell me things were like that? I could have—"

"No," she said, shaking her head. "There's nothing you could have done."

"There might have been. I could have—"

"No." The finality of the word left nothing for him to do or say. She rose from the couch and crossed the room to stand staring out the living room window into the darkness, her back to him. "It doesn't matter now, anyway. It's over. The farm's gone."

Stephen stared at her, at the straight back, the lifted head—she had known for days, and had not told him. She would have known it was coming for months, and she had kept it to herself. He knew what the place meant to her. If she had told him earlier, he could have loaned her enough to keep the place going for a time, could possibly have arranged an extension on the amount they owed.

Finally, he said, "I'm sorry," knowing the words were terribly inadequate.

He started to rise to go to her, but then her quiet voice froze him onto the couch. "Goddamn the Easons," she said. "Goddamn every last one of them."

Finally he forced his mind to work, and the words to come. "What did you say?" he asked, surprised at how calm his voice sounded. No, she did not know—it was something more.

She turned to look at him, her arms crossed before her chest, as if she did not know what else to do with them. "Oh, I know they're not behind this now. We did this on our own—the economy, the drought—there was no way we could make it. And we're not the only ones. Lots of farms have been lost in recent years. But, everything else they've done to my family; if it had not been for them down through the years, we might never have gotten to this point. They destroyed equipment years ago, destroyed animals, parts of the crop several times—"

"I'm sure the Easons couldn't have done anything like that. They're—" He did not know what he had been about to say, just that he was going to defend his family from some slander she had been told by her grandfather and her father, but he had no chance.

"How can you defend them?" she demanded, anger flashing across her features. "That son-of-a-bitch Buddy Eason tried to murder my grandfather more than once! He had my father beaten, and set fire to my grandfather's crop, and our house! My great-grandfather died fighting a fire in his cotton crop that was set by one of the Easons. How can you—! You don't know them."

He sat in dumbfounded silence. Her chest, beneath the white cotton blouse, rose and fell in angry silence as she met his gaze. He had never seen her like this, had never heard anyone say anything like this, and he knew it was a lie. Stephen was an Eason by blood, and she was—

Suddenly her face softened and she came toward him. "I'm sorry. I know you haven't been in the county for that long. You don't know all that's happened. Most of it even happened before I was born. You don't know what the Easons are like." She sat down beside him and took both his hands in hers, looking up at him with gentleness in her eyes. "I had no right to yell at you. I'm sorry."

"That's all right," he said after a moment, turning his face away. He wanted to tell her that he was an Eason in the eyes of so many people in the county, and in the eyes of his grandfather, that same Buddy Eason she cursed so. He wanted to tell her that it was she who did not know. He wanted to tell her that she should hear all the things his grandfather had to say about her family—the truth for once in her life—but he could not. Not now. Not like this.

He looked into her blue eyes, and knew that telling her, when he did, would be the hardest thing he would ever do—but he would have to do it. Maybe it was best now that she had lost the land when she did. There would be nothing to tie her to Eason County once the land was gone and after she knew the truth. He would ask her to leave with him. Maybe they would marry. They could raise her daughter together, and maybe have children of their own.

They had not made love that night, but had just held each other without the need for sex, until the time came for her to go. She was never able to stay the entire night, anyway, for she had to go home to her daughter and family before too late, but they made the most of their time together, as they always did. After she left, he turned out the lights and sat in the living room in the dark, unable to stop himself from recalling the words she had said:

*"Goddamn the Easons. Goddamn every last one of them."*

Stephen watched as the bank president rose from his chair and came around the desk to shake hands with his grandfather. Stephen sat up and placed the paperweight back on the desk, then rose to his own feet, glad the meeting was finished. He wanted to get home where he could be alone to think. Joanna was coming to his house again tonight, and he would find some way to tell her what he had to tell her—she would have to understand. She would have to.

The banker shook Stephen's hand, and then walked them to the door.

"It was good to see you again, Mr. Eason," the banker said to Stephen, patting him on the shoulder. Stephen accepted the name, and the "Mr.," from a man twenty years his senior, without saying a word. He was growing accustomed to it.

He opened the office door and started through, then turned back at the sound of his grandfather's voice.

"Go tell them to bring the van up," Buddy Eason said as he guided the electric wheelchair through the doorway, barely clearing either side of the frame.

"Whatever you want, Grandfather," Stephen said, and then turned in preparation to go for the driver, and then froze where he stood.

Joanna stood a few yards away, an older woman and a little girl at her either side. For an instant there was a look of pleasure on her face as she met his eyes—and something more. Then her gaze took in Stephen's grandfather in the wheelchair just behind where Stephen stood, and a terrible recognition came over her face. Her eyes rose again to Stephen—there was a knowledge there, an awareness, that he

had hoped never to see. His own words echoed in his ears—
*"Whatever you want, Grandfather."*

~

Joanna's hands were suddenly shaking so badly that she had to clench
them tightly into fists at her sides to still their trembling—but he
would not see her hands shaking. He would not.

*Grandfather*—the grandfather Stephen had told her about was
Buddy Eason. She had heard him say it. She could see the truth in his
eyes, could even see now a resemblance to the bloated man in the
wheelchair. Stephen was Buddy Eason's grandson.

He was an Eason.

He had known all along who she was. He had used her, and she felt
filthy. She was such a fool—after all the Easons had done to her family
through the years, to have allowed herself to be used by one of them
was somehow the worst thing of all. Each time he had touched her,
each time he had looked at her, made love to her—it was all a lie, all
part of that same cruel insanity the Easons had used against her family
for generations.

"Joanna?"

She heard her grandma's voice at her one side, and felt her
daughter's hand in hers at the other, but she could not stop staring at
Stephen.

"Joanna, I—" Stephen said, coming toward her, those gray eyes
mocking her with every word she had ever said to him. Once she had
even imagined what a child of theirs might look like, with his gray eyes
and her reddish hair. "You don't—"

"Goddamn you!" She spat the words at him and slapped him hard
across the face. She tried to drive the trembling away, out of her body,
but she could not. He was an Eason. He had used her, betrayed her—
and he was an Eason.

She saw him raise a hand to his cheek, saw the reddened mark her
palm had left there, but she did not care. His eyes showed pain, and
she gloried in it.

"You goddamn—" But she suddenly realized Katie was there, and she forced the words to stop. She hated him—she hated him and every lie he had made her believe. She hated him—and she wished she could see him dead.

Suddenly she knew she was going to cry. She had thought that she was beyond such foolishness—but she was going to cry, and there was nothing she could do to stop it.

"Damn you to hell," she said, hearing her own voice break.

She fled toward the back entrance of the bank, where she, her grandmother, and Katie had entered such a short time before. She held tightly to Katie's hand, dragging the little girl along, leaving her grandmother behind. Tears coursed down her cheeks—but he had not seen. He would not know how much he had hurt her. She would never give an Eason that satisfaction.

Elise Sanders stood facing the young man her granddaughter had cursed and slapped—Buddy Eason's grandson, though Joanna had not known until now.

The young man started after Joanna, but Elise stepped into his path. She heard the rear door of the bank slam. Only then did she move her eyes to Buddy Eason in his wheelchair.

Buddy's insane laughter followed her as she turned to walk away.

# 25

JOANNA HAD NEVER KNOWN such hurt or such a sense of betrayal. As the days passed into weeks, she expected it to diminish, but it did not. It grew and strengthened inside her, as did the hatred she now felt. Stephen called repeatedly until they had to leave the phone off the hook and finally had the number changed to a new, unlisted one. But he somehow found the new number and the calls resumed. He wrote letters and stuffed them into the mailbox, but she burned them unopened. He even dared to come to the house to try to see her, and left only after her father's temper finally exploded to send him sprawling into the yard with what she hoped was a broken nose. Joanna had not spoken his name since that day in the bank, and she hoped never to see him again.

Her father and grandfather both threatened to kill him. Her grandfather even went so far as to load a rifle, but her grandmother and mother would not let him leave the house.

"It's over," her grandma said, trying to take the rifle from his hands.

"It ain't over," Janson told her, angrier than Joanna had seen him in years. "It ain't never gonna be over so long as Buddy Eason's alive."

"He's not worth it," Joanna told him, "and neither is his grandson."

Her mother asked outright: "You were sleeping with him, weren't you?" and Joanna had told her the truth.

She could imagine Buddy Eason asking his beloved grandson for details:

*"Does she scream out your name?"*

*"Is she good?"*

*"Did you use a condom?"*

They hadn't.

She was not pregnant—thank God—for she had gone on the pill when she admitted to herself she was eventually going to sleep with him. Stephen had never asked about birth control, and she bitterly wondered now if his intention had been to leave her pregnant when he told her who he was. What a triumph that would have been for Buddy Eason, what a victory, to leave Janson Sanders's granddaughter pregnant and abandoned by Buddy Eason's grandson, with the county to know the truth of how she had been used. What a fool she'd been. What a goddamn fool.

She could not sleep without nightmares. In those nightmares it was Buddy Eason who took her, the bloated, sick, twisted old man, smothering her beneath his weight.

Or it would be Stephen who became his grandfather during the act.

She would be pregnant from what they had done. Stephen/Buddy's child would be a twisted monster, with Buddy Eason's face, who would rip her open at its birth—and she would wake in a cold sweat, her heart racing as she stared into the darkness.

She sickened knowing she had once allowed herself to wonder what a child they had together might look like, when she knew now that it would be Buddy Eason's great-grandchild.

When they had to leave the farm, they moved into a six-room, rented house in the mill village in Pine. Joanna knew what leaving did to her grandfather, and she wondered if Janson Sanders would live a year after they left the land. He had been such a part of it for so many years, and it of him, that she could not imagine one existing without the other.

Her father had taken a job in a plant, and her mother was working part-time for a lawyer in Wells. They both came home, tired and exhausted at the end of the day, as did Joanna, who took a temporary job bookkeeping for Hess Furniture. She had no idea what she would do after the auction of their land, but she would stay in Pine until then, until their land and her home was sold to another owner. Her father's friend, Mr. Betts, had called to offer her a job again, and she thought she would take it; before long there would be no reason for her to stay in Eason County, except for her family.

And she never wanted to take the chance she might see Stephen Dawes Eason again.

~

Stephen sat in his grandfather's den at twelve-thirty on a Thursday afternoon, waiting to be called through the closed doors into the living room to see the old man. Buddy had called his house that morning before daylight, waking Stephen from a sound sleep to tell him to dress and come to the house so they could speak.

Stephen had done just as he had been told, had shaved and showered and dressed as quickly as he could, but had been waiting for hours now to see the old man—as he would keep waiting until his grandfather had time to talk to him. He was hungry, not having eaten since early the evening before, and the hunger was now edging toward nausea, but Stephen would not even go to the old man's kitchen to find something to eat. His grandfather might look for him while he was gone, and not believe Stephen had done exactly as he had been told, and Stephen would not have his grandfather believe he had disobeyed his direct order.

Things had been so much better between Stephen and his grandfather since the day at the bank. His grandfather believed Stephen had gotten close to Joanna simply to please the old man—and Buddy Eason had found great pleasure in it. He had clasped his hands in delight the moment Joanna ran from the building, tears filling her eyes. A cackling laugh had escaped the old man as he rocked back and forth in his wheelchair, clapping his hands over and over again after Elise Sanders walked away.

"Goddamn—Sanders's granddaughter!" Buddy Eason laughed, rocking so much now that the wheelchair rolled slightly forward, and then again. "You've been getting at her, haven't you boy?" he demanded, so loudly that people in the bank were turning to look at them. "What's she like, boy? What's she like? Was she any good?"

The old man was still grinning broadly in the van as they left the bank's parking lot. He picked at Stephen's coat sleeve, plucking it up, and then smoothing it down, over and over again, at last beginning absently to pet Stephen's arm, almost as if he were a dog, until Stephen pulled away.

"You made her love you, didn't you?" his grandfather said, cackling again. "Oh, I wish I could see that goddamn red nigger's face when he finds out. Oh, I wish—I bet she's good, huh, boy? I bet she's good."

Buddy's behavior toward his grandson changed that day. The change was subtle at first, but Stephen had noticed—his grandfather was pleased with him. His grandfather was pleased, and even in his shame at what he had done to Joanna, Stephen couldn't help enjoying his grandfather's approval.

"You did something I could never do," his grandfather had said that day, just before the van's lift lowered him to the ground. He reached up to take hold of Stephen's suit coat at the shoulder, pulling him down until they were face to face. His grandfather stared at him through dark glasses. "You got right to the heart of them, boy. You used her and got to them—you did good, boy. You did so good."

And then Buddy Eason pulled him forward and kissed him full on the mouth, startling Stephen so that he pulled away quickly and hit his head on the van's door opening, shooting stars through his vision for a moment before it cleared. By then they had lowered the old man to the ground and he could do nothing but stare.

Now he waited outside his grandfather's door, the hunger beginning to make him lightheaded. At last the door opened and one of the male nurses stepped through. The man did not speak, but stood there until Stephen realized he was being summoned inside. Stephen rose from the leather sofa and walked past the husky man and into the living room, hearing the heavy door close after him to leave him alone with his grandfather.

Stephen waited until the old man motioned to one of the chairs in the room before he sat down, and, once seated, he waited to find out what his grandfather wanted of him.

"I have a job I want you to do for me," Buddy Eason said.

"A job?"

"Yes." Buddy reached up to rub one side of his thick neck, a ring glittering in the light from the desk lamp, catching Stephen's eye. "You are going to buy something for me," Buddy said.

Nervousness tightened Stephen's stomach muscles. His grandfather's tone was light, but Stephen had the sudden impression that he was about to be asked to do something illegal. His grandfather had done so much for him. Stephen owed him everything—but he had become increasingly uncomfortable with Buddy's business dealings and dreaded the possibility that he might be asked to get involved in an unknown something in repayment.

His grandfather's sudden laughter took him by surprise, and he jumped when the old man slapped an open palm down on the desktop before him. "Don't worry, boy," Buddy Eason said, reading the worry in his expression. "You don't have to kill anybody. I just want you to buy something for me."

His grandfather's assurance did not dispel the tension inside of him.

"What do you want me to buy, Grandfather?" he asked, knowing that he sounded again like the child he had once been. Stephen's entire field of vision was focused on his grandfather sitting there in the wheelchair beyond the cherry wood desk.

Buddy Eason watched him for a long moment, and then spoke again, his voice very quiet. "You're going to buy Janson Sanders's farm for me."

When Stephen found his voice, after a sharp intake of breath, he could get out only one word—"But—" before his grandfather interrupted.

"The auction will be this Saturday. I'm going with you, but you'll be the one who does the bidding. Sanders will be there—he has to be—" There was a sound of desperation to the last words. "If he sees me buy the place, it would be bad enough, but you buying it would rub their noses in what you did to her—rub their noses in it," he repeated with a cackle, scrubbing his hands together before him. "You had his granddaughter—he has to know that. He has to picture it, day after day, you with her, the things you did. And her grandmother— she has to know; she has to think about it all the time. I always—" He fell silent and was staring away now, hardly aware Stephen was even in the room.

"Grandfather—" Stephen reached out after a moment to him and Buddy Eason brought his eyes back, turning the dark glasses toward his grandson.

"You'll buy the place for me," he said, very quietly now, a sound of pleasure in his voice. "We'll burn the house and buildings to the ground and sow the fields with salt. I'll have it paved over and turned into a parking lot there in the middle of nowhere so no one will ever farm it again. No one—it will kill him," he continued, a rising tone of excitement in his voice, "seeing it gone, seeing it gone to me, seeing it taken by you, just like you took his granddaughter—"

"But—"

"No buts. You know where your loyalty is. You know—"

"Yes, Grandfather." And he did. He owed Buddy Eason everything—everything, the best education that could be had, the roof over his head every night, everything he had ever had in his life from the age of five.

"I know." There was satisfaction and pleasure in Buddy's voice. He opened a folder on his desk and drew a paper that he pushed across the desk toward his grandson. "This is a cashier's check for more than the place will ever go for. Whatever you can bid in under this, you keep the rest. A little bonus—" The word was followed by a chuckle.

Stephen stared at the numbers on the check—so much money. Far more than it would ever take to buy the Sanders land, their home, everything Joanna had told him about.

He knew he owed the old man more than he could ever repay. He owed his grandfather so much, for all the years that Buddy Eason had looked after him. Buddy's had been a strange love, but it was the only love Stephen had ever known.

He lifted his eyes from the check, to the face of his grandfather, realizing how much he did resemble the old man—they were of the same blood, so much the same. He met his grandfather's gaze through the dark glasses, then heard his voice speaking, even before he thought. "You tried to kill Janson Sanders , didn't you?"

For a moment the heavy face was impassive. "Yes."

"Several times?"

Only a moment's silence. "Yes, I did."

"And his father?"

The face showed nothing, his grandfather's expression changing not in the slightest. "I heard he had a heart attack fighting a fire in his cotton crop."

Stephen watched him. "You had someone set the fire?"

There was just a flicker across the features. Memory. Satisfaction. "I set it myself."

"And you've wrecked their equipment through the years, killed their cattle, destroyed their crops?" He was surprised to hear how rational the words sounded, the concepts.

"Or had it done." Buddy's voice was the same—so normal, so unfeeling. The face Stephen stared at was unmoved—and they carried the same genes, were so much the same, and his grandfather had done so much for him. Stephen could never repay it all. Never.

"You know where your loyalty is, don't you, boy?" his grandfather asked again, his voice low.

Stephen looked back down at the check his grandfather offered. "Yes, Grandfather. I know where my loyalty is."

Buddy Eason smiled warmly at his grandson for the first time that Stephen could ever recall, a smile of acceptance, of something near to respect, what Stephen had longed to see there for as long as he could remember.

"I knew you would, Stephen."

It was the first time the old man had ever called him anything other than 'boy,' the first time he had ever used his name. Stephen felt a lump rise in his throat to choke him as he reached out and took the check.

"Thank you, Grandfather," he said quietly, swallowing the lump back—so much to repay.

$\sim$

Elise Sanders sat on the front porch of the house they had rented, watching the sun rise that Saturday morning over the tops of mill houses to the east. When they moved from this village in 1946, she had never expected to watch another sunrise over these quiet streets, had never thought she would go to bed or sleep beneath a roof other than the one Janson had dreamed of for so long—but here she was, watching the sun rise over the Eason mill village.

She had been restless through the night, tossing and turning in the bed she shared with Janson, until she rose before dawn to keep from waking him, and came out onto the porch to watch for the sun to rise on the day when the land would be auctioned to someone else. She could understand now why Janson had left the county before the auction could take place when he lost the land the first time in 1927— they had met shortly thereafter, their meeting a direct result of his losing the land. So good did come of that loss.

But nothing good would come from this day. Elise feared what this was doing to Janson, and she worried for Henry and Joanna— Janson had reared Henry on the dream of the land, on the promise of having it back for him, as well as for Henry's children. Janson had accomplished that, finally.

But the land would never be regained this time. This was no longer a world where dreams had value. People lived for money now, for having something they believed would appear better in the eyes of someone else.

She was tired. Old age had given her a reduced need for sleep, but also a feeling of being tired all the time. But there was nothing she had in particular to do this morning, she told herself. She would sit here on the porch and watch the sun rise, then she would go in and begin breakfast for the family, bacon and eggs, because Janson loved bacon and eggs, biscuits and grits, and coffee to which Janson would add milk but no sugar.

She was surprised to hear the door open. She turned to see Janson slowly step out over the threshold and onto the porch. He was looking at her, slowly maneuvering his way out through the open doorway.

"I wondered where you was when I woke up," he said. He eased the screen door shut behind himself to keep it from slamming to wake the remainder of the household, then turned to look at her again. "You're gonna catch your death, sittin' out here in th' cool."

"It feels good to me," she said, rising to go to him.

"You better come in an' get dressed. You ought not be sittin' out here in your nightgown and robe where everybody can see you; you know better'n that."

Elise smiled, knowing he was concerned that some man might be looking at her—as if some other man would be interested in looking at a woman on the high side of seventy who was sitting on her porch in a cotton nightgown and bathrobe that covered the worn slippers on her feet.

"I'm coming in," she said, taking his arm. He turned back toward the screen door.

"Could you help me find some clean overalls?" he asked. "I been a farmer all my life. I ain't goin' t' th' auction today dressed up lookin' like somethin' other than what I am."

"Janson, you don't have to—" she said, and stopped to stare up at him.

"Yeah, I do," he told her, meeting her eyes. There were lines in his face now that sometimes surprised her, and she reached up and ran her fingers over them, down toward his mouth. "Yeah, I do," he said again, bringing one hand up to capture hers and hold it tightly.

His knuckles were swollen, and she knew how painful his hands were now much of the time, and especially in the mornings—but still he held her hand, squeezing it in his own, as he had through the years.

"I'm too old t' run away now," he said, his voice quiet as he stared into her eyes. "I run away back then. I didn't stay t' watch th' land go t' somebody else."

"Janson—"

But he shook his head, stilling her voice. "It's no different than leavin' so you don't have t' watch somebody you love die."

Elise had to blink back a tear. She did not like hearing him talk like that.

"I won't get th' land back this time—I know that. I'm too old—"

"No—"

He smiled. "You are, too." And she smiled. "I don't think Henry will ever get it back, or Joanna either—but I'm not runnin' away this time. I'm gonna see it go. I owe my pa that, an' my ma, an' t' Henry an' Joanna. I'm gonna see it—"

Elise nodded, knowing there was nothing else she could do.

He pulled open the screen door, entering the house before her.

⁓

There were people already on the land when they arrived, cars and trucks, many with out-of-state tags, parked in the drive before the house, along one side of the road, and at the edge of a field that Janson knew he would never see grow a crop again. Henry pulled the LTD up into the yard in front of the barn, and Janson got out slowly, followed by Elise, and Joanna. Olivia had stayed with Katie so the little girl would not have to see this. Children had a right to dreams, not to the knowledge that a lifetime of dreaming and planning could be taken by bad luck, weather, and hard times.

Elise came around the car to Janson's side and took his arm. He was glad to have her there, glad for the support she gave him—as she always had.

"Are you okay, Grandpa?" Joanna asked, coming to stand by him, looking so young, and so much as Elise had looked when he first brought her to live here so many years ago.

Janson started to speak, but his eyes drifted away, to the house where he had been born, the wide porch, now bare, the windows vacant and staring. So much living had gone on in that house, so many years of watching his family grow and of loving Elise.

He gently freed his arm from Elise's hand and walked alone to the front of the house to gaze at the place he had spent so much of his life. For a moment he was certain he heard a voice, felt a touch, saw something just at the edge of his vision. There was the smell of biscuits cooking in an old wood stove, the sound of a man singing an old hymn, the ring of an ax as it rose and fell, and he closed his eyes, feeling that he could hear his mother's voice calling him—

Then Elise was there, her hand slipping through his arm again, and he opened his eyes and looked at her—*It's all right*, he told her with a smile. *I'm all right*—and then he turned his eyes to the field where men had gathered to buy his life.

There were faces he recognized and others he did not. At the edge of the yard stood a group of farmers the Sanders knew well and were known well by, men and women with sun-baked skin and faded clothes and work-hardened hands. Some were in little better shape financially than the Sanders family, a few had already lost farms, others were barely hanging on, waiting for the next act of God or man that might drive them from their own land. There had been talk of trying to block the sale, but Henry had asked that nothing be done. There was no need of anyone getting in trouble trying to block something that no one could stop.

Janson looked down to the rough ground to be certain of his footing as they reached the field where the auction would take place. After only a few steps, Elise tightened her hand on his arm and said his name softly, bringing his eyes up to hers. She nodded her head in the direction of the people already gathered in the field and to a small group right in their path. Janson followed her gaze. There was Buddy Eason's massive bulk, and Janson wondered how it was that Buddy had gotten there over the rough ground of the field, then he noticed the heavy-shouldered men adjusting the wheelchair. One bent to lock the brakes on Buddy's chair. Another reached to adjust the lap robe that had slipped to show the shapeless legs beneath, in their dark trousers, but Buddy slapped his hands away.

The attendants left, except for one who remained standing at Buddy's side, a tall young man with curling brown hair and eyes, as Janson drew near enough to see them, that reminded him of Buddy's. Janson looked down at Buddy as he walked past. He could see himself reflected in the lenses of Buddy's dark glasses. Buddy was smiling.

"They picked the right place to hold the auction, didn't they?" Buddy said in a low voice.

Janson did not reply.

"This is the field I burned that killed your father," Buddy said, staring at him. "It's just right I take your land from this same field."

Janson halted—but he realized that he had already known. Buddy had burned half of downtown Pine decades ago. He had tried to burn the house and cotton in Janson's first year back on the land. Buddy had been setting fires in Eason County since he was a small child.

Janson guessed he would be burning in Hell before too long.

He refused to react, but Buddy's next words were not directed at Janson but to Joanna.

"Stephen said you're pretty good in bed," Buddy told her, loudly. "Maybe you can find a way to make a living now on your back."

Janson noticed Buddy's grandson tense beside him, and realized why an instant later as Henry's fist slammed into the boy's mouth, followed immediately by the other being driven into his stomach, doubling him over. Stephen coughed and gagged, and almost went to his knees—but Henry had him by the hair at one side of his head, drawing him up short, dragging him forward until his face was only inches from that of Henry Sanders.

"You ever touch my daughter again, you even mention her name or anything about her and I'll castrate you and feed you your balls—do you understand me?" Henry demanded, hissing in Stephen's face as he tightened his fingers in the boy's hair.

Buddy Eason's grandson did not respond. He met Henry's eyes.

"Do you understand me?" Henry hissed again. When he still did not respond, Henry released him with a shove that sent him back against his grandfather's wheelchair, rocking it and causing Stephen to almost lose his footing. His eyes moved to touch on Joanna, and then moved away as her father started back toward him.

"No, Daddy—he's not worth it," Joanna said, "and neither is his grandfather." She had Henry's arm, pulling him away. Janson was certain that she looked directly at Buddy Eason for a moment, for he saw Buddy pucker his lips as if blowing her a kiss, and then Joanna turned away, a sick look on her face as Buddy began to laugh.

Other people were open-mouthed around the spectacle. Janson knew they had all heard Buddy Eason's words.

"Come on, Henry," Janson said. Joanna's cheeks were flame red, torment written on her face as she looked at her grandfather, her eyes pleading for him to do something—anything—that would just get this over.

Elise had Joanna's arm now, and Henry's. Under her firm insistence they moved on, distancing themselves from Buddy Eason and his grandson. Janson followed.

Stephen stood mutely by Buddy, and Buddy reached up to pat his hand, laughing still, it appeared now only to himself.

Elise took Janson's arm when they stopped. Henry turned to stare at Buddy Eason and Buddy's grandson until Joanna slipped her hand in his and brought his eyes to her instead. Janson watched them all, watched Henry relax slightly, and Joanna take a deep breath as the auction of their land and home began.

A moment later Stephen Dawes Eason made his first bid.

# 26

SEVERAL OF THE PROSPECTIVE county buyers grew silent as Buddy Eason's grandson entered the bidding. Joanna watched their faces, seeing their feelings, watching those feelings being quickly masked—they were bidding against Buddy Eason, and they knew it.

And they all knew the man all too well.

More fell silent as the bidding continued, seeing the angry looks directed their way by the massive man in the wheelchair, until the bidding was between Stephen and several men Joanna had never seen before, men who must have come from outside the county. They looked to be businessmen, not farmers, men who would break the land up into little lots, or operate it as part of a corporation from somewhere far outside the Southeast—and she found herself praying for one of them to win the final bid to keep the land out of Eason hands. She looked at her grandfather's face, and found him looking at her. Then Janson Sanders's eyes moved toward Stephen as the bidding continued.

Her father's face had lost some of its color but his jaw was clenched, a muscle jumping in his cheek. She knew Henry Sanders was keeping his emotions in tight control. Her grandmother was holding her grandfather's arm, and Joanna wondering which was supporting the other. Tears welled in Elise Sanders's eyes as she watched the auctioneer—it was gone, Joanna thought. Joanna's dreams were gone, her father's, her grandfather's, even the dreams of the great-grandfather she had never known. All was over. The land, her home, all the years of work—gone for nothing. Everything Elise and Janson Sanders had worked toward most of their lives, and her father for all of his, and what she had planned for as long as she could remember—with the final fall of the gavel, a lifetime, everything, would be gone—and Stephen was doing it. Stephen, at his grandfather's bidding.

Which was the same reason he had gone to bed with her. The same—and she hated him for it. Oh, how she hated him.

When the bidding was complete, a silence fell over the place. People were beginning to leave the field to return to their cars when Stephen walked to the auctioneer to shake his hand, a smile now on his face. She could see the look of triumph on Buddy Eason's face, that look of satisfaction as he stared at her, at her grandfather, and her father. She wished that she could kill them both.

The knot of pain rose in her. She felt unsteady on her feet, as if she had been struck, felt her father take her arm, and saw her grandparents' concerned faces—*but I should be comforting them*, Joanna thought. Her father and grandparents had lost more today than she could ever know. They had had decades here, a lifetime of memories and dreams that now would be left behind. Joanna felt a tear move down her cheek, and she cursed herself for the weakness, cursed herself for the pain, cursed herself that she had ever cared for Stephen and that she had thought she had to come here to see this happen when she could have stayed away.

Stephen started back in his grandfather's direction, the paperwork for his purchase now in his hands—he had bought everything, down to the last piece of equipment they owned. The land. Her home.

It was over.

Joanna looked away from him to the red fields, the pines, the land rolling into woods and hills beyond. She had loved this place for so long, and it seemed such a part of her, but she forced her eyes away from it and back toward Buddy Eason and his grandson as Stephen came at last to stand before the wheelchair bearing the old man.

Buddy reached out, a smile on his face as he prepared to take the deed to what had belonged to Janson Sanders, and to his family, for so long—the Easons had won. After all the years, all the stories Joanna had heard, all the times that Buddy Eason had come up against her grandfather—and the Easons had finally won. Buddy Eason had won.

And Janson Sanders was there to see it.

Joanna turned her face away, the tears coming freely now, until she could no longer even wipe them away—she could not watch, could not see this happen. Could not—

"*No—!*"

The loud exclamation filled the silence, drawing the attention of all those still present to the two men. Buddy Eason glared in disbelief up at his grandson. The smile of triumph was gone.

"What did you say to me, boy?" Buddy asked.

"I said no, Grandfather."

When Buddy responded his voice was high and angry. "You used my money, boy. You—"

"I used my own money, every cent I had, but it's mine." Stephen reached into his pocket and held a folded check out toward his grandfather. When Buddy did not reach to take it, he dropped it on the ground at the old man's feet. "There's your money."

Buddy stared down at the check, and then back up at his grandson. Rage contorted his features.

"It's over," Stephen said, "everything you've done to these people all these years, it's over. You'll leave them alone from now on, or you'll answer to me—and you don't want to answer to me. I'm your grandson; everything I know, I learned from you."

"Do you know what you're saying to me, boy?" Buddy Eason's voice was low now, filled with threat. "You're an Eason—"

"Yes, I am, partly, and because of that part I owe more of a debt to these people than I could repay in a lifetime." He met his grandfather's eyes through the dark glasses, and then turned away.

Joanna watched in disbelief as he walked to where she stood with her family. He stopped before her and reached out to take her hand, into which he put the paperwork, closing her fingers firmly around it. A scream of rage broke from Buddy Eason behind him.

"It's yours," Stephen said, not turning to look at his grandfather, though Buddy was shaking the wheelchair in fury, trying to move toward them.

Stephen looked at her for a moment longer, and then released her hands, leaving the paperwork with her as he moved to stand before her father.

"My name is Stephen Dawes," he said, meeting Henry Sanders's eyes, "and I hope one day to marry your daughter."

When supper was ready to go on the table that night in the old mill village house, Elise left Olivia and Katie dishing food into bowls and went to look for Janson. It was unusual for him not to be in the kitchen by then, prying into plate-covered bowls on the kitchen table, taking just a taste of something with a spoon or fork that he would leave sitting in the middle of his plate until everyone else joined him at the table.

Elise found him in the living room, peeping out the curtain covering the front window. She stopped and stared at him, and at Henry, who was peeking out the other side of that same curtain to where Elise knew Joanna was sitting with Stephen Dawes in the front porch swing.

She could hear the slow screak of the old swing, and the voices of the two young people, and Elise smiled to herself just before she asked, "Why don't you just go outside where you can stare at them openly?"

Janson glanced her way, though Henry did not move. It was a long moment before he spoke, and, when he did, Elise wondered if he were speaking to himself, the words were so quiet.

"I don't like this," Henry said, still staring out the gap in the curtain. "If he thinks I'm just going to stand aside and—" His words trailed off.

Elise crossed the room to place a hand on Henry's arm. She parted the curtains slightly with her other hand to look out, and she smiled—they were an attractive couple, in their own way, though there was the unfortunate resemblance between Stephen and Buddy Eason. Stephen was holding Joanna's hand now, her fingers securely intertwined with his and resting on his thigh. Joanna had seemed uncertain of him at first, Elise noticed—but that uncertainty was now gone. She could see that the two young people had made their peace. Joanna smiled, and Stephen leaned closer and kissed her briefly.

Elise felt Henry stir uncomfortably at her side.

"Leave them alone, Henry," she said, letting the curtain come together before her and reaching out to take hold of both men's shirt sleeves and draw them away from the window. "It's none of your business," she said after she had drawn them several steps into the room.

"Like hell it's not. She's my daughter." He looked back toward the window.

"She's a grown woman, and there's nothing you can do about it."

"I'm not—"

"Leave 'em be."

It was Janson who had spoken this time, and Elise turned to look at him. Of the two, she had thought he would be the most reluctant to have an Eason in the family—a part-Eason, anyway, not to mention the fact that he was a blood descendant of both Helene and Cassandra Price.

"There ain't nothin' you can do about it. You cain't keep 'em apart, not if they're meant t' be together. Th' only thing you will do is drive your daughter away—"

"I'll be damned if I—"

"No," Janson said.

So many times in the past, Elise had looked at her son and realized how much he looked like Janson. But in that instant, it was her own father that he reminded her of. She could see something of that same determination there, that same hatred that she had seen in William Whitley's face when he had looked at Janson all those years before. When Janson spoke again, she knew he also saw it.

"Your mama's pa never held you in his arms when you was a baby," Janson said quietly, staring at their son. "William Whitley never looked int' your face t' go beyond what he could see 'a me there, t' see somethin' 'a himself. He loved your grandma' Whitley—I don't have no doubt 'a that—but he kept her from seein' you an' your mama 'til th' day she died. You can't stop what's meant t' be; all you can do is give up your part in it. All you can do is give up th' chance t' look int' a face, t' go beyond what you see 'a Buddy Eason there, t' see yourself as well. Nobody could'a kept me an' Elise apart; nobody could'a kept you an' Olivia apart—don't make Joanna choose between you an' Buddy Eason's gran'son. You won't like her choice."

Henry stared at his father, and then moved back to peep out again through a narrow gap at the side of the front curtain.

"I'll give him one chance," he said at last.

Elise looked at Janson and smiled.

One chance was all they had ever needed.

# Epilogue

JOANNA SANDERS LEE AND
Stephen Dawes were married beneath flowering dogwoods in the
Sanders side yard, near the old kitchen Buddy Eason had tried to burn
so long before. The household's kitchen had been moved years ago
into a back room in the house, and most recently that separate
structure, attached to the house by a covered and elevated walkway,
had served as living space for Stephen Dawes, for Henry Sanders
would not allow his future son-in-law to spend even one night in the
house until he and Joanna were properly married by a minister in the
presence of her family.

Andrew Betts performed the ceremony, and his brother, Isaac,
came all the way from Georgia to attend the wedding. Joanna's
brothers were there, their wives, and their children, including a baby
who began to cry part-way through the ceremony, though nobody
seemed to mind.

Joanna had both her father and her grandfather give the bride
away, one walking at her either side, and, though Buddy Eason could
not see Janson Sanders's face from where he sat in his van parked so
far away on the dirt road that cut through Sanders land, Buddy was
sure it was the happiest day of Janson Sanders's life.

Buddy had intended to do something to stop the wedding, to ruin
the day for the Sanders family, but he found that he could not. His
head hurt horribly, and there was a searing pain in his eyes as he stared
through dark glasses and watched his only grandson marry Janson

Sanders's granddaughter. There was tingling and numbness in one of his hands, and he kept rubbing at one eye, until he knocked the glasses from his face and had to get the driver to find them.

His headache had worsened by evening. He could hardly see through one of his eyes, and he was almost certain he had done it himself as he kept rubbing it—but that did not matter. He was alone—so completely alone—for he had fired the nurses, and dismissed his driver as well, when he got home, showing them to the door with a revolver.

Now he sat in the huge, old house that had sheltered Easons for generations, drinking, trying to make himself drunk, as he thought about all he would do to his grandson and to Janson Sanders's granddaughter—*what God has joined together, Buddy Eason will pull asunder*, he kept thinking. *What God has—*

But there was no God, only Buddy and the things he would do. He lit a cigarette with an engraved lighter, then sat for a moment studying its flame before he flicked the top shut and set it on the cherry wood desk. He took a deep drag on the cigarette, and then rested that hand back on the arm of the wheelchair, thinking of all he would do, and of how he would make his grandson suffer before he was through with him.

*What God has—*

The hand holding the cigarette was going numb. The cigarette fell from his fingers and rolled into the broad expanse of his lap, then onto the floor, coming to rest in folds of the blanket covering his wasted legs.

Before long the blanket was smoldering. Buddy's face was drawing down on one side by then, the muscles pulling, twisting the side of his mouth, and his head hurt so bad that he thought he would die even before the blanket was fully in flames.

Buddy Eason was conscious, fully awake and knowing, when the fire reached him at last.

# ABOUT THE AUTHOR

Charlotte Miller was born in Roanoke, Alabama, in 1959, and has never lived outside the South. She began writing her Sanders family trilogy while a student at Auburn University, where she received a degree in business administration. Today, she works as a certified public accountant to pay the bills, and writes late into the night because she must. *There Is a River* completes her multi-generational saga of the agricultural and cotton mill South that began with *Behold, This Dreamer* (2000) and continued with *Through a Glass, Darkly* (2001). She is presently working on a fourth novel, which is expected in Fall 2003. One of her short stories, "An Alabama Christmas," was included in the bestselling 1999 regional collection, *Ordinary & Sacred As Blood: Alabama Women Speak*. She is a member of the Georgia Writers and the National League of American Pen Women. She lives in Opelika, Alabama, and has one son, Justin.